For Nicki and Vernon, with love

ONE

Georgina parked on the gravelled drive outside Little Wenborough Manor, ready to collect Sybbie and Cesca for their trip to Rosa Wines.

No matter how many times she visited Sybbie, she always fell in love with the house all over again: a red-brick Elizabethan manor house, built in the shape of an E, with stepped gable ends, stone mullioned windows, a red-tiled roof and barley-sugar twist chimneys. Wisteria grew round the doorway of the porch, though as a friend Georgina was more used to going to the back of the house and knocking on the kitchen door.

'I'll be two minutes, tops,' she told Bert, her springer spaniel, whose harness was clipped into the seatbelt on the back seat. He thumped his tail against the seat as she scratched the top of his head and lowered the side window to give him some air.

At the back of the house, the gardens stretched out from the terrace. Sybbie's famous national collection of azaleas had finished flowering, but there was plenty of colour in the herbaceous borders; some of the roses were on their second flush, perfuming the air with their gorgeous scent. There were troughs of lavender on the patio, and fat bumblebees buzzed lazily over them, while butterflies flitted in the sunshine.

Georgina knocked on the kitchen door before opening it. 'Morning!' she called.

'We're almost ready, dear girl,' Sybbie said with a broad smile, coming to meet her.

'Good, because I've left Bert in the car,' Georgina said.

'I'm holding you up because I'm *waddling* everywhere,' Francesca, Sybbie's daughter-in-law, said ruefully.

'You look blooming, to me,' Georgina said.

'I'm glad the morning sickness is over,' Francesca admitted.

'Max, Jet, go and find Bernard and Giles,' Sybbie told her two black Labradors. 'I'll be back soon.' She gave Francesca a grin. 'And don't bother teasing me about talking to the dogs. Georgie talks to Bert just as much as I talk to the boys.'

'Wouldn't dream of teasing you,' Francesca said, laughing.

They all headed out to Georgina's car, where Sybbie opened the front passenger door for Cesca.

'I don't mind sitting in the back,' Cesca said.

'You're pregnant. You get the most comfortable seat. No arguments,' Sybbie said, and climbed into the back seat next to Bert. 'Hello, gorgeous boy. You're so patient.'

Bert licked her and leaned against her.

'This looks like a perfect day for your photo shoot, Georgie,' Sybbie said. 'The sun's shining, there isn't a cloud in the sky, and the vines will be in neat little rows, marching across the valley – well, as much of a valley as you get in Norfolk.' She smiled. 'And, with any luck, we'll also get to try a glass or two of very delicious wine from Cesca's favourite supplier.'

'Only one sip for me – I'm driving,' Georgina reminded her friend.

'And no sips for me at all,' Francesca said sadly, clipping on her seatbelt next to Georgina and laying a protective hand on her bump.

'Is Doris here?' Sybbie asked.

'She says yes,' Georgina said. After months of keeping quiet about the ghost who lived in her house – Doris Beauchamp, the young woman who'd died there just over half a century before – Georgina had finally told her friends that she could hear the ghost through her hearing aids. She'd half expected them not to believe her, but they'd listened to her story and immediately supported her. Colin, Georgina's partner, was rather less open-minded about the situation, but they'd reached an awkward truce on the subject. 'She also says she hopes Bert doesn't need to dig anywhere.'

'If he does, just blink twice and we'll run interference,' Sybbie said.

'Except, dearest ma-in-law,' Francesca drawled, 'as you just said, it's sunny. How are we going to see Georgie blink behind her sunglasses?'

'That's a very valid point. Tap your nose, then, Georgie,' Sybbie said.

Georgina laughed. 'That's *so* unsubtle, Sybbie. Anyway, let's get this road trip started. I'm going to take photos of Gabrielle Edwards for *Veritas* magazine – they focus mainly on wine, but apparently they're going to start looking at cheese and delis as well – Doris is joining us for a trip out, Cesca's coming to take a look at Rosa Wines' newest vintage for the farm shop, and you...' They all knew why Sybbie was really there. To keep an eye on Francesca, who was six months pregnant and had a tendency to overdo things. 'You're in charge of Bert,' Georgina finished brightly.

'Who's a very good boy and, if I'm right, is cuddled up to Doris right now,' Sybbie said.

'He is,' Georgina confirmed on Doris's behalf.

'It's a shame Jodie's not with us,' Francesca said, referring to the youngest member of their group, who came with them to the Thursday Pilates class at the village hall, worked part-time in Francesca's shop and her brother's pub, and also cleaned the barn that Georgina rented out as a holiday home. 'It would've been a nice trip for the four of us. But there's a function at the Red Lion at lunchtime today, so Mike needs her help.'

It really was a perfect late August day; the wide Norfolk skies were a shade somewhere between azure and cobalt. Queen Anne's lace frothed along the sides of the narrow country roads, and the spring wheat had ripened to gold in the fields.

'According to the magazine's brief, Gabrielle Edwards is twenty-five, and she's one of the best up-and-coming vineyard managers in the country. They're doing a feature on her because she's aiming to get organic status for Rosa Wines. She won a fairly prestigious award last year for her wine, and they reckon she's got a good chance of scooping it again this year,' Georgina said. 'Obviously I've had a look through the vineyard's website, and I like what I've read. You said you've been buying from her for the last four years, Cesca?'

'Yes, though Rosa Wines has been going for a lot longer than that. Gaby's gran, Rosemary, set up the vineyard as a hobby project in the 1990s, after her husband died,' Francesca explained. 'The vineyard's named after Rosemary. Gaby basically grew up following in her gran's footsteps. And her wines really are good.'

'But we're meeting her at Willow Farm Wines, not Rosa Wines,' Georgina said. 'Which threw me a bit.'

'It's a bit complicated,' Francesca said. 'Gaby's dad owns Willow Farm, and he set up the other vineyard next to Rosa Wines. When Gaby's gran died, he took over Rosa Wines. Although Gaby's trying to carry on what her gran did, she has to run everything past him. The two vineyards share an office. But Willow Farm Wines caters for a different market to Gaby's, and the way her dad produces the wine is pretty much the opposite to everything Rosa Wines does. Gaby's an artisanal winemaker and does everything by hand.'

'Father versus daughter – and taking opposite approaches,' Sybbie mused. 'That must be a bit awkward.'

'I'll need to tread carefully, then,' Georgina said. It wouldn't be the first time she'd had a tricky assignment. Six months before, she'd been commissioned to take photographs of developer Eliot Manson and the lighthouse he was renovating. Then she'd discovered that the developer was universally disliked by both his workforce and the communities where he'd bought up the land. Hopefully this commission wouldn't be quite as difficult as the lighthouse had been.

'You'll probably need a bit of tact. But I wouldn't worry too much. You're good with people, Georgie,' Francesca said.

'Thank you. I try,' Georgina said, pleased by the compliment.

As they drew nearer to the village of Ashingham, where the vineyards were situated, the gold in the fields gave way to green, with neat rows of vines stretching across the landscape. Georgina turned the car in to a wide opening next to the sign saying *Willow Farm*, and followed the gravelled drive up to the farmhouse. Like many of the farmhouses in the area, Willow Farm was a low, two-storey building made from clay lump, painted white, with a thatched roof and two large chimneys. It looked to her as if the original part of the house was seventeenth century, with Victorian additions and a pretty porch with roses twining round the door. Next to the farmhouse was a converted brick barn with a glass front and a red-tiled roof, sporting a sign saying *Willow Farm Wines*, which Georgina assumed housed the office where she'd arranged to meet Gaby.

They parked in a gravelled area labelled *Visitors*. As they climbed out of the car, a young woman who looked to be in her mid-twenties came out of the barn to meet them. She was wearing black jeans, Doc Martens and a bright pink T-shirt; her shoulder-length blonde hair was loose, cut into a bob, and she'd tucked a few strands behind one ear. Georgina recognised her from photographs on the vineyard's website as Gabrielle Edwards.

'You must be Mrs Drake. Welcome to Willow Farm,' the younger woman said with a wide smile. 'And an especial welcome to Rosa Wines.'

'Thank you, Ms Edwards,' Georgina said. 'And thank you for agreeing to let me bring Bert. Obviously you already know Cesca and Sybbie.'

'I've known them both for years,' Gaby confirmed. 'Good to see you both. And I'm dying for you to sample the new vintage, Cesca, even if it's just a single sip and you spit it out after you taste it – we're just about ready to release it, and I think it's even better than the one that won the award.'

'Sybbie will have to step in for me, I'm afraid,' Francesca said ruefully. 'I'm over the morning sickness now, but I'm not drinking.'

'Of course. I'm sorry, Cesca. Another three months to go, isn't it?' Gaby asked.

'Three months of being nagged and fussed over too much,' Francesca said, patting Sybbie's shoulder. 'Just as well I love my mother-in-law. But keep her away from those roses round the front door of the farmhouse, Gaby. She keeps secateurs in her pocket.'

'I do *not* have secateurs in my pocket,' Sybbie protested, albeit with a longing look cast towards the roses.

'That's because today they're in her handbag instead,' Georgina said in a stage whisper, and Francesca laughed.

Gaby bent down to make a fuss of the spaniel. 'Hello, Bert. You're a lovely boy, aren't you?' She straightened up. 'He reminds me of Monty, my mum's spaniel. He used to be the official mascot of Rosa Wines.'

Georgina noticed the past tense and decided to be very tactful. The loss of a pet could cut very deeply. Bert had been with her for more than a year now, and she loved him dearly; she was aware that, coming up to eight years old, he was in the middle of his life, and she really didn't want to think beyond that to the inevitable parting. Though at least she knew he'd have Doris to look after him when he left her.

'Where would you like to start, Mrs Drake?' Gaby asked.

'Do call me Georgie – and may I call you Gaby, Ms Edwards?'

'Absolutely,' Gaby said with a smile.

'As the weather's nice, I thought it might be nice to take some outdoor shots of you among the vines – I assume that'll be the Rosa Wines vines rather than Willow Farm's?'

'Yes,' Gaby said.

'OK. And then maybe we can take some in the winery itself. Is there a particular stage of production that'd make an interesting photo? Otherwise maybe I can take photographs of you opening a bottle, pouring a glass and tasting?' Georgina suggested. 'And I'd like a picture of you holding your trophy, too.'

'We can do all of that. Let me give you a quick tour of the fields, first, and I can tell you all about Rosa. If you see a good spot for photographs along the way, we can stop to take some,' Gaby said brightly. 'Cesca, are you OK to walk with us, or would you rather have a comfy chair in the office and I'll ask someone to bring you a drink while you wait for us?'

'I'm very happy to walk. Exercise is good for me,' Francesca said, her tone making it clear that she wasn't going to accept any unnecessary fuss on the grounds of her pregnancy. 'But a cup of tea while you're tasting the wine would be very welcome. And I brought cake.'

'Your lemon drizzle cake?' Gaby asked.

Francesca chuckled. 'You're a businesswoman. Know thy customers. Of course it's lemon.'

'Wonderful,' Gaby said with a grin.

Georgina fetched her camera bag from the car, Sybbie took charge of Bert's lead and they all followed Gaby down the path behind the office to the vineyard.

Just as Sybbie had suggested, the vines were all laid out in neat rows, spreading across the landscape. Between the vines, there were strips of grass and what looked like purple clover, and at the edges of the field there was a strip of land filled with pinkish-purple, cream and yellow wildflowers.

'Cesca told me you basically grew up working with grapes, Gaby,' Georgina said.

'Pretty much,' Gaby agreed. 'Gran set up the vineyard about five years before I was born. I took my first steps among these vines, and one of my earliest memories is helping her to pick the grapes. We've always done it by hand rather than by machine at Rosa Wines.'

'Is there much of a difference in the way you produce the wine?' Georgina asked. 'Not that I'm doubting you, I should add; I'm interested in how it all works.' And she'd also learned early on in her career that when you got people talking about their passion, they relaxed, making it easier to take a really good photograph of them.

'Gran taught me that minimal intervention makes better wine,' Gaby said. 'You start with the best quality grapes you can, but every process you add takes a little bit more away from that. Letting nature do its job means it takes a bit longer to produce the wine, but Gran always said it was worth it for the quality of the final product, and I agree with her.'

'I agree, too,' Francesca said. 'And so do the farm shop customers.'

'I try to keep everything as non-mechanised as possible. Everything from pruning to harvesting – because the machines tend to mush the fruit, and in my view whole fruit that's been gently pressed makes better wine than what you get if you put mushy fruit through a centrifuge machine,' Gaby said. 'It takes about nine months to clear our wines naturally after fermentation, because we let gravity do it all, though not all producers like to wait that long. It depends on your market. If you want to speed up the process – say you're looking to sell bigger volumes at a lower price point – you can clarify your wine in a fortnight by adding finings to the tank.'

'Finings?' Georgina asked.

'Usually pigs' trotters or fish guts.' She wrinkled her nose. 'Me, I'd rather stick to just the fruit and a bit of yeast, and let the process take a few months longer.'

Francesca's face turned a little bit green at the mention of fish guts. 'Gaby, can we...?'

'Sorry!' Gaby patted her arm. 'I'll get off my hobby horse. Anyway, while I was still in my teens, Gran taught me everything she knew about growing grapes, and then I did a degree in viticulture. The plan was, I'd come back here after I graduated, then Gran would retire after a couple of years and hand Rosa over to Mum and me.' She looked sad. 'Except Gran died just before I graduated, so it didn't quite work out as we planned. I miss her so much. I would've loved to talk about these new varietals with her, to see what she thought of them. And I wish she'd been here when we scooped that award for the Solaris. She would've been chuffed to bits that the very first wine she let me make on my own, when I was still a student, did so well.' She bit her lip, suddenly looking vulnerable. 'Still, at least I had Mum there at the awards do with me.'

'You work with your mum?' Georgina asked.

'I used to,' Gaby said. 'It was always supposed to be the three of us at Rosa Wines. Three generations of women winemakers. Except now it's just me.' She looked sad. 'I can't change the past, so there's no point dwelling on it.'

There was clearly a story there. Either Gaby had lost her mum as well as her gran, Georgina thought, and it would be unkind to ask and bring the sad memories back, or there had been some kind of falling out. Maybe Francesca could fill her in later. 'Let me take a shot of you here, with all the vines behind you,' she said. 'Keep talking. Tell me what you love about the land,' she added, and took several shots of Gaby looking enthusiastic and gesticulating as she talked her guests through how her grandmother had chosen the site for the vines and the quality of the soil, and how the aspect and the soil had influenced their choice of grapes.

'We measure our carbon footprint and we're trying to become carbon neutral by the end of the decade,' she said. 'And we sow grass and alfalfa between the rows as a kind of green fertiliser – we only cut it after nesting season.'

So that was what the purple clover-like flowers were, Georgina thought.

'Plus we're looking at the diversity of the plants on the perimeters of the vineyard – mallow, yarrow and red campion, which is good for the local fauna,' Gaby continued. 'We're working with the local conservation trusts to encourage beneficial insects and pollinators – and that naturally decreases the harmful ones.'

Georgina could see the wildflowers at the edge of the field. 'Let's get some shots of you sitting here, with the flowers behind you,' she said. 'And if you give me your permission, I can spend a while here maybe later in the week, and photograph the insect life.'

'That'd be great,' Gaby said. 'My brother Ash has drawn some gorgeous pictures of dragonflies, if you wanted to include them.'

'We'll see what the magazine says,' Georgina promised.

Gaby submitted to Georgina taking various shots at various angles.

'Tell me about these new varietals you're looking at,'

Georgina encouraged her when they were back among the vines.

'I've been converting Rosa's fields to organic status, and I planted some test vines, the year Gran died. They're disease-resistant hybrids, meaning you don't have to spray them with chemicals,' Gaby explained. 'It takes three years for a vine to be developed enough to make wine, so we harvested the first crop last year, and the wine we made from them is just about ready for tasting now. If it's as good as I hope it is, I'll scale up and plant a full field.' She smiled. 'I'm about halfway to persuading Dad into making the change. The government's introduced a scheme for sustainable farming, and the new grape meets all the criteria to let us get the grant. I've applied for it – obviously in Dad's name, because he's the landowner – and I'm really hoping it'll work for us.'

'Your dad's in charge of Rosa Wines as well as Willow Farm?' Georgina checked.

'Since Gran died, yes.' Gaby winced. 'The only thing is, he wants to retire.'

'Maybe he'll put you in charge of Rosa Wines,' Francesca suggested.

'Sadly not.' Gaby gritted her teeth. 'The way he sees it, I'm a girl, and I'm young.'

Clearly that stung, and Georgina could understand why. 'Those points are both in your favour, as far as *Veritas* magazine is concerned. That's why they want to run this feature on you,' Georgina reminded her.

'I wasn't fishing, but thank you.' Gaby gave a nod of acknowledgement. 'The thing is, Dad's already decided to put Nathan – that's my other brother, the oldest one – in charge of Willow Farm Wines.'

'Does that mean he'll be in charge of Rosa Wines, too?' Sybbie asked.

'Nathan thinks so, but I'm trying to persuade Dad to give me a bit of time,' Gaby said.

Not wanting Gaby to feel awkward and clam up on her, Georgina asked, 'What about your other brother – the one who draws dragonflies?'

'Ashley's the middle child – I'm the youngest,' she said. 'But Ash doesn't work in the business.'

Was it her imagination, or was there a slightly protective look on Gaby's face as she spoke about her artist brother? Georgina wondered.

'So it's you and Nathan working on the vineyards?' Sybbie asked.

'Yes, but not together. Nathan and I are about as opposite as you can get,' Gaby admitted, 'and there isn't a way to compromise. You're either organic or you're not. There's no in-between. He thinks organic is a waste of time, and he's all about cutting costs and expanding yields. I mean, the way he'd prune my fields, it'd take one person and a tractor a couple of days to chop the lot, whereas I prune by hand, which means we need three people for four or five months. That's a big difference in staff costs alone.' She shook herself. 'Sorry. I don't mean to slag him off. We just see things in different ways. And we make very different wines.'

'But surely you winning that award would make your dad back you?' Francesca asked.

'I guess I need to try a bit harder,' Gaby said, and squared her shoulders. 'Anyway, I want to be positive. I'd like to show you what we do here and how we're conquering the challenges of modern farming. This month has been the driest August we've had in twenty years. Irrigation's an issue – and moisture in August can lead to mould, so we have to be careful – but the new varietals are a bit more robust. And we were very precise about the planting, to get the shade in the right place so it's no more than halfway up the next canopy.'

'You know that running-interference business the others were talking about in the car?' Doris murmured in Georgina's ear.

Georgina started. She'd been so caught up in Gaby's story that she'd almost forgotten Doris was with them. 'Mmm-hmm,' she muttered beneath her breath.

'Sybbie needs to drop Bert's lead,' Doris said. 'Tap your nose.'

Georgina caught Sybbie's gaze, tapped her nose and gave a single nod in the direction of Bert.

Sybbie looked momentarily surprised, then clearly caught on to what Georgina was suggesting and gave an almost imperceptible nod in reply. 'Gaby, it's the gardener in me being terribly nosy, but would you talk me through the pruning of the vines? Plus I'm half tempted to try growing grapes at Little Wenborough Manor, so I'd love to know your thoughts on where I should start.'

'Of course,' Gaby said with a smile.

Sybbie waited until the dog was halfway down the row before saying, 'Oh, no! Gaby, I'm so sorry – I've dropped Bert's lead.'

'I'll go and collect him,' Georgina said.

'I'm sure he won't do any harm,' Gaby said. 'It's fine.'

Francesca's eyebrows rose briefly, telling Georgina that the younger woman had picked up the signals, too, and would join Sybbie in distracting Gaby for as long as necessary.

Bert's plumy tail wagged as he trotted down towards the far end of the field.

'Maybe he wants a drink and can smell the pond,' Gaby said. 'The water's perfectly safe for him to drink, Georgie. As I said, we don't spray Rosa Wines' fields, so there's nothing nasty in the pond that could make him ill.'

'Thank you. I'll go and fetch him anyway,' Georgina said with a smile.

As soon as they were out of earshot, she said to Doris, 'Is there a body?'

'There's a skeleton in the pond,' Doris confirmed. 'As Gaby said, it's been a very dry August. The water's dried up and the skeleton's quite near the edge. Bert won't have to dig very far.'

Georgina had worked with Doris on several occasions now to find out the truth behind an unexpected death. Although part of her was glad of the opportunity to help right a past wrong, part of her still felt upset that a family had lost someone they loved, and the killer had got away with it for years.

'What can you tell me about the bones?' Georgina asked.

'They're the remains of Percy Ramsey, who used to farm the land here back in the 1930s,' Doris said. 'He remembers being in a fight, of someone landing a punch – and then nothing.'

'And that was it? He was killed by a single punch?' Georgina asked.

'It seems so,' Doris agreed.

'Why was he in a fight?' Georgina asked. 'Who hit him?' Then she sighed. 'Sorry. I should know how this works, by now. Until we find out something from the records to jog his memory, he's not going to be able to tell us anything more, is he?'

'No,' Doris confirmed.

Bert was happily digging at the edge of the pond, ignoring the dragonflies that glided round him, and he soon uncovered what Georgina had been expecting since the moment Doris had whispered in her ear.

Bones.

TWO

'Good boy. You found him,' Georgina said softly, and made a fuss of Bert. 'Doris, please can you tell Percy we'll do what we can to find out what happened to him?' She paused, remembering the way previous cases had panned out. 'Do you need to be here at the vineyard to be able to talk to him?'

'That's how it's been in the past,' Doris said. 'But something feels different – I'm not sure what, but it does,' she added, sounding puzzled. 'Like when I was first able to leave Rookery Farm, after years of being stuck there. Hopefully now Percy's made contact with me, he'll be able to talk to me away from here. Otherwise you might need an excuse to come back.'

'Got it. I'd better tell the others; then we'll call the police,' Georgina said.

'Georgie, this isn't going to make things more difficult between you and Colin, is it?' Doris asked.

Colin didn't believe in ghosts and hadn't reacted well when Georgina had finally told him that she could hear Doris through her hearing aids. It had caused a rift between them, but they were trying to mend it. 'I hope not,' Georgina admitted. Her relationship with Colin still wasn't quite back to where it had been before she'd made the revelation, but she didn't want to worry Doris or make her friend feel guilty. She and Colin would just have to work a bit harder at finding a compromise. 'I think he's coming to terms with things a bit more,' she said instead.

'Hmm,' Doris said. 'I don't want to come between you.'

'You won't,' Georgina reassured her. She picked up Bert's lead and walked him back through the vines to where Sybbie and Francesca were still running interference with Gaby.

'Everything all right, dear girl?' Sybbie enquired.

'Actually, no. I'm afraid it isn't,' Georgina said. 'I'm really sorry, Gaby. We need to call the police.'

'The *police*?' Gaby's eyes widened in shock. 'Why? What's happened?'

'I'm afraid Bert's uncovered some human remains,' Georgina said.

'Oh, my God. There's a dead body in my fields?' Gaby put a hand to her mouth.

'It looks like a skeleton, so I think they're the remains of someone who died a while ago,' Georgina said quickly. 'Bert isn't a sniffer dog, but he has found, um, bones before now.'

'A skeleton.' Gaby was clearly still trying to take it in. 'But how? And why didn't anyone find the bones when the vines were planted?'

'They're at the edge of the pond,' Georgina said. 'You said it had been a really dry August. Maybe it's only this year that the bones have come so close to the edge of the pond?'

'Dry Augusts seem to be the norm, nowadays,' Gaby said. 'I'm still surprised nobody found it before. Unless' – she looked horrified as the thought struck her – 'the poor person died *after* we planted this field.'

'All the skeletons that Bert has found before have been designated "bones of antiquity" by the police. I'm sure this one will be the same,' Sybbie said, clearly trying to be helpful.

'I've learned a bit about bones, but not enough to say things with any certainty. They look old, though, to me,' Georgina added. 'But the police will call in an expert to take a look and recover the skeleton, and then they'll be able to tell you more.'

'OK,' Gaby said, her face still pinched with shock. 'Do we need to – I don't know, cordon off the area, or something?'

'The police will do that if they think it's necessary,' Georgina said. 'I assume this bit of the vineyard isn't usually open to the public?'

'Only as part of a tour,' Gaby confirmed. 'And they're only at weekends.'

'So nobody's likely to walk around here until the remains are recovered properly. Good. Though it might be worth asking your staff to avoid the area until after the experts have had the chance to take a look,' Georgina said.

'Let's go back to the office. I'll tell the staff to stay away, and we can call the police,' Gaby said.

Except, as they reached the courtyard behind the office, they could see a flashing blue light. An ambulance, its doors open, was parked in the courtyard. Half a dozen people, whom Georgina assumed worked at the vineyard, were gathered outside one of the buildings, talking in low voices and looking anxious.

'What's an ambulance doing here? Oh, my God. *Dad.*' Gaby's face blanched. 'What's happened? Where's Dad?' she called.

'Gaby!' A middle-aged man broke away from the group and put his arms out to stop her going any further into the courtyard. 'Gaby, love, don't go in with the fermentation tanks.'

'Why?' She shivered. 'Oh, no. Del – please tell me it's not Dad. He hasn't had a heart attack or something? He's all right?'

'It's not him,' Del reassured her, but then added, 'We don't actually know where your dad is, at the moment, and he's not answering his phone.'

'What's happened?' Gaby asked again.

'There's been, um, an accident,' Del said, looking worried and as if he had no idea how to break some seriously bad news.

Georgina noticed that his clothes were wet in places and he smelled strongly of wine.

Something had clearly happened in the winery.

'Who?' Gaby asked.

'Nathan. Love, I'm sorry, there isn't a way to put this nicely,' he warned. 'We tried to get hold of you straight after we called the ambulance, but your phone must've been on silent or out of coverage.'

'There's no signal in the vineyard,' Gaby said. There were still a lot of pockets in Norfolk where mobile phone coverage was spotty. 'I was giving Georgina, Cesca and Sybbie a tour and Georgina was taking photos for that magazine,' she explained. 'You said Nathan had an accident. Is he badly hurt?'

Del's face looked pinched, showing his distress. 'He fell into a vat of red wine. I'm so sorry, love. Nobody realised he was there. He – he drowned. Harry and I pulled him out.'

'Drowned? But... he can't have done!' She shook her head, clearly unable to take it in. 'Where's Ash?'

'He's not answering his phone, either. I've sent Harry over to the studio to find him,' Del said. 'I was kind of hoping you'd gone to have a cup of tea with him, the way you normally do in the mornings, and he'd got chatting.'

'I haven't seen him today. I wanted to be here on time for the photo shoot, and I needed to do a few things among the vines, first. You know what Ash is like when he gets going,' Gaby said.

Del looked awkward. 'Sorry, love. I forgot about the photo shoot.'

Gaby dragged a hand through her hair, suddenly looking a lot younger than her twenty-five years. 'Nathan's d—' Her face was anguished as she cut the word off. 'Oh, my God. No, Del. He *can't* be.'

Obviously, despite their differences when it came to business, Gaby loved her older brother, Georgina thought.

'If I... if we'd come in here to do the photos first, instead of going to the fields, he might still have been alive. We might've been here when he fell in. I could've—' A sob choked off the rest of her words.

'No, you couldn't. I think he'd been in the tank for a while, love,' Del said. 'Don't blame yourself. It wasn't your fault. All of us could say we should've been here, but you know what it's like at this time of year. We're busy checking the fruit.'

Georgina went over to them and took the younger woman's hand, squeezing it gently for comfort. 'Come and sit down, love. I'll see if I can rustle up a mug of tea from somewhere, and I promise it will help.' She gave the older man a small smile. 'I'm Georgie, the photographer. You said you've already called the police?'

'Yes, and I've called everyone out of production to wait here in the courtyard, out of the way. Nobody's been allowed in with the fermentation tanks. I'm Del, Nathan's second-in-command,' he said. 'That's a good idea, some hot sweet tea for our girl. There's a kitchen in the next room.'

Georgina's first thought had been to comfort Gaby. But, as a policeman's girlfriend, she was very aware of procedures and the reasons behind not touching anything near the scene of an unexpected death. There might be some kind of trace evidence in the kitchen, and the last thing she wanted was to affect it. 'On second thoughts, maybe I'd better not use the kitchen until the police have taken a look. Until they say otherwise, it's probably best to treat the whole area as...' There wasn't a tactful way to say 'a crime scene'. Even if it had been an accident rather than deliberate, there would need to be some kind of investigation. '... out of bounds,' she finished. 'Gaby, do you live on the farm?'

Gaby shook her head. 'I lived with Mum and Gran, but after Gran died...' She looked awkward. 'I moved into the village.'

'I'm Sybbie Walters,' Sybbie said, coming over to them. 'Cesca, my daughter-in-law, is—'

'—one of Rosa's long-term buyers. Little Wenborough Manor's farm shop,' Del said, clearly knowing exactly who they were.

'Indeed,' Sybbie said with a smile. 'Georgie's partner is with the police, and he's a friend of ours, so we're rather used to difficult situations. You said the police are on their way?'

Del nodded.

'And the paramedics are waiting for the police and looking after Nathan's body?'

Del swallowed hard. 'Yes.'

'Then come and sit in the car with us, Gaby, until the police get here,' Sybbie suggested.

Gaby, looking dazed, agreed. But before Sybbie could shepherd her towards Georgina's car, another of the Willow Farm employees – wearing a black polo shirt with the Willow Farm Wines logo on it – came over to them.

'Gaby! I'm so glad you're all right,' he said, looking relieved.

He, too, had wet clothing and smelled of wine; he must've been the man who'd helped Del get Nathan out of the tank and then gone to fetch Ashley, Gaby's middle brother, from the studio, Georgina thought.

'Harry, why isn't Ash with you?' Gaby asked. 'Or did he refuse to come?'

Why would Ashley refuse to come to the winery? Georgina wondered.

'He wasn't at the studio,' Harry said carefully.

'Are you sure?' When he nodded, Gaby narrowed her eyes at him. 'What aren't you telling us?'

'I...' He shook his head.

'Spit it out, lad,' Del said, though his tone wasn't unkind.

'His studio's a mess – and I don't mean the way it normally looks a tip,' Harry explained. 'It's different. Things have been smashed. It looks as to me if there's been some kind of fight. And there's... It looks like blood on the floor,' he said, his voice dropping to a near-whisper. 'It might be paint,' he added swiftly, his face lighting up with momentary hope.

'I doubt it. He's sculpting, not painting, right now,' Gaby said softly, and the light in Harry's eyes vanished.

'I'm so sorry, Gaby.' Harry looked haunted.

One brother dead, the other missing and with blood on the floor of his studio – poor Gaby's world had just been ripped apart. And it sounded as if Colin was going to have a difficult case ahead of him, Georgina thought.

'Is there someone we can call for you, Gaby?' she asked gently.

'Dad. Dad should be here.' Gaby grabbed her phone and tried calling him, then shook her head. 'Voicemail,' she muttered. 'Dad, it's Gaby. Please ring me urgently. Something awful's happened at the winery. Just – please ring me as soon as you get this.' She ended the call and bit her lip. 'I have no idea where he is, or how long it'll be until he's back.'

'Then call Diana, love,' Del said. 'Obviously you've got my full support, but I think right now you need your mum rather than anyone else.'

Gaby looked torn. 'But if Dad comes back when she's still here...'

'Nathan was her son, too. If your dad gets shirty about it, I'll tell him it was my idea,' Del said.

So Gaby's mum was still alive; that answered one of Georgina's questions. But Gaby had intimated that she'd worked with her grandmother and her mother. That they were a team. Why did Gaby's mum no longer work at Rosa Wines? Georgina wondered. Why had Gaby moved out of her grandmother's house? Why would Nick Edwards be angry if Diana was here – and why would he take it out on Gaby?

Not that it was any of Georgina's business.

Though Colin would probably ask the same questions. Maybe after the time she'd spent in Colin's company, she'd started thinking the same way that he did.

Gaby made another call. 'Mum? It's me. I...' Her voice juddered, and tears spilled down her cheeks. 'Oh, Mum. There's been an accident. Nathan—' She dragged in a breath. 'Nathan's dead. I don't know what happened, just that they found him in one of the vats. And Ash has gone missing. And...' It sounded as if her mother had cut in with a question. 'No, Dad's not here. He went out on business, earlier today.' A tiny sob escaped her. 'Oh, Mum. Would you? Please? But don't – you'd better not bring Shaun.'

Who was Shaun? Georgina wondered. And why would it be a problem if he accompanied Gaby's mum?

'All right. I'll see you soon. Love you, too,' Gaby said. 'And I'm so sorry.' She hung up, and gratefully took the tissue Sybbie offered her.

'We'll take her over to sit in my car until the police or one of her parents get here,' Georgina said quietly to Del.

'Thank you.' He sighed. 'Poor kid. I've known her since she was knee-high to a grasshopper. I just hope the boss thinks of her before he has a hissy fit about Diana being here.'

'Or maybe,' Georgina said, 'I can find a very gentle way of reminding him that I'm working for a magazine and Cesca and Sybbie are customers.'

'They're Gaby's customers, not his,' Del said. 'But maybe you're right and he won't give the girl a hard time in front of you.'

Nick Edwards sounded like a difficult man, Georgina thought. But you caught more flies with honey than you did with vinegar. Hopefully she could help Gaby. And there was still the body in the vineyard to sort out.

As she headed over to join Sybbie, Cesca and Gaby, she caught sight of a grey car she recognised coming up the driveway, and her heart gave a little leap of relief.

Colin.

THREE

Colin caught sight of Georgina's car on the gravelled car park as he drove towards Willow Farm Wines.

'I hope Georgie isn't mixed up in this,' he said to Mo Tesfaye, his DS, and Larissa Foulkes, his DC. 'Could you give me a second to have a quick word?'

'Of course, guv,' they said.

He pulled up next to Georgina's car and turned off the engine, then climbed out of the car to talk to her. She got out of her car, too.

'I wasn't expecting to see you here,' he said.

'This was the job I told you about, last week,' she said. 'I'm taking Gaby's photograph for a wine magazine.'

He looked at her, and then at Bert in the back seat of her car.

Sybbie and Francesca gave him a little wave, both looking slightly awkward. The fracturing of his relationship with Georgina a few months ago had affected his friendship with Sybbie and Cesca, too. They were very protective of Georgie; he was glad they were supporting her, but at the same time he regretted the way things had cooled between them all.

'Tell me you didn't find the body,' he said.

'Well, not the one that was called in to you,' she said. 'But since you mention it...'

And this, he thought, was where things were all going to fall apart again. Because no doubt she was going to tell him that Doris had talked to whatever skeleton she'd found and had information to share. He was trying to be open-minded, he really was, but he simply couldn't get his head round the idea that Georgina was friends with a ghost.

Clearly his feelings showed on his face, because she sighed. 'I'm going to text you with what I know, before I even start researching the case – just so *you* know, too. But, yes, please. I'd appreciate it if you could call Rowena Langham to have a look at the bones.' The county's finds liaison officer had worked with them both on previous discoveries of bodies. 'Or I could call her, if you like.'

Georgina knew about the tricky moment a year or so back, when Rowena had made tentative overtures towards Colin which he'd awkwardly rebuffed, but she seemed to think he was making a fuss over nothing. Particularly as, over the last few months, Georgina and Rowena had become friends.

'Probably best to go through official channels. I'll call her and keep you posted,' he said. 'Do you know anything about what's happened here?' Georgina was observant and shrewd, and he valued her thoughts – well, on everything except ghosts. That was still a no-go area.

'A little bit. Gaby's oldest brother, Nathan, was in charge of the vineyard. He's the one you've been called out for. Del, one of the team here, found the body in a vat of red wine. He told us Nathan had drowned. Gaby's middle brother, Ashley, is an artist, I gather. One of the vineyard team went to his studio, which I assume is reasonably close by, but he seems to have disappeared and the guy who went to find him – Harry – reported that the studio looks as though there was a fight, with things smashed, and possibly blood on the floor,' Georgina said. 'Nick, their father, is out somewhere with a client and nobody can get hold of him, though both Del and Gaby have left messages on his voicemail. Del has gathered all the staff in the courtyard, out of the way, and told Gaby to call her mum. Diana – Gaby's mum – is on her way. There's tension between Nick and Diana, but I don't know the full story. Gaby told me that Diana used to work here when Gaby's grandmother was still alive, but she didn't say when her mum stopped working here, or why.'

'Thank you,' Colin said, appreciating the succinct way she gave him the information.

'Obviously I won't ask Gaby anything more until after you've interviewed her. She's sitting in the back of my car at the moment because we wanted to get her away from the spot where her brother died. It sounds to me as if there was a bit of an acrimonious divorce, so Sybbie and I will try to defuse things if Gaby's parents look as if they're about to start having a row,' Georgina said.

'Thank you. That'd be helpful,' Colin said. He paused. 'You might as well tell me about the skeleton, while you're here.'

Georgina looked shocked, as if she hadn't expected him to discuss it with her, and he felt a flare of guilt. Of *course* he was interested in the case. She'd solved several cold cases now, and he knew she was good at working things out and finding the evidence. Though it was a bit awkward trying to discuss the situation without bringing up the subject of Doris.

'He was at the edge of the pond. Gaby was surprised nobody had discovered the bones while they were planting the vines,' Georgina added, 'but it might be that the skeleton has only become visible right now because the pond has dried up a bit more than usual, this month.'

'That's reasonable,' Colin said.

'His name's Percy Ramsey, he farmed here in the 1930s, and somebody hit him.'

'With what?'

'I don't know.' She shrugged. 'Presumably a fist, unless they came armed with some kind of club or a cricket bat.' She raised her eyebrows and gave him a challenging look. 'I'm going to text this to you, right now, to time stamp the information. And I confirm now that I haven't had time to look up any newspapers or find any documents yet.'

'You don't have to do that. I don't want to fight with you, Georgie,' he said softly.

'I'm just being thorough,' she said. 'Because then maybe, just maybe, when I find the documents to prove what I'm saying to you now, you'll believe me that I have a different source of information.'

Just what he'd been dreading: another argument over Doris. 'I don't believe in ghosts,' he said, 'but I do believe in you. More than that.' His voice deepened. 'I believe in *us*.' They just needed to find a place where they could both compromise. He reached over to squeeze her hand. 'Finding a skeleton and then discovering a very recent death – I know it's happened to you before, but it's something nobody ever really gets used to. Are you all right?'

'I'm fine. Just... poor Gaby, Colin. She and Nathan apparently had completely opposite approaches to the business,' Georgina said, 'but she clearly loved her brother anyway. She's devastated by his death.'

Colin knew that Georgina, having a kind heart, would want to help Gaby. 'OK. I'll go and see what the situation is, and I'll call Rowena Langham about your skeleton, too.'

'Thank you,' she said.

He rapped on Sybbie's window, and she wound it down.

'Hello, dear boy. Fancy seeing you here,' she drawled, with a wide smile.

'Fancy,' he agreed, his own smile rather more wry. Sybbie had been involved with previous cases, too, and Colin liked her and her husband enormously. 'Cesca,' he said with another smile, acknowledging another friend. He turned to the third person in the car: a young woman who looked as if her world had just been turned upside down and she didn't have a clue where to start getting things back to anywhere near resembling normality. He'd met plenty of people in her situation, over the years. 'Miss Edwards, I'm very sorry for your loss,' he said, keeping his voice gentle. 'I'm DI Colin Bradshaw. I'll do my best to find out exactly what happened to your brother, but one of my team will need to take a statement from you this morning. We'll call in a family liaison officer to support you, and make sure you know who to talk to if you have any questions.'

'Thank you, DI Bradshaw,' she said, her voice hoarse.

'We would have gone to the staff kitchen and made tea,' Sybbie said, 'but Georgie reminded us you might not want people...' She stopped, but Colin knew exactly what she meant. Compromising a potential crime scene. 'Well. We thought here might be a better place to wait,' she finished.

And it also meant Gaby wouldn't have the heartbreak of seeing her brother's dead body being removed to the ambulance. Trust Georgie and Sybbie to think of that, and find a tactful way of helping. 'You did absolutely the right thing,' he reassured her. 'Thank you.'

Bert had climbed onto Sybbie's lap and stuck his head out of the open window, desperate to say hello to his friend. 'Hello to you, too, and stop squashing poor Sybbie,' Colin said, scratching the spaniel behind his ears. Bert gave a wriggle of joy and wagged his tail.

'I'll see you soon,' he said to Georgina, and went round to the passenger side of his own car.

Larissa and Mo got out of the car so he could lock the door.

'So what's the situation, guv?' Larissa asked, keeping her voice low.

He gave her a succinct rundown of what Georgina had told him.

'So this guy just fell in a vat of wine and drowned?' Larissa asked.

'That's what we need to establish. It *sounds* like a work-related accident.'

'But it might not be,' Mo chimed in. 'And because it's an unexpected death at work, we have to investigate anyway.'

'Do you want me to call forensics?' Larissa asked.

'Hold off for a few minutes, until we've spoken to the man who found him,' Colin said. 'We also need to find the whereabouts of the other brother and take a look at his studio. If it's blood rather than paint in the room, we need to know whose blood it is, what happened, and where he is now. And we need to keep both sites secure, so we'll call for extra help now.' He sighed. 'Plus we need to talk to Rowena, because Bert—'

'—has found yet another skeleton?' Larissa cut in, raising her eyebrows. 'He really ought to be our official police dog, the way he's going.'

'He should,' Colin said lightly. It was much easier to go along with the joke than it would be to tell his team that a ghost guided the dog to dig for bones, which was why Georgina had become involved in so many cold cases. Then again, even that far-fetched story was more believable than the possibility that Georgina was some kind of time-travelling serial killer.

He asked Mo to call in for reinforcements, and called the Health and Safety Executive contact himself to update them on the situation. Once they'd found their way to the courtyard where everyone was waiting, talking quietly among themselves and looking anxious, he had a quick word with the paramedics; they confirmed that the body of a thirty-five-year-old man identified by the production manager as Nathan Edwards had been pulled out of a vat of wine. They also confirmed that life was extinct, but the cause of death would need to be determined by a doctor.

'Everyone, thank you for waiting here,' Colin said. 'I'm DI Colin Bradshaw, and my colleagues are DS Mo Tesfaye and DC Larissa Foulkes. I'm sorry for your loss. We need to investigate what happened to Nathan Edwards, and I believe there's also a question mark over the whereabouts of Ashley Edwards. We'll be taking statements from everyone – not because anyone here is necessarily a suspect in Nathan's death or Ashley's disappearance, but because we need to investigate the cause of the accident and trace people's movements,' he explained. 'If anyone knows where Ashley might be, or has seen or heard anything that might be helpful, however small, please let us know. We'll keep everything confidential. In the meantime, if I could ask for your patience – please don't go to Ashley's studio or the area where the fermentation tanks are, and please don't talk to each other about what you'll discuss with us in your statements. Again, it's not that we think anyone's a suspect,' he said, 'but we want everyone to keep their memories clear. If you talk about it between yourselves, then your memories will start to blur with something you heard someone else say, and we might lose a small but important detail as a result.'

There were a few murmurs, but everyone nodded.

'The people in the fields – can they keep working?' one of the team asked. 'Because they wouldn't have seen or heard anything. And, at this time of year, things are really busy.'

'I'm sorry, but no,' Colin said. 'If someone could go and fetch everyone and explain what I said about no discussion, I'd appreciate it. And we'll be as quick as we can, taking statements.'

'If you want to start with me,' the man said, 'I'm Del Turnbull, the production manager. Then I'll help manage the team.'

'Thank you, Del,' Colin said.

'I'll call the pathologist,' Larissa said, 'then Mo and I will start taking statements. Is there a quiet location we can use, Mr Turnbull?'

'The offices and the reception area,' Del said, gesturing to the barn behind them.

'Thank you,' Colin said again, and followed him into a neat room with large windows and polished wooden floorboards. The two light-coloured wooden desks were immaculately tidy, with only a desk blotter, a lamp and a pen pot on them; Colin assumed that whoever usually sat there had either taken their laptop with them or locked them in one of the drawers. There were posters on the white walls advertising Willow Farm Wines; a large Swiss cheese plant sat in a ceramic pot by the glass sliding doors.

'Please take a seat,' Del said, gesturing to the desks. 'Can I get you anything?'

'Thank you, but no,' Colin said, sitting down and getting his notebook out while Del moved one of the office chairs to sit opposite him. 'Before we start, Mr Turnbull, is there any CCTV in the building?'

'Not in the area with the tanks,' Del said. 'The insurance company asked, but Nick pointed out that nobody's going to come and steal wine that's not in a drinkable state. The finished stock's covered, but it's in a different building.'

'What about the office?' Colin asked.

'No. It's alarmed, but that's it.'

'What about the gates to the premises?'

'No.'

'I'd appreciate sight of the CCTV you do have. At this stage, it might be relevant, or it might not,' Colin said.

'I'll arrange it,' Del said.

'I believe you found the body, Mr Turnbull?'

'Yes,' Del confirmed.

'Can you talk me through what happened, in your own words?'

'I was checking that everyone was clear on what they were doing today,' Del said. He was talking calmly, though the way he was clicking the button on his ballpoint pen betrayed his agitation. 'Some of the team were in the field, checking the condition of the vines and assessing the grapes; others were bottling, so we'll have the tanks clear before harvest, ready for the new crop. Nick – the boss – was out with a client. Gaby wasn't around; she works on the Rosa Wines fields, and she normally has a cup of tea with Ashley in his studio before she starts work in the mornings.'

It sounded as if Gaby was very close to her middle brother, perhaps more so than to her oldest sibling, Colin thought.

'I assumed Nathan was in the office, reviewing the latest lab analyses. But when I came back from seeing the staff, put the kettle on and went to see if Nathan wanted a mug of tea, he wasn't there,' Del said. 'So I wondered if he might be in with the fermentation tanks, taking samples. As soon as I saw the ladder lying across the floor, I knew something was wrong. It should either have been up against the platform by the top of the tanks, or put away on the rack by the wall. We don't leave things lying around where they can cause an accident.' His face twisted in recognition that an accident had happened anyway. 'I called his name, but there was no answer. That's when I thought maybe he'd fallen into a tank and was in trouble.' He dragged in a breath. 'I put the ladder back up against the platform so I could check the open tanks, and he was floating face-down in the third one. I went into the bottling area to get help, and Harry came with me to help get a rope round Nathan and pull him out of the tank. We lowered him down to the floor. Nathan wasn't breathing and he didn't have a pulse. Harry called the ambulance and we tried giving Nathan mouth to mouth, but I knew it wouldn't work.'

Colin made rapid notes. 'Is it normal for someone to take samples on their own?'

'Yes,' Del said. 'It's an easy job. You drop the dipper in on the chain so it goes to the middle of the tank, then pull the dipper up and fill the sample bottle.'

'I'm sure I've read about people drowning in wine before – something to do with gases, I think,' Colin mused.

Del nodded. 'There've been a few cases over the years. During fermentation, carbon dioxide is released from the grapes and it depletes the oxygen in the tank. Anyone who's worked in the business knows better than to stick their head over a tank and take a deep breath, because they'll probably be overcome by fumes. Nathan has – *had*,' he corrected himself, 'been working here with his dad for years. He was experienced enough to know what he was doing.' He shook his head. 'The only thing I can think of is maybe he was distracted about something and not concentrating on what he should've been doing.'

'What about the ladder?' Colin asked.

Del shook his head. 'I don't know. The only thing I can think of is that he leaned over the tank, was overcome by the fumes, and when he fell in, he knocked the ladder away from the tank and it fell across the floor.'

'And nobody heard a large metal ladder crash onto a concrete floor?' Colin checked.

'The team in the bottling plant like working with the radio on,' Del said. 'Let's just say they have it up loud enough to cover machinery noise. They wouldn't have heard a thing. That's why I went into the plant to get help – I knew it was pointless yelling, because nobody would hear me.'

'What about you? You didn't hear anything?' Colin asked.

'No. I don't know when he fell into the tank. If it happened when I was in the fields, I would've been too far away to hear. As I said, it's too noisy in the bottling plant to hear anything else,' Del said.

Which all made a kind of sense, Colin thought. This could be a straightforward industrial accident.

But.

Nowadays, employers paid a great deal of attention to health and safety – if for no other reason than to avoid being sued over an industrial accident. Nathan's family owned the winery, so they'd hardly sue themselves; but surely they'd still think about procedures to protect their workers? And there was still the question over the missing brother and the possible blood on the floor of the studio.

'Were you aware of any tensions between Nathan and anyone else at the vineyard?' Colin asked.

Del blew out a breath. 'Well, yes – but there are tensions in any workplace. I'm sure you find the same in your job. It's very rare for someone to get on with absolutely every other person they work with.' He frowned. 'This was an accident, though. Who'd want to kill Nathan?'

'Can you think of anyone?'

Del shook his head emphatically. 'Of course not.'

'I believe there were some tensions between Nathan and his sister,' Colin said quietly.

Del sighed. 'Well, yeah – though that's the boss's fault. But you can't possibly think Gaby would try to kill him. Nathan is – *was*,' he corrected himself, 'built like a rugby player. No way could she have pushed him in. She wouldn't even have been able to move the ladder with him at the top.'

'You said the tension was Nick's fault,' Colin said, keeping his tone light. 'Can you explain what you meant?'

Del looked awkward. 'It doesn't feel right, gossiping about my boss.'

'You're not gossiping. You're helping the police with enquiries, and I'm trying to establish whether Nathan's death really was an accident, or if someone might've had a motive to make sure Nathan fell in that vat,' Colin said.

The production manager was silent for a while, as if weighing up what to say. Finally, he nodded. 'It all goes back to when Rosemary Edwards, Nick's mum, set up the vineyard. It was just after Terence, his dad, died, in the mid-1990s. I guess she started the vineyard to keep herself busy and help herself get over losing him; I mean, English wine wasn't that much of a thing, back then, not like it is now. Diana – that's the children's mum – worked with her. It's not often you get mother-in-law and daughter-in-law getting on well, but them two always did.' He gave a wry huff of laughter. 'I sometimes think Rosemary liked Diana more than she liked her own son. Nick was a bit of a chip off the old block.' He wrinkled his nose. 'Let's just say he had an eye for the ladies. Diana divorced him over it, in the end, and Nick wasn't happy that his mum let Diana keep her job here. That's when he set up Willow Farm Wines, to prove to his mum that he could make wines just as good as she and Diana did.'

Colin stayed silent, giving Del space to talk.

'Nathan would've been about fifteen at the time. Nick had been training him up to join the family firm when he left school, the following year,' Del said. 'Nick had to get rid of the dairy herd when foot and mouth hit in 2001, and he never went back to farming cattle. The farm had been producing wheat, barley and oilseed rape, but then Nick got a bee in his bonnet about the vineyard and decided to turn some of the barley fields over to vines. When Nathan left school, he worked on the arable side, but Nick brought him in on the vineyard after Rosemary died. Everyone thought Rosemary was going to leave her vineyard to Gaby, but...' He spread his hands. 'Maybe she thought it would cause too much aggro with Nick if she did that, so she left it to him instead. He had to wait for probate to be settled, but as soon as that was sorted and Gaby was back home from uni, Nick reorganised everything so Diana didn't have a job anymore.'

Which sounded very much like constructive dismissal, to Colin. Had Nick relied on his ex-wife going quietly because she wouldn't want to make things difficult with the children?

'The reorganisation meant Nick was in charge of Rosa Wines as well as Willow Farm. For the last four years, Gaby's had to answer to him for everything, and she's had to fight her case to keep making wine the way her gran taught her, instead of letting her dad use the grapes for Willow Farm's produce.' Del wrinkled his nose. 'It's been hard for her, but that girl really does know what she's doing. She's a born winemaker.'

'With Nick being in charge, didn't it cause tension between father and daughter rather than between brother and sister?' Colin asked.

'Yes,' Del agreed. 'Though Nick backed off a bit when she won that award, last year. We thought everything was going to settle down. But he's been talking recently about retiring, and last month he put Nathan in charge of Willow Farm Wines. Nathan's made it very clear he plans to integrate Rosa into Willow Farm. He was going to stop the move to organic, and Rosa wouldn't be an artisanal producer anymore. The label would die out.'

Now Colin understood what the problem was.

'If Nathan wasn't around,' he said quietly, 'would Nick have put Gaby in charge of Rosa?'

'You'll have to ask him,' Del said. 'I can't speak for the boss.'

Where did Del's loyalty lie? Colin wondered. With Nick or with Gaby?

'Did anyone else have issues with Nathan?' he asked.

'His ex and her new partner,' Del admitted. 'I don't think Nathan ever forgave Kelly for divorcing him.'

Another divorce, Colin thought. 'Why did she divorce him?'

Del winced. 'He was seeing someone else. And he was

furious when the judge gave her custody of the girls. But she hardly ever comes to the farm. He picks them up from hers and drops them off there. Though, even if she had been here, there's no way she would've been able to push him into the tank.'

'Can you think of anyone who clashed with Nathan who would also have been strong enough to move the ladder?' Colin asked.

'No.'

Colin wasn't sure that Del was being entirely honest with him, but at the moment this wasn't a useful line of enquiry. 'What can you tell me about Ashley Edwards?' he asked instead. 'Does he work in the family business?'

Del shook his head. 'He's an artist. Sensitive,' he said. 'If you ask me, he would've been better off being brought up by Diana rather than Nick.'

'Nick brought the children up?' Colin asked, surprised.

'Nick brought the boys up,' Del confirmed. 'Gaby stayed with her mum. Diana wanted her boys as well, but Nick's lawyer made sure he got custody of them.'

Interesting, Colin thought. Another possible reason for tension between Gaby and Nick – and between Gaby and her brothers. Had Gaby felt that their father had favoured his sons, or had her brothers felt jealous that she'd had their mother's undivided attention?

'And Ashley has a studio here?' he asked.

'Nick converted one of the barns for him,' Del said. 'Like I said, Gaby usually calls in to see Ash before she comes to the office and has a cup of tea with him, but today she had the photo shoot so she said she came straight here.'

'She's close to Ashley, then?' Colin checked.

Del nodded. 'She's the one who talked Nick into letting Ashley have the studio. He... Well, that's not relevant.'

'It might be,' Colin said. 'Remember, you're not gossiping.

You're helping the police build a picture of what's happened, and so far the evidence seems to suggest that Ashley's missing.'

'Ashley often goes missing, though. He tends to take himself off when things get too much for him,' Del said. 'Like I said earlier, he's sensitive. Nick doesn't have a lot of patience with him, and neither does Nathan.'

Sensitive. Often went missing. Mental health issues? Colin made a note. 'Do you know where he usually goes?'

'I think he stays with friends. Which could be anywhere,' Del said. 'Gaby would know where he's most likely to go. To be fair, he usually leaves her or their mum a message when he takes off. He doesn't just off and let them worry.'

Colin added Diana Edwards to the list of people he wanted to talk to.

'Has he had the studio for long?'

'Since he left art school,' Del said.

'When was that?' Colin asked.

Del narrowed his eyes, clearly thinking about it. 'About eight years ago, I think.' He wrinkled his nose. 'Ash is happy when he's doing his art stuff.'

'What kind of artwork does he do?' Colin asked.

'Painting and sculpture.' Del grimaced. 'To be honest, quite a bit of it gives me the creeps. There's a lot of stuff with hands. But they're... well, they're not normal hands. They're *weird*. You'll see for yourself when you go to the studio. And it's a shame, because he can draw so beautifully when he wants to. Gaby got him to do the Rosa Wines logo and it's lovely – a rose that when you look at it, is actually a letter R. It's clever.'

Del obviously had traditional tastes in art, Colin thought, and it sounded as if Ashley Edwards's work was quite avant-garde. 'Did Ashley get on well with Nathan?'

'They're very different people. Nathan didn't have patience with him, the way Gaby does,' Del said.

A diplomatic way of saying no. And Colin noted that

Nathan seemed to have a lot in common with his father: lack of patience with Ashley, being divorced for infidelity, resenting not having custody of his daughters. 'Is Ashley particularly strong?' Colin enquired. Didn't sculptors have to haul blocks of stone about?

'I couldn't tell you. He doesn't do anything on the farm or the vineyard,' Del said. 'Not that I'm saying he's lazy. He works all hours in his studio. He just isn't part of the business.'

'Thank you,' Colin said, wrapping up the conversation. 'That's been really helpful.'

He asked similar questions of Harry, who confirmed everything Del said and added a bit more. 'Ashley had a breakdown when he was in sixth form. He had to resit his exams, but he managed to get into an art school in London. We all think he would've been better off staying there, but he came back and had another breakdown. It's why Gaby goes to check on him every morning.' He sighed. 'Except *this* morning she didn't.'

'You went into the studio? It wasn't locked?' Colin checked.

'It wasn't locked,' Harry confirmed. 'Sorry. You'll have my fingerprints on the door handle and what have you. I didn't think about it at the time. When I knocked and called his name and he didn't answer, I assumed he'd got headphones on or something and hadn't heard me. I tried the door and it wasn't locked, so I went in. The studio was even messier than usual, as if there had been some kind of fight. A few things were smashed. I mean, Ash isn't very good at keeping stuff tidy, but he's careful with his art. And there was a pool of what looked like blood in the middle of the room, though it *might* be red paint,' he added. 'I could smell chemicals and wine – Gaby reckons Ash uses wine as paint, sometimes – but it... I dunno. Something about it didn't feel right.'

'We'll check it out,' Colin said. 'I assume Ashley wasn't there?'

'I checked the other rooms, and he definitely wasn't there,' Harry said.

One man drowned in wine; another who'd disappeared and left behind what looked like a pool of blood. Were they separate cases, Colin wondered, or was there a connection, other than the two potential victims being brothers?

FOUR

'That's Mum,' Gaby said as a battered and slightly muddy four-by-four parked next to Colin's car. She climbed out of Georgina's car and waved both hands frantically. 'Mum!'

The woman who came over to them was an older version of Gaby, Georgina thought: blonde, pretty and slender. She wore absolutely no make-up, her face was ashen, and her eyes were reddened, betraying the fact she'd been crying, though she was clearly trying to hold it together and be a support for her daughter.

'Gaby.' Diana wrapped her arms round Gaby and held her tight. 'I'm here, darling. It's going to be all right.' Though her mouth looked pinched, as if she didn't believe a word she was saying. How could things possibly be all right, with one of her sons dead and the other missing?

'Mum, this is Georgina, Sybbie and Cesca,' Gaby said. 'They've been looking after me.'

'Thank you,' Diana said. She sounded like she was operating on autopilot. Just as Georgina thought she'd be, herself, if she'd heard such terrible news about her own children.

'It was the least we could do,' Georgina said. 'I'm Georgina

Drake, the photographer from *Veritas* magazine. Cesca and Sybbie are Gaby's customers.'

'I apologise for not knowing who you are,' Diana said to Cesca and Sybbie, 'but you clearly started buying from us after my time at Rosa Wines.'

'I'm so sorry for your loss,' Georgina said.

'Thank you.' Diana looked at Gaby. 'Has Ash turned up yet?'

Gaby shook her head.

Diana gave a tight nod, as if she was used to this and had a plan for tracking him down. 'OK. We'll have to start thinking about where he might have gone. What about Nathan? Can I see him?'

'The police are keeping people out for now, Mum,' Gaby said gently. 'They're investigating.'

Diana raked a hand through her hair. 'Of course they need to look at things, first.' She shook her head. 'Sorry. I'm all over the place.'

'That's understandable,' Sybbie said. 'Anyone would be, in your shoes.'

Diana grimaced. 'I assume Nick still isn't back from visiting his' – she paused, almost as if she were making air-quotes – '*customer?*'

Clearly Diana didn't think Nick was visiting a client.

'No,' Georgina said. 'Del did say he'd look out for Gaby when...' She stopped, realising that what she was about to say was far from tactful.

'When my ex comes back to find me darkening his doorstep?' Diana rolled her eyes. 'Del's right. He probably *will* kick off. But that's Nick for you. It's why I told Shaun to stay put. He wanted to come with me, to check on Gaby.'

'Shaun?' Georgina asked.

'We... work together,' Diana said carefully.

Gaby had said that her mum no longer worked here. It

sounded as if Diana had gone to work with a competitor, who Georgina assumed was Shaun. But the fact that Shaun had wanted to come with her and the expression on Diana's face hinted that it wasn't just a business relationship. 'Got you,' Georgina said.

'Do you know what happened?' Diana asked.

'No. DI Colin Bradshaw and his team are talking to Del and the team here, to establish what happened,' Georgina said. 'For the sake of transparency, Colin's my partner.'

'He can be a bit stuffy,' Sybbie added, 'but his heart's in the right place. He'll be sensitive.'

'That's good to know,' Diana said.

'And we found a skeleton in the fields, Mum,' Gaby said. 'At the edge of the pond.'

'A *skeleton*?' Diana looked shocked. 'Whose?'

'I don't know,' Gaby said.

'Colin's going to speak to Rowena, the finds liaison officer,' Georgina said. 'She'll be able to tell us a bit more. If the skeleton's more than fifty years old, the police will class it as "bones of antiquity" and won't need to investigate.' She paused. 'I realise this isn't the best time to ask, and I apologise for that, but do you know much about the people who farmed the land before your mother-in-law planted the vines?'

'Actually,' Diana said, 'I could do with something to distract me. Because if I let myself think about what happened to Nathan, I'm going to fall apart. Which isn't going to help anyone.' She shuddered. 'The farm's been in Nick's family for generations. Ernest and Ivy – Nick's grandparents – farmed here before handing over to Terence and Rosemary, who then handed over to Nick and me,' she added. 'I knew Ivy when she was a very old lady, though Ernest died years before I met Nick.'

Had Percy been a farmhand here, perhaps? Georgina wondered. But now wasn't the right time to ask. Georgina was aware that she'd probably already overstepped the boundaries. 'Let me introduce you to Colin and ask if he'll let you see Nathan,' she said instead.

'We'll stay here with Bert,' Sybbie said.

'Bert. That's a good name for a spaniel,' Diana said, making a brief fuss of Bert. 'You look like a bit like my Monty, though he's an old boy, now. Fourteen, and he still skips about like a puppy when the mood takes him.'

Georgina realised that she'd got the wrong end of the stick when Gaby had talked about Monty being their former mascot. Obviously Gaby had meant that he wasn't part of Rosa Wines anymore, not that he'd died. 'The joy of the zoomies,' Georgina said, smiling back. 'Even after a long walk.'

'I loved it when Monty used to leap down the field like a gazelle,' Diana said. 'It doesn't happen very often, now.'

Having bonded with Diana over the dog, Georgina went with her and Gaby through to the courtyard behind the offices. Colin was talking to Larissa, and Georgina went over to introduce Diana to him.

'I'm sorry for your loss, Mrs Edwards,' Colin said.

'Thank you. When can I see Nathan?' Diana asked.

'Soon,' Colin said. 'Could we perhaps have an informal chat, first?'

'All right,' Diana said. 'Though if Nick comes back any time soon, you need to be aware that he might not take very kindly to me being here.'

'Understood,' Colin said. 'Though he doesn't have the legal right to harass you. You're here on police business.'

'Thank you,' Diana said. 'Gaby, can we use the office?'

'Of course you can, Mum,' Gaby said.

'I'd like a chat with you afterwards, Miss Edwards, if you wouldn't mind,' Colin said.

'That's fine,' Gaby said. 'Are we allowed to use the office kitchen?'

'Perhaps not just yet,' Colin said. 'I'm sorry.'

Gaby's eyes widened as she made the connection. 'Are you saying Nathan's death wasn't an accident?' she asked, sounding shocked and as if it hadn't occurred to her that it could be anything else.

'Right now,' Colin said, 'we're treating it as a work-related incident. Because he died unexpectedly, the police were called out first. I'm liaising with Health and Safety, but we need to find out what actually happened to your brother. I promise I'll tell you as soon as I have something to say.'

Gaby's shoulders drooped, but she nodded.

'Please take a seat, Mrs Edwards,' Colin said when they went through to the office.

'Diana will do, Inspector,' she said. 'I went back to my maiden name after the divorce. It's Murray.'

Colin gave her a nod of acknowledgement. When she sat behind the desk, he sat in the chair Del had used and opened his notebook.

'Despite what you said to Gaby, you obviously don't think Nathan's death was an accident,' Diana said.

'Not necessarily. Any industrial accident needs investigating,' Colin said. 'But I was hoping you could fill in some background for me.'

'I... Sure.' She shook her head, as if to clear it. 'Sorry. I can't quite get my head round this. Nathan's dead and Ash is missing. I just...' She scrubbed the back of her hand across her eyes, obviously dashing away tears. 'I can't believe I'll never speak to Nathan again,' she said, her voice cracking. 'And what if something bad's happened to Ash?'

'We're trying to find him,' Colin said. 'And whatever you tell me will help build a picture.'

'I...' She squared her shoulders. 'OK. Background, you said.

I assume someone's already explained to you that I used to work with Rosemary, Gaby's gran – Nick's mum,' Diana said.

'Yes, but if you'd like to tell me in your own words,' Colin said.

'Rosemary set up Rosa Wines not long after Terence died – that was the same year Ashley was born. I'd worked in marketing before I had the boys, and she suggested that I could work with her – my hours would be flexible and fit round the children. Nick was in charge of the farm, and things were going OK until the dairy herd was hit by foot and mouth in 2001. Things were a bit tricky financially, after that, and he didn't replace the herd. But he kept going on the arable side, and Rosemary was doing well with the wine.'

It confirmed everything Colin had already been told so far, and the corroboration was useful. 'But you're no longer part of Rosa Wines?' he checked.

'No. I divorced Nick in 2005, when Gaby was five, Ash was ten and Nathan was fifteen.' She blew out a breath. 'Nick was a serial adulterer, and I'd had enough of it. We had a fight over custody of the kids, but he could afford better lawyers than mine, and the judge let him have the boys.'

'Right,' Colin said, making notes.

'Rosemary kept me on at Rosa Wines, and she let me and Gaby stay in one of the farm cottages. I hoped we could keep it civil for the children's sake, but Nick's not an easy man.' She sighed. 'That's when he decided to set up Willow Farm Wines.' She wrinkled her nose. 'Maybe I'm being unfair to him, and he'd looked at the figures and thought a vineyard would be more profitable than the arable farming.'

'But?' Colin prompted.

'I think he wanted to prove to himself that he could make more money out of his vineyard than Rosemary and I could out of Rosa Wines,' she said drily. 'He took a different approach – more commercial. Which isn't me being snobby about it: as a winemaker, you decide on your market and you use the best production method to suit that market's needs. Rosa Wines doesn't have the same market as Willow Farm.'

'How do the children fit into the business?' Colin asked.

'Gaby came to work with Rosemary and me. Ash was always a dreamer, so he does his own thing with his art. Nathan left school as soon as he could to work at Willow Farm – Nick was spitting feathers that the school leaving age changed and Nathan had to stay on for another year,' Diana said. 'Nathan originally focused on the arable side, but when Rosemary died and left Rosa Wines to Nick, Nick brought Nathan over to the vineyard side.' She shook her head. 'You more or less said to Gaby that you don't think it was an accident. I agree. I don't understand how Nathan could've drowned in the fermentation tank. He's not stupid, and he wouldn't have been reckless enough to take samples without someone knowing where he was – if he didn't come back with the samples in a few minutes, someone would go and check on him,' Diana said. 'Just in case he'd been affected by the carbon dioxide.'

Colin nodded. 'Del explained about the carbon dioxide.' He paused. 'I know this isn't a very nice question, but was Nathan on bad terms with anyone?'

Diana wrinkled her nose. 'I don't want to throw his ex under a bus. Kelly's a nice woman.' She frowned. 'But I'm afraid my son followed in his father's footsteps – and his grandfather's, come to that – and he couldn't keep his trousers zipped. She divorced him a couple of years ago and got custody of the girls, and Nathan wasn't happy about it. He was even less happy when she and Miles – her new partner – got engaged last summer. But she's always insisted that they try to be civil for the girls' sakes, and to give them both credit, they've done a much better job of it than Nick and I did.'

'What about Miles?'

'He stays out of Nathan's way,' Diana said. 'Though I'm pretty sure he'd stand up for Kelly if Nathan tried to bully her.'

'Did Nathan have any clashes with anyone at work?' Colin asked.

'I wouldn't know. I don't work here anymore,' Diana said quietly. 'Nick reorganised Rosa Wines when he inherited it and took great pleasure in making me redundant, as well as giving me notice to leave the cottage. I probably could've taken him to tribunal for constructive dismissal, and I really thought about doing it, to teach him he can't just trample over people, but then I thought he'd probably take it out on Gaby. For her sake, I left without making a fuss. He's not happy that I'm working with a competitor now.' She rolled her eyes. 'Though he only has himself to blame for that one. If he hadn't forced me out, I wouldn't be working elsewhere. It'd be stupid to let thirty years of experience go down the drain.'

Colin waited, giving her the chance to elaborate in the same way that Del had. And Diana's response was very interesting indeed.

'Rosemary was going to leave Rosa Wines to Gaby,' Diana said. 'But she died before she could sign the will.'

'I'm sorry,' Colin said.

Diana sighed. 'So am I. Not just because I lost a good friend – Rosemary was a brilliant mother-in-law and grandmother. She'd be horrified by what Nathan planned. Nathan wants – *wanted*,' she corrected herself with a gulp, 'to integrate Rosa Wines into Willow Farm Wines, and get rid of the organic side. If that happens, the Rosa label will be gone for good. Hopefully Gaby will be able to persuade her father otherwise.'

'Was Nathan in charge of both wineries?'

'Not *quite*. Nick put Nathan in charge of Willow Farm, last month. The implication was that Rosa would be next,' Diana said. 'If Nathan had sprayed those fields, revoking the organic status, then Gaby would've left here and come to work with me and Shaun.'

'So there was tension between Gaby and Nathan?' Colin already knew that, but he was interested in seeing their mother's viewpoint.

'Nathan is his father's mini-me. He wants his own way, all the time.' Diana's lips tightened. 'I wish I'd had a better lawyer when I divorced Nick. If the boys had grown up with me instead of him, things might've been very different. Even though I lived on the estate, I didn't have any say in their upbringing – Nick followed the custody agreement to the letter of the law.' She shook her head. 'Don't get me wrong. I loved Nathan, but I didn't always like him. He gave Ash quite a hard time when they were teenagers. I did try talking to Nick and asking him to be a bit firmer with Nathan, but he wouldn't have it. And there was a fine line to walk.'

'How do you mean?' Colin asked.

'This stays with you?' she checked. 'Because it's not something I want shared with Nick, for Ashley's sake.'

'I'll be as tactful as I can,' Colin said, 'but if it's something material to what happened to Nathan, I can't promise to keep it from the court.'

Diana sighed heavily. 'This is personal. And you need to understand that Nick has some funny ideas about – well, what makes a man a *man*.' She rolled her eyes.

'I'll do my best,' Colin said.

'Nick had a very good housekeeper when the boys were young,' Diana said quietly. 'She told me confidentially that Ash wet the bed, most nights. I tried getting Ash to talk to me about it – I wondered if it was a reaction to the divorce, because he's always been sensitive, and I felt guilty about it – but he just said that Nathan could be mean to him. He wouldn't elaborate. Rita, the housekeeper, washed the bedding without a fuss and made sure Nick didn't know. She realised Nick would've gone on and on about how Ash needed to be a man instead of a bedwetter, and it would only have made things worse.'

'Got you,' Colin said, feeling sorry for the child, caught between two warring parents and with an older brother who bullied him.

Diana bit her lip. 'Sometimes I wonder if I should've just put up with Nick's behaviour, for the kids' sake. Or fought harder to get custody of Ash, at least.' A tear leaked from her eye and she brushed it away. 'The worst was when Ash was sixteen and had a breakdown. But the treatment seemed to help. He got through his A levels and went to art school in London, and things were easier. Nathan met Kelly, and he seemed to get on better with everyone after that. I thought things had finally turned around. After they married and the girls were born, I hoped that love and becoming a dad had changed him.' She shook her head sadly. 'But Nathan was just like Nick. It wasn't enough for him.'

Again, Colin waited, giving her the chance to talk.

'I'm sorry. All this stuff about my family… it's just me wittering on. I can't believe my boy's dead. And Ash is missing, so he's obviously having an episode. I've tried calling him, but there's no answer.'

'Episode?' Colin prompted gently.

'Every so often, things get too much for him and he goes off grid for a bit,' Diana said. 'Gaby's good with him. She checks in on him every day, and makes him feel like he matters. She can normally tell if he's building up to a meltdown and lets me know, but she hasn't said anything to me, this time. This has come out of nowhere.' She raked a hand through her hair. 'Right now I need to be strong for my daughter, but it feels as if I've forgotten how to put one foot in front of the other.'

One drowned man, one missing man, and what looked like a potential scene of a fight, with smashed things and blood. The studio was the next thing he needed to look at, Colin decided.

. . .

'Georgie, I'll need a witness statement from you, if you don't mind,' Mo said.

'Of course,' Georgina said. 'I know the drill. Sybbie and Cesca are in my car. Do you want me to get them to come and see you when you're done with me?'

'Yes, please,' he said gratefully.

She took him through what had happened that morning and signed her statement; just as she and Mo were walking back into the courtyard, she became aware of a lot of shouting.

'Excuse me, Georgie. I'd better sort this,' Mo said, and strode quickly over to the man who was gesticulating wildly.

'What the hell is going on here?' the man demanded.

Gaby was white-faced. 'Dad. I *called* you. I left you loads of messages, but you didn't ring me back.'

'My phone's out of charge,' he snarled at her. 'And you're not in charge of me, so don't you—'

'Dad, will you just stop and listen?' she cut in urgently. 'Nathan's *dead*!'

'What?' Nick stiffened. 'How? He can't be.'

'That's why I was calling you,' Gaby said. 'He fell into one of the vats and drowned.'

'Mr Edwards, I'm Detective Sergeant Mo Tesfaye,' Mo said. 'We were called here earlier.'

'My son.' Nick shook his head as if to clear it, obviously shocked by the news. 'He can't be dead.'

'I'm very sorry,' Mo said. 'The paramedics were unable to revive him.'

'He can't be dead,' Nick said again. He started at Gaby. 'How could you let this happen?'

'It wasn't her fault, Nick,' Del interjected. 'It was a horrible, unlucky accident.'

'My *son*,' Nick began through gritted teeth.

'Mr Edwards,' Mo cut in, 'Detective Inspector Bradshaw is talking to Gaby's moth—'

Frantically Gaby shook her head at him to warn him not to say anything, but it was too late.

'Gaby's *what*?' Nick glared at him. 'Are you telling me that woman's here?' He turned on Gaby again. 'You called her?'

'It was my idea,' Del cut in swiftly. 'Nathan was her boy, too, Nick.'

'She walked out on us,' Nick said, his tone bitter and sharp. 'As for you, you're on a warning. One more step out of line, and you're out.'

'Dad, that's not f—' Gaby began.

'Where are they?' Nick demanded, ignoring his daughter's protest.

'The office,' Gaby said. 'But you can't—'

It was too late. Nick was already stomping towards the office, and flung the door open so hard that it banged against the wall.

'What the hell is going on in my vineyard?' A man Colin judged to be maybe ten years older than himself stormed into the office. 'And why are *you* here, when you know you're not welcome?' He jabbed his finger at Diana, a sneer on his face.

'Nicholas Edwards, I presume,' Colin said quietly, standing up.

The other man turned towards him. 'What's it to you? As for you,' he said, glaring at Diana, '*get* out.'

Colin knew that the ambulance was still outside, and someone – Gaby, Del or one of his own team – would have told Nick what had happened to Nathan. 'Ms Murray is currently helping me with our enquiries into your son's death,' he said. 'I'm Detective Inspector Bradshaw.'

Nick scoffed. 'You're not needed here. It seems my son was

careless and fell into the wine. He drowned. End of story. And *you*,' he said, turning to Diana, 'are not wanted here. At all.'

She'd predicted her ex's reaction very accurately, Colin thought. 'Naturally you're upset about your son's death, Mr Edwards, and I offer my condolences,' he said, 'but I would advise you very seriously to calm down.'

'Or what?' Nick challenged.

Colin sighed inwardly. If this was the 'old block' everyone seemed to say Nathan was a chip off, he could quite understand why Nathan had clashed with people. 'Or I'll arrest you for wilful obstruction of an investigation.'

'You can't do that.' Nick sneered at him. 'You're not investigating. No crime's been committed.'

'An unexpected death at work is either an industrial accident or a potential homicide, both of which – by law – need police investigation,' Colin said, keeping his voice even. Why was Nick so insistent that Nathan's death was an accident? Did he have something to hide? 'I'll need to interview you, when I've finished with Ms Murray.'

'She isn't wanted here, either. I told Del he's on a warning for letting her in here,' Nick snarled.

'Your daughter,' Colin said quietly, 'needs a bit of parental support. She's just lost one brother, and her other brother is missing.'

Nick scoffed. 'Ashley's a waste of space. I don't know why I let him have that barn when I could've rented it out and made some money out of the place. I was soft in the head, letting Gaby talk me into it.'

'Mr Edwards, I understand that you're upset,' Colin said. 'Anyone would be, in your shoes.'

'And what would *you* know about it?'

'More than thirty years of experience at my job,' Colin replied, keeping his voice calmer and more patient than he actually felt. Maybe anger was the only thing stopping Nick

Edwards from collapsing in a heap; regardless, snapping back at him wouldn't be helpful. 'If you could wait outside, please, I'll come and see you when I've finished interviewing Ms Murray.'

'This is *my* office,' Nick said, his eyes narrowing. '*I* say who stays and who goes.'

'In your absence, Mr Edwards, your production manager suggested that this would be a suitable place for conducting interviews,' Colin said. Given that Nick had raised the subject of money, maybe that was the way to get through to him. 'However, if you prefer, we can arrange transport for your entire workforce – and yourself – to the station, where we can continue the interviews. And then we'll transport everyone back when we've finished.'

'That's outrageous. You can't just hijack my staff and keep them off work for God knows how long! I have a business to run,' Nick said, his face flushing dangerously red.

'And I have a legal duty to fulfil. Should you continue obstructing that duty, then I will arrest you. Or we can all save a lot of time by you letting me do my job,' Colin said. Hopefully Nick would accept the offer Colin was about to make, to let him save face. 'If you'd prefer me to conduct interviews in another part of the building rather than your office, that's fine. Perhaps you can direct me there.'

'I – you...' Nick swore loudly. 'Oh, do what you bloody want.'

'Thank you. I'll continue my interview here,' Colin said. 'Please keep yourself available, Mr Edwards. I'll talk to you next.'

Nick glared at him, and stomped off.

'Well, that told him.' Diana gave a mirthless laugh. 'You're the first person in forever to stand up to him.'

'I'm simply doing my job,' Colin said. 'Which means not taking sides. And I'm sure you're anxious to get back to Gaby, so shall we continue? We were talking about Ashley. Did he clash with Nathan?'

'He avoided Nathan, because he didn't like fighting,' Diana said.

'I'm sorry to ask this, but is that the case even when he's not well?' Colin asked.

'Even then,' Diana confirmed. 'Ash wouldn't hurt a fly. He made pets of the calves, and he's refused to eat meat since he was seven years old.'

'Do you have any idea where he might be?'

Diana shook her head. 'He hasn't answered his phone or messaged me, and he always tells me if he's leaving the farm. Gaby and I were going to start ringing his friends in Norwich, in case he's with them, and if they don't know anything, then we'll try his London friends.'

'Thank you, Ms Murray,' Colin said formally. 'I'll write up what you've told me, and then if you could check it, ask me to make any corrections and then sign it, I'll escort you back to Gaby.'

'I hope Nick's not shouting at her for asking me to come here. He was always a bit difficult, but he's got worse with age,' Diana said. 'If he'd been that much of a bully when we first got together, I would never have married him.' She sighed. 'His dad was a bit that way, too, but his mum was so nice. I really hoped Nick would take after her instead of Terence.'

There was nothing Colin could say to that. 'If you'll excuse me, Ms Murray, I'll sort out your statement,' he said.

'One last thing,' she said. 'This client he went to see. He's not going to want to admit it, but she's not a client.'

Colin blinked in surprised. 'You know who he was visiting?'

'Not the name, but I know the type,' Diana said. 'It's the line he always used on me, until I'd had enough of the affairs and walked out on him.'

'Got you,' Colin said dryly.

When he'd finished writing up the statement and Diana had checked it and signed it, he took her back out to the courtyard. Gaby looked pale but uncowed, and went straight into her mother's arms. Georgina gave him an unobtrusive nod; either she'd picked up some information she'd share with him later, or she was telling him that Nick had calmed down a bit.

It seemed to be the latter, because this time Nick glowered but didn't start shouting at Diana; instead, he went quietly to the office with Colin.

FIVE

'Was Dad very bad?' Gaby asked. 'We tried to stop him bursting in on you, but you know what he's like when he's got a bee in his bonnet.'

'He's been worse,' Diana said drily. 'Are you all right?'

Gaby nodded. 'Del stuck up for me.'

'Thank you, Del,' Diana said. 'And your Colin's very good, Georgina. Calm and unflappable.'

Except where ghosts were concerned, Georgina thought. 'He has his moments,' she said lightly.

'Honestly. All the men in this family are bad-tempered and never listen, with the exception of Ash,' Gaby said. 'I don't remember Grandad Terence, but Ash said he used to be a bit shouty. Dad always shouts first and asks questions later, and Nathan's just as... Well.' She blew out a breath. 'I know you shouldn't speak ill of the dead, but he was a pig to Kelly, at times.' She swallowed hard. 'Oh, God. How are we going to tell the girls that their dad's died?'

'Kelly should be the one to do that,' Diana said. 'With support. I'll go and see her.'

'We'll see her together,' Gaby said. 'And between us we need to ring round Ash's friends to see if he's turned up with one of them.' She bit her lip. 'We need to sort out the skeleton in the pond, too.'

'I might be able to help you with the skeleton,' Georgina said. 'My daughter's an actress; when she's resting, she works for a probate genealogy company. She's taught me how to look things up in records, and I've helped Colin with some cold cases in the past. Once Rowena – she's the finds liaison officer, and also a friend of mine – gives you an idea of how old the skeleton is, if it's classed as bones of antiquity, we'll have a starting point.' A starting point she already had, thanks to Doris, but now wasn't the time or place to discuss that.

'Thank you,' Diana said. 'The obvious place to start is with who worked here over the years and their families. I know Rosemary had some papers about the farm from Nick's grandmother; they might be of some help, but I'm afraid I have no idea where they are.'

'I do. They're in a couple of boxes in my spare room,' Gaby said. 'After Dad sacked Mum and evicted her, I moved out as well. I rented a cottage in the village,' she explained to Georgina. 'I liberated Gran's papers when I moved, because I'd like to write a history of the vineyard in my spare time – not that I've had time to go through the papers yet. All my time's been spent in the vineyard, or working out forecasts and grant applications that stop Dad sacking me permanently and handing everything over to Nathan.'

'Sacking you permanently?' Georgina queried.

'He sacks me at least once a month,' Gaby said, as if it were perfectly normal behaviour. 'Only I ignore him and just carry on with my work, and he's usually changed his mind by the next day. Not that he'll ever say sorry, because that isn't who Dad is. He just pretends nothing happened, and it's easier to go along with him.' She blew out a breath. 'I have no idea what's going to happen now. Only that it's going to be tough.'

'One step at a time, darling,' Diana said, squeezing her shoulders. 'And if your father's difficult, you know you'll always have a home with me. And a job. You can walk away any time you choose.'

'Thanks, Mum. I appreciate the offer, but no. I'm fighting Rosa's corner,' Gaby said. 'What we've been doing here is good for the land and good for the business. I've got the figures to prove it. And I'm *not* letting Gran's name be wiped out just because Dad's throwing a tantrum.'

'That's my girl,' Diana said softly.

Nick Edwards didn't apologise for his outburst of temper – not that Colin expected him to – but at least now he wasn't shouting.

'I never expected this,' he said instead. 'Why didn't Nathan yell for help when he fell in?'

'He might have already been too woozy from the carbon dioxide,' Colin said. 'Or he might have hit his head as he fell and was knocked unconscious. The pathologist will have a better idea of what happened.' He paused. 'I know this will seem insensitive and intrusive, but it's not meant to be. I need to investigate as part of my job. Can I ask you to talk me through your day?'

'I've been out seeing a client,' Nick said shortly.

Colin noticed Nick didn't offer a name. It looked as if Diana's supposition had been right. 'What time did you leave Willow Farm?'

'Early,' Nick said. 'It was a breakfast meeting.'

'Did anyone see you?'

'I have no idea,' Nick said. He looked at Colin. 'Are you accusing me of something?'

'No. I'm trying to establish facts,' Colin said. 'Mr Edwards, I'm simply an officer of the law, doing my job. And I'd like to remind you that I'm neutral.' Even though sometimes it was hard to resist the temptation to take sides.

'What did she tell you about me?' Nick demanded.

'Very little,' Colin said, suppressing a sigh. 'I asked her the same question I'm going to ask you. Was Nathan on bad terms with anyone?'

'Not in the way you mean. You always get workers moaning about the boss,' Nick said. 'People want money for doing nothing.' He rolled his eyes. 'If they do their job properly, there isn't a problem.'

It rather depended on whose viewpoint you were using, Colin thought. 'Had Nathan had difficulties with anyone recently?'

'No.'

'Was there any tension between him and his siblings?'

'Kids always squabble, whether they're toddlers or grownups,' Nick said. 'Look, Nathan's always been about the bottom line. He looks at cutting production costs and maximising profit. Ashley's arty-farty and wafts around, and Nathan doesn't have time or patience with that. Gaby's all holier-than-thou about organic and artisanal methods.' He flapped a dismissive hand. 'If there are any squabbles, they sort themselves out, one way or another.'

It certainly seemed like they had, Colin thought, because Nathan was dead.

'Look, everyone knows the oldest kid is the one who takes over the family business,' Nick said. 'I was going to retire, this year. Travel the world. Nathan was going to take over the farm and the winery.'

'Both Willow Farm and Rosa Wines?' Colin asked.

'That's commercially sensitive information,' Nick said.

Colin's gut instinct said that Gaby wasn't a killer; but he couldn't deny that the prospect of losing the vineyard she'd helped her mother and grandmother build up was a very strong motivation for getting Nathan out of the way. As for the means, she knew about the effect of carbon dioxide and the risk of drowning in fermenting wine. Depending on what the pathologist told him regarding the time of death, Gaby might also have had the opportunity to kill her brother. Had she perhaps worked together with Ashley to do that and make both their lives easier?

'I assume someone's told you that Ashley's missing?' Colin asked.

Nick rolled his eyes. 'He always runs off when he's not getting his own way. He'll be back when it suits him.'

'There's a potential crime scene at his studio,' Colin said.

'How do you mean?' Nick demanded.

'His artwork's been smashed up and there's blood in the studio.'

'Probably him having a temper tantrum,' Nick said.

Which wasn't the impression everyone else had given Colin. Was Ashley highly strung? Or was Nick trying to justify his own temper?

'Oh, wait – let me get the phrase right,' Nick said. 'He's a sensitive, *artistic* soul.' The words were said with a sneer, and Colin felt even more sorry for Ashley. It couldn't be easy, having to deal with such negative attitudes every single day – particularly if you didn't have a thick skin.

'Do you have any idea where Ashley might be?' Colin asked.

Nick shook his head. 'I don't have a clue what goes on in his head. Ask Gaby. They're thick as thieves.'

Colin wasn't sure whether Nick resented the closeness between his younger two children, or whether he was trying to hide something. Did he think Ashley could be involved in Nathan's death, perhaps, and was trying to direct suspicion away from him – even if that directed suspicion towards Gaby?

But that was as much information as Colin was able to extract from him. Nick clearly had no intention of being helpful or volunteering information; every line of questioning was shut down instantly. He might just as well have sat there saying, 'No comment,' to everything.

'Thank you for your time, Mr Edwards. I might have more questions, further into the investigation,' Colin said. 'In the meantime, I'll write up what you told me and ask you to check it, advise me of any changes you need me to make, and sign it.'

And he really hoped that Gaby would be more forthcoming.

Gaby corroborated everything Diana had told Colin. 'Don't get me wrong – I loved my brother. But Nathan could sometimes be a bit difficult. He was Dad's mini-me.' She smiled wryly. 'Luckily the two of them usually saw things the same way. If they'd ever disagreed, I think the rows would've been heard in Australia.' She sighed. 'Mum shielded us from the worst of it, but looking back I'm pretty sure Dad wasn't the best of husbands. Nathan was the same. And they both bullied Ash. If I challenged them, they'd claim they were "only joking" – but it's not funny when someone's always the butt of their jokes. And they'd get really huffy if I asked them to explain exactly how it was funny, saying I was a woman so I didn't have a sense of humour.' She shrugged. 'Still. It didn't bother me when they sniped at me. I'd rather they picked on me than on Ash, because I could cope with it.'

'You're close to Ashley?' Colin asked.

'Yes. I always feel as if he's the baby of the family, not me. Nathan's the oldest – he's ten years older than me – and Ash is in the middle. I'm worried about him disappearing today. He hasn't had a wobble for a couple of years now, and I can normally tell if his mood's dipping. That's when we need to get him some extra help, usually some talking treatment and sometimes a residential stay,' she said. 'He trusts me. And there haven't been any signs of him going haywire. This is completely out of nowhere.'

'Is it possible he could've had a fight with Nathan?' Colin asked.

She blinked. 'You mean, you think he might've pushed Nathan into the tank?'

'At the moment,' Colin said, 'I'm simply investigating possibilities and trying to find out what happened. If they'd had an argument, might that have tipped the balance and made Ashley want to get away from the farm for a bit?'

'Maybe. He was scared of Nathan,' she admitted. 'Though I really don't think he would've pushed Nathan into the vat. Ash is as nonviolent as you can get. But I'm worried about his studio being in a mess. Well, more of a mess than usual,' she qualified. 'Ash lives by the volcano principle – if it's important, it'll come to the surface. I've helped him with his filing, but within a week his place is usually a tip again.'

'He lives in his studio?'

'There's a bedroom, a bathroom and a small kitchen in the barn as well. But, yeah, he lives for his art. And he's good at what he does.' She bit her lip. 'That's why I'm worried. Harry said stuff had been smashed, and Ash never breaks things. He's messy, yes, but he's really careful with his artwork.' She looked at Colin, her eyes haunted. 'There is one thing I've been thinking about, though – this pool of blood Harry said he saw. A few years back, Ash became a bit obsessed with this artist who sculpts his own head out of blood.'

'Sculptures made out of blood?' Colin asked, surprised.

'I think he makes some kind of cast, turns that into a silicon mould, then fills it with his own blood and freezes it. The heads are in special exhibit cases so people can see them, but they stay frozen,' Gaby explained.

Colin waited, giving her the space to fill.

'Ash was doing experiments along the same sort of lines. Not his head – according to him, it takes ten pints of blood to fill a life-size mould of a head, and he would've had to take a bit of blood every so often and freeze it – it would've taken too long.'

Colin frowned. 'Ten pints? But there are only eight pints of blood in the human body.'

'I thought the same, at first. But then Ash pointed out that an actual head has more than just blood in it – there are bones, brains and muscles as well. It made me curious, so I looked up measuring the volume of a human head on the internet.' She shrugged. 'And it seems it really does take ten pints to fill the mould of a head and neck.'

Colin made a note. 'You said he was doing experiments with similar things – not the head. What was he doing?'

'Ash does things with hands. Always the left hand.'

Colin remembered Del describing Ashley's pictures of hands and saying they were weird. 'Is there any particular reason for his interest in hands?'

'I don't know. He's always focused on hands, ever since I can remember,' Gaby said. 'Mum might be able to tell you more about when it started.'

'So he draws hands? Or he sculpts them?' Colin asked.

'Both,' Gaby said. 'After he saw that exhibition, he made a cast of his hand, then made a silicon mould and filled it with...' She winced. 'Well, he's done a few of them now, and I know he kept them in a freezer in the studio. He made some with red wine, because it looks like blood. I think others were a mix of wine and blood. I saw bruises on his arms once and he admitted he'd taken blood samples. Not because he was self-harming or anything like that, but because he was interested in the texture and colours of blood, and whether it changed after it had frozen.

I think he got a microscope from somewhere to check.' Then she leaned forward across the desk and looked Colin in the eye. 'Don't judge him, please. It might not be what you're used to, but Ash is wired a bit differently from the rest of us. I think most artists are.'

'Noted,' Colin said gently. 'It's not my job to judge. I'm looking at facts. Do you think that's what might be the pool of blood Harry saw? The frozen sculptures had melted?'

'I don't know. I kind of hope so, because then it means that Ash hasn't been hurt by someone – not that I can think of anyone who'd want to hurt him. On the other hand, if someone thawed his work, that could've upset him enough to tip him into an episode.' She shook her head in frustration. 'While you were with Dad, Mum and I started calling Ash's friends, to see if he's gone to see any of them or if they've heard from him over the last couple of days. So far, we've left five voicemails and we've managed to talk to one of his friends. They said they hadn't heard from him.'

'OK. Can you take me through your movements today, please?' Colin asked Gaby.

'I was busy in the fields, first thing, checking a spot I'm keeping an eye on and taking samples to check the sugar content of the grapes and see if they had the flavour profile I want. Then I showered at the office and changed, ready for the photo session with Georgina.' She bit her lip. 'I normally drop in on Ash and have a cup of tea with him in the mornings; it's part of our daily routine. If I'd done that today, maybe whatever happened at his studio – well, wouldn't have happened.'

'You can't know that,' he said gently. 'Did you see anyone?'

'Nobody was in the office, at that point,' she said.

'You didn't see Nathan?'

'I tried to stay out of his way, today,' she said. 'Mainly because if he'd remembered it was the photo shoot, he would've picked a fight with me to make sure I was all ruffled before the photographer arrived.' She blew out a breath. 'Now I feel bad. If I'd walked through the tanks this morning, I might've found him in time.'

'The pathologist will tell us more, but my instinct says you would've been too late,' he said. 'Don't blame yourself.'

'Maybe.' She bit her lip. 'And I hate the fact we were at odds and never managed to patch it up before he died.'

'At odds?' Colin asked gently.

'He wanted to take over Rosa Wines and treat it as part of Willow Farm. I wanted to keep to what Gran, Mum and I were doing and turn our fields fully organic. He has – *had*,' she corrected herself, 'a short fuse like Dad, so we argued a lot.' She sighed. 'It was getting to the point where I was just going to give in and walk away. Shaun offered me a job.'

'Shaun?' Colin checked. Diana had already told him, but he was interested in hearing Gaby's take.

'Mum's boss. But I think he's always had a soft spot for her, and they finally got together a couple of years ago. He's a nice guy, and he's good to Mum.'

And that, Colin realised, was the most important thing to Gaby. 'What was the job?' he asked.

'Winemaking. It'd mean working with Mum again and doing what I wanted to do here. I'd love that.' She shook her head. 'But walking away from Rosa Wines means I'd be letting Gran down, and it means leaving Ash. Dad'll see me working with Mum again as a betrayal and he'll take it out on Ash, which isn't fair.'

Which was exactly why Diana had left without a fuss: to stop Nick taking it out on the children, Colin thought.

'So I was just knuckling down, getting my figures sorted and trying to persuade Dad to do the right thing and make Nathan back off.' She closed her eyes for a moment. 'And now my brother's dead. The fight's over. It was a horrible accident, and even though I know I had nothing to do with it, I feel guilty.'

'I know I keep saying it, but we'll know more when we have the pathologist's report,' Colin said. 'Until then, the best thing you can do to help is to take me through your day today.'

'OK.' She swallowed hard. 'Georgina, Sybbie and Cesca were here for ten, as we'd arranged. I took them out to the fields, and talked them through what we're doing at Rosa. Georgina took photographs. Then Sybbie dropped Bert's lead by accident and he disappeared in the direction of the pond. When Georgina went to fetch him, he'd found a skeleton.'

'She's reported that to me,' he said. 'The finds liaison officer will come out to advise the next steps.'

She gave him a brief nod of acknowledgement. 'Then we went back to the office. We were going to call the police about the skeleton and then take some shots in the winery – but then we saw the ambulance. I thought they might be here for Dad, that maybe he'd had a heart attack – I mean, he eats terribly, he smokes and he drinks too much, but if you try and suggest he does something to be a bit healthier, he'll bite your head off – but Del told us it wasn't Dad. He said Nathan was dead and Ash was missing. And then you arrived. And I called Mum.'

'Thank you,' Colin said. 'Since you know your brother's studio well, perhaps I can ask you to come with me and take a look?'

'So I can see if anything's missing or been moved, you mean? Of course.' She looked worried. 'Anything that might help us find him. I want him home safely. If he's got himself in a state, he's vulnerable.'

That was what worried Colin, too. 'I'll have to ask you to put on a paper suit and foot coverings, so we don't compromise any evidence that might help us find him,' he said.

'All right,' Gaby said.

Colin wrote up Gaby's statement and she checked and signed it. Then they made a quick detour by his car to pick up forensic suits and boots, and he sent a message to Mo and Larissa to let them know what they were doing.

Ashley's studio was in a converted barn, tucked away behind the farmhouse. The top of one wall was made of glass, but the windows weren't low enough to see inside. 'It's like weaver's windows at the top, and it gives lots of north light for his work, but because the windows are high, it also means his workspace is private,' Gaby explained. 'Gran and I talked Dad into converting the barn like this for Ash when he came back from art school. And I've persuaded Ash to do some commercial stuff for us that looks good on his portfolio – he redid our labels.'

When they walked inside, she gasped. 'No!'

The place was chaotic, but from Gaby's reaction the state of the room clearly wasn't the norm. There were papers piled up on the desk, the sink was covered with blobs of clay and paint, and there appeared to be some kind of sculpture in progress. Colin had no idea if this was normal for artists, because he didn't really know any, apart from Georgina; her darkroom was meticulously neat because she worked with chemicals and light-sensitive paper that could easily be ruined.

But if you ignored the general untidiness in Ashley's studio, it was clear that *something* out of the ordinary had happened. Pieces of torn-up papers were strewn around the room, and it looked as if some sculptures had been smashed, with chunks of what looked like... were they *fingers*? Bones? Del had described Ashley's artwork as being about strange hands.

And then, in the middle of the room, there was the pool of dark red liquid Harry had noted. Colin could smell wine, and chemicals that were no doubt part of the artist's raw materials; but he could also smell the distinctive coppery tang of blood.

'This – this isn't how Ash does things,' Gaby said. 'I mean – the sink, the messy papers on his desk, *that's* him.' She sounded indulgent rather than judgemental. 'But his work's all smashed up. The hands.' She looked horrified. 'Ash never destroys his work. Even stuff he's not happy with, he files away. And that stuff in the middle of the floor... It smells of wine.' She bit her lip. 'And blood.'

Was it frozen blood from the artwork, the way she'd described him making them? Or fresh blood from Ashley, because someone had hurt him? Colin wrinkled his nose. 'And there's something chemical.'

'Thinners and linseed oil. Standard art supplies,' she said. 'As for the wine, Ash doesn't drink. I think someone must've taken his sculptures out of the freezer and let them melt. Some of them would've been wine-based and some of them a mix of red wine and blood, like I said earlier.' She shook her head. 'And he wouldn't ever have done that. He spent so much time making those pieces. Literally with his own blood. Even if he'd taken them out of the freezer briefly to photograph them or something, he would never have left them out to melt.'

'Who might have done something like that?' Colin asked.

Gaby's eyes widened, as if she'd had some kind of revelation. 'I don't know.'

Colin didn't believe her. 'What about those screwed-up papers?' he asked.

'I don't know.'

That sounded more honest, he thought. Could Nathan perhaps have had a row with Ashley? It sounded as if Nathan had been a bit of a bully; might he have thawed Ashley's artwork? Though the only person who could tell them was Ashley himself.

Colin checked the rooms through the doors leading off the studio; the bedroom, kitchen and bathroom were all untidy but unoccupied, and there were no signs of the havoc wreaked in the studio itself.

'We'll leave this for the forensics team,' he said, and took a couple of snaps of the scene on his phone. 'Let's go back to your family. And I'll need the details of Nathan's wife, please, because we'll need to break the news to her.'

'Mum and I were going to see her together,' Gaby said.

'It's good that you're offering her support, but we can give the whole family support via a family liaison officer,' Colin said gently.

'I guess,' Gaby said.

SIX

Diana wrapped Gaby in the fiercest hug when Colin brought her back to the courtyard. 'Can we see Nathan now, Inspector Bradshaw?' Diana asked.

'I think,' Colin said gently, 'given how he died, it might be better if you wait until after the post-mortem before you see him.'

Diana's eyes filled with tears. 'But...' Her voice tailed off, as if she didn't know what to say.

'I've seen a lot of people in your shoes, over the years,' Colin said. 'I understand how much you want to see him, but please trust me on this. It'd be better to wait just a little longer, rather than seeing him as he is right now. When the pathology team has finished, he'll just look as if he's asleep, and you can spend as much time with him as you need.'

'He's right,' Georgina said, taking Diana's hand and squeezing it briefly. 'My husband died of a heart attack, a couple of years ago. I was the one who found him, and it took a long time before I was able to stop seeing that image. It'd be better to wait.'

Diana's chin wobbled, as if she was fighting back the tears, but eventually she nodded. 'It's the waiting I find hard to handle. I'm used to...'

'... being a human dynamo,' Gaby said, giving her a rueful smile. 'Mum always does six things at once.'

Diana gave an awkward shrug. 'It's just how I am. I like being busy. If we can't see Nathan, then we'll just concentrate on trying to find Ash.'

Keeping busy and concentrating on a task as a way of ignoring grief, Georgina thought. She'd done that enough herself, in the past.

'Are we free to go, Inspector Bradshaw?' Diana asked.

'For now, but I might need to ask you more questions in the future,' Colin said. 'I've been talking to Gaby about Nathan's ex. We'll break the news to her and offer support through the family liaison officer, so you don't have to do the hardest bit. We'll let you know as soon as we've spoken with her.'

'Thank you,' she said. 'I'll be with Gaby at her place while we ring round Ash's friends. I'll let you know if we have any news of him.'

'Thank you,' he said.

'We'll be going, too,' Georgina said. 'Colin, the three of us have given our statements to Mo.'

'Understood,' he said. 'I'll be in touch later.'

'Did you want to take Gran's papers with you, Georgie?' Gaby asked.

'Yes, please, if you don't mind,' Georgina said. 'If I could get you and your mum to talk me through some of the family history, too, that would be useful.'

'Of course,' Diana said. 'Gaby, let's take my car.'

Georgina explained the situation to Sybbie and Francesca when she got back to her own car. 'I'll try to be as quick as I can,' she said.

'Take the time you need,' Sybbie said. 'We'll help.'

'Absolutely,' Francesca said. 'I'm covered at the farm shop.'

'Thanks,' Georgina said, and drove the three of them and Bert into Ashingham.

Gaby's cottage was at the edge of the village, a small flint-and-brick building with a red-tiled roof, roses climbing round the door, and an old-fashioned cottage garden in the front full of lavender, deep blue delphiniums, rose campion and white alyssum.

'What a gorgeous garden,' Sybbie said, looking enraptured.

'Thank you, but I can't take the credit,' Gaby said. 'It's all my next-door neighbour. We help each other out.'

Inside, Sybbie helped Gaby make tea and unwrapped the lemon drizzle cake Francesca had brought with her as a treat after the photo shoot, while Georgina talked to Diana and made notes. Francesca submitted to sitting still, and Bert clearly picked up that Diana needed comfort because he went to sit by her and leaned against her.

'Nick's parents were Rosemary and Terence,' Diana said, 'and Terence's parents were Ernest and Ivy. Ernest died before I met Nick, but I remember Ivy. She was in her eighties when I first met her, and she was tough – she'd grown up a farmer's daughter, so she worked on the land and with the cattle.'

'Early morning milking,' Doris murmured, 'when you'd get up in winter and there would be ice on the inside of the windows.'

'Ivy's brothers were killed in the First World War,' Diana said, 'and I'm sorry, I can't remember their names. Just that there were two of them. Mary, her mum, died in the flu epidemic in 1918, so then it was just Ivy and her dad. His name's on the tip of my tongue.'

'Douglas Cooper,' Gaby said, coming in with a tray of tea and cake. 'Gran said she thinks he never got over losing his wife and sons, and he drank himself to death. Ivy kept the farm going. Ernest was the man Douglas hired to help out, after the war, and he and Ivy fell in love.'

'No, they didn't,' Doris murmured. 'Percy's very clear about that. Ivy wasn't in love with Ernest. She married him, yes, but she didn't love him.'

And how did Percy know that? Georgina wondered. Not that she could ask. Yet.

'Has your family always been at Willow Farm, Gaby?' Francesca asked.

'For well over a hundred years, and probably longer than that,' Gaby said. 'Douglas's parents were Len and Nancy. Gran told me they died in a flu epidemic in the late 1800s. Mary was the daughter of the village doctor – that's how she met Douglas. She was helping her dad get medicine out to people.'

'I knew about the flu epidemic of 1918, but I didn't realise there had been another epidemic before then,' Sybbie said.

'One of my friends is a medical historian,' Gaby said. 'She told me the flu epidemic of 1889 was the first one that spread rapidly round the world – from ships and trains. It wasn't as deadly as the 1918 flu epidemic, but apparently it affected nearly half the world's population.'

'Right,' Georgina said. So far, Gaby hadn't mentioned Percy. But from his reaction to Gaby's comments, it sounded as if he'd known Ivy – perhaps had even been in love with her, himself. Had Ernest been the one who'd hit him and killed him?

But she was getting ahead of herself.

After Gaby had dished out the tea and cake, she smiled. 'I'll just go and dig out Gran's papers,' she said.

'She's a good girl,' Diana said when Gaby had left the room. 'I've been so lucky, having her as a daughter.' She bit her lip. 'I just wish I'd fought Nick a bit harder for Nathan and Ashley. Maybe Nathan wouldn't have been so combative and Ash would have found life easier.'

'Artists often have a sensitive temperament,' Georgina said lightly.

Diana nodded. 'Ash was the worst-affected by the divorce.

That's really why I stayed at the vineyard, to be close to him. Rosemary was sympathetic, and it meant I got to see more of the boys.' She rolled her eyes. 'I knew Nick wasn't happy about his mum letting me keep working with her after the divorce. It's why he set up Willow Farm Wines, a few months later, to be in competition with us and prove he was a better winemaker – even though he wasn't. When his mum died, four years ago, he was delighted to use the excuse of a restructure to get rid of me.'

'You didn't think of taking him to tribunal for constructive dismissal?' Sybbie asked.

'Oh, I more than thought about it. I talked to a solicitor,' Diana said. 'But then I realised that was what he wanted me to do; then he could blame me for the tension and use it as a wedge to get between me and the kids. And I didn't want to make things hard for them again, so I let it go. Though I admit I'd love Gaby to come and work with Shaun and me. She'd fit in really well at Chalk Valley – and if she'd worked for another vineyard, it would have stopped all the tension between her and Nathan.' She sighed. 'On the other hand, Nick would probably have considered her a traitor.'

'Shaun's your partner?' Francesca asked.

'Yes. We were just friends – he used to work at Rosa Wines, years back,' Diana explained. 'When I split up with Nick, he was very supportive. Nick noticed, and made life difficult for him, so Shaun went to work for Chalk Valley Wines and eventually bought the vineyard. When Rosemary died and Nick pushed me out, Shaun offered me a job.' Colour tinged her cheeks. 'We really were just friends – unlike Nick, I believed in my marriage vows, and after the divorce I didn't think I had it in me to date again – but we finally got together a couple of years ago. It took me a while to tell the kids, but Gaby and Ash were pleased for us.'

Georgina noticed that Diana hadn't mentioned Nathan's

reaction. Clearly her oldest son hadn't shared his siblings' views. And she'd just bet that Nick was furious about it, too.

Gaby returned with a box of papers. 'There's a second box, if you have room in the car for it,' she said to Georgina.

'I have – thank you,' Georgina said. 'And I promise I'll take great care of them.' She smiled at Diana. 'We'd better let you get on ringing round Ashley's friends. I hope he's with one of them and he's just lost track of time and forgot to check in with you.'

'I hope so, too,' Diana said. 'It was lovely to meet you. And if you've got any more questions about the farm and Gaby can't answer them, let me know and I'll try to help.'

'I'll keep Gaby posted with what I find out about the skeleton,' Georgina promised.

On the way back to Little Wenborough, Georgina filled Sybbie and Francesca in on what Doris had told her.

'Percy obviously knew Ivy and her family,' Francesca said. 'Was he her age, do you think?'

'Until Rowena's looked at the bones, we don't know,' Georgina reminded her.

'He said Ivy wasn't in love with Ernest. She married him, but she didn't love him. Does that mean that Ivy was in love with Percy?' Sybbie asked.

'Or that Percy was in love with her?' Francesca asked.

'Or both? We're asking questions, but we need to find evidence and let that guide us. I need to look at the census records to see if Percy lived in Ashingham in 1911 or 1921,' Georgina said.

'Actually Percy stuck around when we left the farm,' Doris said.

So Doris's odd feeling that something was different had turned out to be accurate; they didn't have to be near the place where Percy died for Doris to talk to him, Georgina thought.

'I asked him if he remembered Douglas, Mary and their children,' Doris said. 'He says he went to school with Ivy's brothers, Sid and Len. Sid was a couple of years older, and Len was in his class. They were friends. Sid joined up in 1915, when he was eighteen, and Len and Percy were called up in 1917.'

Georgina relayed the information to the others.

'So we know that Percy's a couple of years older than Ivy, and probably born around 1899, if he was eighteen when he was called up,' Francesca said. 'As Bert found his skeleton, obviously he survived the war – or at least he wasn't killed in France. Though we know from Diana that Len and Sid died.'

'With his grandad being a doctor, they made Sid a stretcher-bearer,' Doris said. 'There was a chlorine gas attack. They could see this thick greenish-yellow cloud drifting towards them across No Man's Land and heard it sizzling. It smelled a bit like pepper. Sid knew if you went down in a trench, you'd be done for, because the gas would sink and be more concentrated there. But if you went above the trenches to get away from the gas, that'd make you an easy target for the enemy. One of his friends climbed a tree and was all right. Those who got caught in the gas couldn't see – their eyes were streaming and painful, and all they could do was put a roll of bandage round their eyes. They were sent back from the trenches and you'd see them all in a line of up to a dozen men. The one who could see best went first, and the ones behind them put a hand on the shoulder of the man in front.'

'That's horrific,' Georgina said.

'The medics told the stretcher-bearers to pee on their handkerchiefs and use them to cover their faces when they went to rescue the men. The urea in their urine was a base, so it'd help to neutralise the acid in the chlorine,' Doris said. 'But it was bad for those who got a lungful of the stuff. It took people days to die. They just lay there, gasping for breath, and nothing could be done,' she continued. 'And the fear of the gas made it worse. In the early days, all the troops were given was a pad of cotton wool covered by gauze and with elastic attached at the top and bottom, to cover their nose and mouth – but after a couple of minutes using the masks, the men just couldn't breathe. They pushed it up over their foreheads to get some air.'

'And, just when they were vulnerable, they ended up breathing in the gas,' Georgina said. 'Did Sid join you and tell you this?'

'No. Percy says Sid wrote home about it,' Doris said.

'Is Percy here with us?' Francesca asked when Georgina relayed what Doris had said.

'Yes, he is,' Doris confirmed.

'Then welcome, Percy, and we're sorry you're here in such sad circumstances,' Francesca said.

'Let me budge up a bit to give you more room,' Sybbie added, getting Bert to move closer to her, too.

'Welcome, Percy,' Georgina said. 'I can't even begin to imagine how horrible the trenches must've been, for all of them.'

'Percy says it was pretty grim. From Sid's letters, he and Len knew what they were going to face when they joined up. Mary was in bits, because she didn't want Len to go to France. She said she didn't want to risk losing him, too. Percy's mum, Mabel, said the same – they'd already lost enough young men in the village, and Percy and Len were both needed on the farms. But Percy and Len were adamant that it was their duty. Sid was out there, and they wanted to support him,' Georgina said.

'What happened?' Sybbie asked. 'Obviously, we know Percy came back from the trenches, and I'm glad about that.'

'Percy says Len died at Ypres, after a gas and shell attack – he'd only been at the front a couple of months. Sid died two months later, killed by a shell as he was taking wounded men back to the camp.' Doris paused. 'I get the sense Percy hasn't really forgiven himself for being the only one of the three of them to make home at the end of the war.'

'Survivor guilt,' Sybbie said quietly when Georgina filled them in. 'He'd been through years of war, and came home to all these gaps in the village where his friends should've been. It must've been dreadful.'

'It makes me wonder about the person who punched Percy,' Georgina said. 'Was it someone who resented the fact he'd come home from the war when so many hadn't?'

'Will we ever find out?' Francesca asked. 'Surely there won't be any evidence.'

'Hopefully the records will tell us enough to help Percy remember more,' Georgina said, 'and then we'll be closer to finding out the truth. Cesca, can you jot down what Doris told us, please?'

'Sure – and then I'll email it to you,' Francesca said. 'Poor Percy. I really hope we can find out the truth for him.'

SEVEN

When Georgina parked outside the farm shop, Sybbie looked torn. 'I want to make Cesca put her feet up for a bit and rest. But I also want to go back to Rookery Farm with you and help you find out more in the records,' she said.

'Go with Georgie,' Francesca said. 'I'm going to have some lunch, then sit in my office and catch up on paperwork. And I know you've already had a word with Beth' – Francesca's assistant – 'and told her to stop me overdoing things, so don't deny it.'

'Busted,' Sybbie said, looking faintly guilty.

'I appreciate you looking out for me,' Francesca said, 'but being pregnant hasn't taken away my common sense. I'm not going to overdo things. Go with Georgie,' she repeated.

'All right. If you're quite sure,' Sybbie said.

Back at Rookery Farm, Georgina and Sybbie brought Rosemary's boxes into the kitchen. Sybbie made coffee while Georgina put together a salad and took a quiche from the fridge; after they'd eaten and cleared away, she collected a notebook, pens and her laptop and they sat down at the ancient oak table. Bert settled at their feet, resting his chin on Georgina's toes.

'I'm just texting Colin, before we start,' Georgina said, and rapidly sent him the facts she had so far about Percy.

> Sybbie and I are starting to research the records now.

'Things are still not right between you two, are they?' Sybbie asked.

'Because he's being narrow-minded,' Georgina said. 'Everyone else believes me about Doris. You, Cesca, the kids – even Jodie, and she's a sceptic.'

Sybbie sighed. 'It's his job, dear girl. He deals with logic.'

'Working on the Sherlock Holmes principle of ruling out the impossible, and what's left has to be the truth, however improbable,' Georgina said. 'Surely by that logic he should believe me?'

'I think that's the problem. Colin's confusing "impossible" and "improbable",' Sybbie said. 'I know he's stuffy at times, but he's got a good heart and he loves you. He worries about you.'

'When there's no need. I'm perfectly capable and competent,' Georgina said.

'Be fair: he did rescue you from a poisoner. Two, in fact,' Sybbie said.

'Yes,' Georgina acknowledged, 'but that has nothing to do with my capability or my competence.'

'Of course it doesn't. I'm not trying to start a fight,' Sybbie said, lifting both hands as if in surrender.

'Good, because we have work to do,' Georgina said.

'I don't want to cause a fight between you and Colin. I'll go away,' Doris said.

'You don't have to go anywhere, Doris,' Georgina said. 'You're my friend and you're welcome here. That's not going to change just because Colin's being narrow-minded.'

'Obviously I'm only able to hear one side of this conversation,' Sybbie said, 'but I can work it out. I'm with Georgie,

Doris. Stay. You need us to help you find out what happened to Percy – and we need you to help direct our search.'

'All right,' Doris said. 'But you need to sort things out with Colin, Georgie.'

'I will. Later,' Georgina said, and pulled up the 1911 census. 'Here we are. Willow Farm, Ashingham. Douglas Cooper, aged forty-two, married, head of household, farmer. Wife Mary, aged forty; son Sidney, aged fourteen, farmworker; son Len, aged twelve, farmworker; daughter Ivy, aged nine, scholar.' She skimmed down the page. 'Two servants living in; three cottages on the same page clearly housing the farmworkers. Cattleman, agricultural labourers, horseman, dairymaid, dairymaid, children... But no Percy Ramsey. He's not one of the workers here. We know he was in Len's class at school, so he must've been aged about twelve, here. The chances are that he lived with his parents, or maybe an uncle and aunt.'

'If he didn't work for the Coopers, maybe they were neighbours,' Sybbie suggested. 'Either he worked at a different farm, or his family weren't in farming.'

Georgina turned to the next page in the census. 'Holm Farm – which I assume is next door to Willow Farm, as it's the next one in the records. Fred Ramsey, aged forty-five, married, head of household, farmer. Wife Mabel, aged forty; son Percy, aged twelve, farmworker; daughters Millicent and Rose, aged ten and eight respectively, scholars.'

'So Percy was the boy next door,' Sybbie said softly.

'He and his sisters probably grew up playing together with Ivy and her brothers, in and out of each other's houses,' Doris said, 'just like Jack and I did with our neighbours. Over the next few years, they might've become sweethearts.'

'They might,' Georgina agreed. She told Sybbie what Doris had suggested. 'Let's see what we've got in 1921,' she continued, and picked out the relevant records from the next census. 'Douglas Cooper, aged fifty-two, widowed, head of household, farmer. Daughter Ivy, aged nineteen, farmworker.' She sucked in a breath. 'Down from a family of five to just two, and only one servant living in now. Cattleman, agricultural labourers – some of the names are missing here, too, so we can assume they didn't come back from the war. We also have Ernest Edwards, aged twenty-seven, farm horseman. He's not the same person who was the farm horseman in the last census, so I'm guessing he replaced someone who was killed in the war. And he's not local, either; he was born in Hendon, Middlesex. I wonder what brought him to Norfolk?'

'Maybe he had family in the area, and he wanted somewhere peaceful rather than the city after the war,' Sybbie suggested. 'At twenty-seven, he was of an age where he would've fought in the war – unless he was exempt, of course.'

'Let's see what the war records say,' Georgina said. 'Doris, do we know which regiment Percy, Len and Sid were in?'

'Norfolk Regiment, eighth battalion,' Doris said promptly.

Georgina looked up Len Cooper. 'Killed in action, 11 August 1917, Ypres. Just like Percy told us.' She took a deep breath and looked up his brother. 'Sid died on 26 October 1917, at Ypres. They're both buried at Tyne Cot, according to this.'

'That's so sad,' Sybbie said. 'What about Mary?'

Georgina looked up the parish records for St Peter's church in Ashingham. 'She died on 17 November 1918. There were three others in the village who died of flu, that week.'

'Mary was the doctor's daughter. I bet, even though she was devastated about losing her sons, she was used to helping sick people in the village, because of her dad. She'd been involved in the last flu epidemic, too,' Sybbie said. 'And maybe she thought helping others would help take her mind off losing her boys. Maybe she went to help families she knew had been stricken down with it.'

'Except she caught the virus, too,' Georgina said.

'Percy says that's what finally tipped Douglas over the edge.

Losing his boys was bad enough, but then Mary as well – he never recovered,' Doris said. 'He started drinking. Percy was worried about the farm. He tried to help, but Douglas threw him out. He accused Percy of trying to take over the farm and turning his daughter against him.'

'Which obviously wasn't the case,' Sybbie said when Georgina filled her in. 'Was Percy in love with her?'

'Yes. Before he even went away, they were getting close. He wrote to her during the war, and kept all the letters she sent to him,' Doris confirmed. 'He tried to get help for Douglas, but Douglas was paranoid from the drinking by then and was convinced that Percy was trying to get rid of him. He banned Percy from seeing Ivy, so they had to meet in secret. Percy knew Douglas would never give permission for Ivy to marry him, so their plan was to wait until she was twenty-one and didn't need permission to get married. And then somehow they'd persuade Douglas to get treatment.'

'But clearly she married Ernest Edwards instead of Percy,' Georgina said. 'And Ernest was eight years older than Ivy. When you're nineteen, that's quite a big gap. Did Ernest sweep her off her feet? Or was there another reason?'

Doris was silent for so long that Georgina was beginning to wonder what was happening. 'Doris?' she asked gently.

'Percy's not with me anymore,' Doris said. 'I asked him about Ernest. He shook his head and left. I get the feeling that he remembers something, but he doesn't want to talk about it.'

'Maybe he needs time to come to terms with whatever it is,' Sybbie suggested. 'In the meantime, we'll carry on with the records and see what we can find.'

Of course Georgina was going to check the records next, Colin thought as he saw her message. And she seemed to be time-stamping all the information she found and sharing it with him.

If what she learned matched with what she'd told him this morning after the skeleton had been discovered – and matched Rowena Langham's report – that would strongly suggest that she had another source of information.

Doris.

If the facts made sense, he wouldn't have a problem with admitting that he'd been wrong and ghosts existed – at least, Georgina's ghost existed. But so far he hadn't seen any proof of ghosts that actually stood up to scientific scrutiny.

He raked a hand through his hair. Right now he was waiting for information on his current case: the pathologist's report on the cause of Nathan Edwards's death, plus the forensic team's report on the fermentation tank area and Ashley Edwards's studio. He had one dead body which was either an industrial accident or a murder, and one vulnerable missing person. He didn't have *time* to spend looking at Georgina's evidence.

Then again, he also had information that would be useful to her. He could take a few seconds to forward it.

He texted back.

> One of the estate workers, Tyler, says his family has worked at Willow Farm for decades. He says his great-gran June Wood is in her 80s, still lives in the village, and is pin-sharp on memories so she might remember something that will help with your research. I have his permission to give you her number. C x

He added in June's number – a landline rather than a mobile – and sent the message.

'That's the last of the interviews done,' Mo said, walking into Nick's office with Larissa.

'Great. Is the forensic team here yet?' Colin asked.

'They are,' Larissa confirmed. 'One lot is looking at the winery, and the other is looking at the studio. And Rowena's on her way to look at the skeleton.'

'Then I think it's time for us to see Kelly, Nathan's ex – Diana gave me her contact details – organise a family liaison officer and go back to base. While we wait for the forensics and pathology reports, we can look at what we have and which leads to follow up,' Colin said.

He let Nick and Del know that they were going back to the station, and asked them to get in touch straight away if they heard anything from Ashley.

He waited until they'd left the farm before he started talking about the case. 'It's either an industrial accident or a murder. Nathan's father thinks he was reckless and/or stupid, whereas his mother thinks Nathan knew better than to take risks. I'm keeping an open mind until we get the forensic and pathology reports, but we also have what looks like some kind of fight in the art studio and the other brother's missing. It could be a coincidence that both things happened at the same time, but I don't like coincidences.'

'Agreed,' Mo said.

'Sum it up for us, guv,' Larissa said.

'There are a lot of family tensions. Rosemary started up Rosa Wines and employed Diana. Nick set up Willow Farms wines as a competitor – in the field next door, too – after Diana divorced him. Fifteen years later, after Rosemary died and left Rosa Wines to him, he reorganised the company to oust Diana.' He frowned. 'Though there's a bit of an anomaly there, too. Diana says she thought Rosemary was leaving the vineyard to Gaby, but died before she could sign the will.'

'Isn't that a bit... convenient?' Larissa asked.

'We need to make some tactful enquiries to find out how Rosemary died,' Colin agreed. 'Putting that to one side, Nick also told me he wants to retire. He put Nathan in charge of Willow Farm Wines last year. Nathan took the opposite approach to Gaby in winemaking, so there were tensions between Gaby and Nathan.'

'According to several of the people I spoke to, he threatened to spray her fields, which would stop her claiming organic status for Rosa Wines next year,' Mo said.

'And that would give her a very strong motive to stop him,' Larissa said. 'Could she have killed him?'

'You saw the body. Nathan was tall and well-built,' Colin said. 'She has a motive – as you say, Larissa, to stop him ruining her vineyard – and the opportunity, because they worked in the same place. That leaves the means. Do we think Gaby was strong enough to push him into the vat and then pull the ladder away?'

'Probably not,' Mo said, 'but we can't rule it out. Firstly, she might've had the advantage of surprise – Nathan wouldn't be expecting her to climb up the ladder, get behind him and push him in. Secondly, Nathan also didn't get on with Ashley. The farmworkers all seem to feel sorry for Ashley, because Nathan and Nick gave him a hard time and they think Ashley's a bit strange but harmless. Gaby stuck up for Ashley. What if she and Ashley joined together to push Nathan into the vat?'

'It's a possibility. Ashley was allegedly scared of Nathan, but the studio was a mess. It looked as if there had been a fight, and Ashley's artwork was smashed up. Some of it had melted – according to Gaby, he'd done some frozen sculptures,' Colin said. 'Everyone says Ashley wasn't violent – that whenever he had a meltdown, it was more like depression and withdrawing than getting angry. But if Nathan had smashed up his work, the things that meant most to him, could that have been the last straw – enough to finally tip Ashley over the edge into anger? And if he was angry at Nick for spoiling his work and for threatening Gaby's work at the vineyard, would that be enough of a motive to make him push Nathan into the wine? Is Gaby perhaps covering for Ashley, rather than working with him?'

'We need to find Ashley and talk to him,' Larissa said.

'What about Nick?' Mo asked. 'He's got a temper – we saw that by the way he reacted to Diana being at the winery.'

'He has no alibi – at least, not one he's prepared to tell us about,' Colin said. 'And his reaction was very odd, at first – he seemed contemptuous of all his children. The way most parents react when they lose a child is shock and upset. They're all over the place. But Nick just seemed to sweep everything under the carpet and ignore it.'

'It could be a front. He struck me as the sort who either shouts his head off, or pretends things aren't happening because he thinks showing emotion makes him look weak,' Larissa said. 'Is there anyone else we need to take a second look at?'

'Who gains from Nathan being out of the way?' Colin asked. 'Nick doesn't, because Nathan being out of the way means that he has to find someone else to take over before he can retire. Gaby gains, because it means he wouldn't be interfering in her vineyard anymore; Ashley gains, because he wouldn't be bullied.' He paused. 'But if they didn't do it – who cared enough about the pair of them to step in and stop Nathan causing problems?'

'Diana,' Mo said, 'but she wasn't there when Nathan was found. Obviously we need to check her alibi.'

'What about Diana's partner, Shaun?' Larissa asked. 'He used to work at Willow Farm, and is now Nick's business competitor; he's also working with Diana, and he's Diana's partner.'

'It might not have been intentional murder,' Mo said. 'Maybe Diana or Shaun tried mediating, and it went wrong.'

'They're all possibilities,' Colin said. 'But we need evidence. As soon as we've seen Kelly Edwards and broken the news, I'll ring Sammy and see if she has anything for us.'

EIGHT

Back in the kitchen at Rookery Farm, Georgina and Sybbie were checking the digitised parish records on Georgina's laptop. 'Let's look up the marriage records, next, and see if we can find Ivy's wedding,' Georgina said. 'It looks as if there were about half a dozen weddings per year in the village. Oh, here we are: 9 April 1922. Marriage solemnised at the church in the parish of St Peter Ashingham in the county of Norfolk. Ernest Edwards, full age, bachelor, farm manager – so he's been promoted from horseman. Residence at the time of marriage: Willow Farm. Father: Terence Edwards, deceased.'

'And here's Ivy. Ivy Cooper, age twenty, spinster. Nothing's listed under her profession, though we know she works on the farm,' Sybbie said. 'Residence: Willow Farm. Father: Douglas Cooper, farmer. Married by banns, by F. Birch. And they've both signed the register with their names – I noticed earlier that some of the witnesses were signing the register with a cross.'

'Not these two. Witnesses: Douglas Cooper and S. Birch,' Georgina said. 'I'm guessing S. Birch is probably the vicar's wife, because it looks as if she's been a witness for other people who had a deceased parent.'

'Douglas's signature looks a bit shaky,' Sybbie commented, peering at the screen. 'Maybe the drink was starting to take its toll. But why did Ivy marry Ernest when she was twenty, when we know that she and Percy had planned to marry as soon as she came of age – which would've been the following year?'

'Pressure from Douglas?' Georgina asked. 'Doris, I know Percy went silent on you, but can you try having another word with him? He might be able to tell us what happened.'

'I'll try,' Doris said.

Georgina continued scanning through the register. 'June 1925: so, three years later, Percy gets married to Winifred Henderson. He's a bachelor, farmworker, aged twenty-six; she's a spinster, aged twenty-three. The same age as Ivy: so it's highly probable they were at school together, maybe even friends. Her dad's the village innkeeper.'

'I wonder if Winifred knew she was Percy's second choice?' Sybbie asked quietly. 'I hope they managed to find some happiness together, at least.'

'I hope so, too,' Georgina said. 'I know we ought to check the deaths, to find Douglas, but I can't quite face it. I need to see something happy.'

'Let's check the baptism registers first,' Sybbie agreed.

There was no mention of a child for Ivy and Ernest before Percy married Winifred. Then, two years later, in June 1927, they found the arrival of Mabel Elsie Ramsey, daughter of Percy and Winifred.

In January 1929, there came another daughter, Hannah Millicent; and in June 1930, another daughter, Sarah Rose.

'Meanwhile, Ivy and Ernest have been married for eight years now, and there's still no sign of a baby,' Sybbie said. 'We know they have a boy, because that was Nick's dad – and he was obviously named after Ernest's dad. But if Nick was like his dad, and Terence was like *his* dad, I'm guessing Ivy's marriage to Ernest really wasn't very happy at this point. Eight years and no heir, while the farmer next door has three daughters. And I'm guessing that Ernest wasn't the type to share the blame of not conceiving, or to be sympathetic.'

'I'm dreading the deaths register,' Georgina said. 'I know miscarriages wouldn't be marked, and maybe not even stillbirths – at least, not before the 1980s. But what if they did have babies, but they died before they could be christened?'

'I hope not. Poor Ivy,' Sybbie said.

'Let's try one more page,' Georgina said, and then dropped her shoulders in relief. 'Here we are. June 1933. Terence Ernest Edwards.' She paused. 'This time, Ernest is listed as a farmer, not a farm manager.'

'Douglas must have died before he saw his grandson, then,' Sybbie said. 'Again, how sad. A baby might've helped give him some hope and stop him drinking.'

'I think I need more coffee before we face the deaths register,' Georgina said, and put the kettle on.

Fortified by a strong brew, she went back to the deaths register. 'We already know Mary died in 1918.' She combed through the pages. 'Douglas died in 1925. The month before Percy married Winifred. And our F. Birch wasn't one of the chatty vicars: he's just put the date and Douglas's age – fifty-six. That's no age at all.'

'Younger than me,' Sybbie said, and shivered.

'No infant burials – not for Ivy and Ernest, anyway,' Georgina said. She carried on looking through the pages. 'And there's nothing for Percy. Well, not that I expected it – otherwise his skeleton wouldn't have been in the pond for Bert to discover.'

'Whoever hit him and killed him was hardly going to turn themselves in at the police station and admit what they'd done,' Sybbie said. 'But someone must've noticed he'd gone missing and reported it. Would Colin have access to any papers, do you think?'

'We already know missing persons cases can be difficult to trace,' Georgina said, thinking of the body Bert had found at the lighthouse and how difficult it had been to trace. 'And this was nearly a hundred years ago. There might not be any missing persons list.'

'But someone would've noticed his disappearance. Like when Timothy Marsden went missing from Little Wenborough Manor,' Sybbie reminded her. 'His sister wrote to Bernard's great-great-great-grandfather.'

'Maybe there's something in the newspapers,' Georgina said.

Her phone pinged with a text, and she checked it. 'Oh. Colin's just given us a lead. One of the farmworkers says his family has worked here for generations and his great-gran lives in the village. She might know more about Ivy and have some idea of what happened to Percy.'

'I'd love to come with you, if she's happy to talk to us,' Sybbie said.

A quick call established that June Wood was very happy to talk to them, and Georgina arranged to visit her the following morning.

Meanwhile, Sybbie had been checking the weather forecast on her phone. 'We'll take my car. She could do with a little run out. And maybe after we've talked to June, we can have lunch in Holt.'

Georgina chuckled, knowing her friend's passion well – and knowing how many antique shops there were in the Georgian market town. 'Didn't Bernard' – Sybbie's husband – 'put a ban on you buying any more Staffordshire china dogs?'

'That was *months* ago, dear girl. He'll have forgotten all about it by now,' Sybbie said confidently.

'Hmm,' Georgina said, not sharing Sybbie's certainty.

'I'll bring cake from Cesca's as a treat for June,' Sybbie said. 'Victoria sponge is a safe bet.'

'And I'll pick up some flowers,' Georgina said. 'I'll drop you home, and then I'd better take Bert for a quadruped constitutional.' But before she left, she texted Colin.

> Thank you for the lead. Seeing June tomorrow.

Then she thought about what both Sybbie and Doris had said. Maybe she'd been a bit combative today with date stamping her evidence, and it was time to offer an olive branch.

> Shall I cook dinner for us tonight? G x

His reply came back relatively quickly.

> Thank you. I'd like that. Let me know what time. C x

> Whenever suits you. Let me know when you're on the way. G x

It still wasn't quite back to full warmth, but it felt better than it had for a while, Georgina thought.

Colin parked on the road outside a neat, semi-detached house in the village next to Ashingham. The front garden had been carefully tended, and the car parked in the driveway had clearly been washed recently.

'Ready to talk to Nathan's wife?' he asked Larissa and Helen, their family liaison officer.

At their nods, he climbed out of the car, locked it when they joined him and rang the doorbell.

The woman who opened the door was in her thirties, slender and pretty, with glossy dark hair pulled back into a ponytail.

'Mrs Kelly Edwards?' Colin asked. At her nod, he said, 'I'm DI Colin Bradshaw, and this is DC Larissa Foulkes and PC Helen Robinson. May we come in, please?'

She looked puzzled, and then worried. 'Has something happened?'

'I'm afraid so,' Colin said. 'And I'd rather you were sitting down when we speak.'

'Oh, my God. The girls!' Kelly clapped a hand to her mouth in horror.

'Not your girls,' he said gently.

'I...' She gave a shuddery breath. 'Sorry. Come in. I'm off duty today.' She stepped aside and ushered them into the living room; the room was small but neat, with framed photographs of two girls on the mantelpiece. 'Please, do sit down.' She perched on the edge of the chair and waited for them all to sit. 'What's happened?' she asked.

'I'm afraid it's Nathan Edwards,' he said. 'He died this morning.'

'Nathan?' Her eyes widened. 'Oh, my God. Does Diana know? And is Gaby all right?'

'Diana and Gaby both know, and they're planning to come and see you very shortly,' Colin said.

'What about Ashley? Because...' Her voice faded, as if she'd been about to tell him that Ashley was fragile and then realised that it might not be for her to say.

'He's missing, I'm afraid,' Colin said. 'So if you've heard from him at all over the last week, or you have any idea where he might be, we'd appreciate your help in locating him.'

'No, I'm sorry.' She shook her head. 'He's missing, and Nathan's dead? I can't believe this.' She frowned. 'How did Nathan die? Did he crash his car or something?'

Interesting that that was her first thought, Colin mused. Had Nathan been a reckless driver – and reckless in other areas of his life, no matter what his mother thought?' 'He drowned in one of the vats,' Colin said.

Kelly blinked hard. 'How on earth...?'

'I'm sorry. I'm aware this will be distressing. Del Turnbull saw a ladder on the floor by one of the fermentation tanks, and went to check. He found Nathan in the tank and got him out, but unfortunately he wasn't able to revive him and neither could the paramedics,' Colin said.

'Drowned. I...' She shook her head again. 'Sorry. I don't mean to repeat things at you. It's just... I didn't...'

Shock often made people incoherent, Colin found. 'Take your time,' he said gently. 'At the moment, we're not able to answer any questions, but Helen's our family liaison officer and she'll be able to help you.'

'I'll start by making a cup of tea,' Helen said, 'if that's all right with you, Mrs Edwards?'

'Kelly,' she said. 'Thank you. The mugs and the tea are in the cupboard above the kettle. Just milk for me, please.' She turned back to Colin. 'The girls will be devastated. I mean – I know I divorced Nathan, and I don't regret doing that because I didn't want the girls growing up thinking it was OK for men to treat them the way their dad treated me, but I wouldn't have wished that on him. And Ash is missing?'

'Yes,' Colin confirmed.

'That's worrying. He's – well, Gaby's probably already told you that he has depression.' Kelly frowned. 'So what happened? Did Nathan start on him and Ash, I dunno, hit back, or something? Not that I can imagine Ash ever hitting back, but...' Her voice tailed off.

'We're waiting for the pathology report to find out what happened,' Colin said. 'Del Turnbull thinks Nathan might have inhaled carbon dioxide when he took a sample from the tank, was overcome by the fumes and fell in.'

'He's worked at Willow Farm for years – well, only on the vineyard side since his gran died, but he's a quick learner. He knows the risks and he wouldn't do anything reckless,' Kelly said, frowning. 'Maybe he had a heart attack or something, and that's why he fell in.' She winced. 'His lifestyle wasn't great. And I'm saying that with my nurse's hat on. He smoked, he drank too much, he ate badly and he really didn't look after himself.'

'I'm sorry to ask,' Colin said, 'but can you think of anyone that Nathan had problems with?'

'Someone who'd want to kill him, you mean?' She sighed. 'He fell out with a lot of people. Including me, and Miles, my fiancé. But we've been trying to keep things as amicable as possible, for the sake of the girls.'

'Did Nathan get on well with Gaby and Ashley, in your opinion?' Colin asked.

Helen came back in with four mugs of tea and doled them out.

'I'm sure someone's already told you that Nathan was unkind to Ash – Ashley's a bit different, and unfortunately Nathan wasn't very tolerant,' Kelly said dryly. 'Nathan argued a lot with Gaby because she wouldn't let him push her around and change the way she runs her vineyard. But there's no way Ash or Gaby would've hurt him. If there was any kind of fight, Ash would be more likely to find somewhere to hide until it's all died down and it's quiet again, while Gaby would stay up all night to come up with a watertight business plan to prove to their dad that she was right and would make more money than if they did things Nathan's way.' She paused. 'I assume you also know that Rosemary was going to leave Gaby the vineyard, but then she died before she could sign her will?'

'It has been mentioned,' Colin said. 'But, if she didn't sign the will, how does everyone know about it?'

'Because Diana was sorting through her post, after Rosemary died – when she was still running Rosa Wines – and there was a letter from the solicitor reminding Rosemary to go and sign the revised will,' Kelly said. 'It made things a bit awkward. Diana rang to advise the solicitor that Rosemary had died, and Nick said she was interfering in something that was his business, not hers.'

'I can imagine. And I'm aware that Nick made Diana redundant,' Colin said. 'Again, forgive me for asking at a difficult time, but do you know the cause of Rosemary's death?'

'Yes. She had a stroke,' Kelly said. 'She was eighty-three, so it kind of went with the territory – though actually she was really fit. She looked after herself and most people thought she was ten or fifteen years younger than she was. I was still living with Nathan at one of the farm cottages when it happened, and I was on maternity leave, so I nursed her through those last couple of weeks. My youngest will join her big sister at first school in September.' She bit her lip. 'She was lovely, Nathan's nan. I got on really well with his mum, too. Diana still sees plenty of the girls and she's always welcome here.'

'What about Nathan's dad? Did you get on with him?'

'I tried,' Kelly said, looking embarrassed. 'The thing is, Nick can be very charming, when he wants to be. But if you cross him – well, he's like a little boy who never grew up and has a tantrum when he doesn't get his own way.' She sighed. 'In some ways, I should've seen that as a warning sign. Nathan could be very much like his dad. But I fell in love with him, and I thought it would be different for us – that love could change him.' She shrugged. 'Sadly I was wrong. And I didn't want to spend years doing what Diana did, putting up with the affairs. After eighteen years and three kids – well, I'm surprised she put up with it for that long.'

'Understood,' Colin said. 'Do you have any questions for me?'

'Do you think it was an accident, or do you think someone killed him?' Kelly asked.

'At the moment, we're still investigating. If it was an industrial accident, we need to know what happened and how, so the business can make sure nothing like that happens again,' Colin said. 'I'll know more when the pathology report comes through.'

'Fair enough,' Kelly said.

'Helen will keep you in the loop, Kelly, but if you have any questions in the meantime, please ask Helen to contact me and I'll do my best to answer.'

'Thank you,' she said.

'I'll tell Diana and Gaby that we've spoken to you,' Colin added. 'And I'm very sorry for your loss.'

When they'd left Kelly's house and he'd spoken to Diana, to let her know he'd seen Kelly and the family liaison officer was there, he rang Sammy Grainger's office to see if she could give him any idea when the pathology report was likely to be ready.

'I was just about to call you,' Sammy said. 'Obviously I need to write this up properly, but Nathan died from drowning.'

'Accident or intentional?' Colin asked, putting her on speakerphone so Larissa could hear.

'There are fresh bruises on his shins, consistent with banging into something – given that a ladder was present, I'd say that was a likely candidate,' Sammy said. 'There's also a bruise on his head, consistent with knocking his head against the side of the vat.'

'So he was standing on the platform, leaned over to take a sample, breathed in the fumes, was overcome, slipped and fell in, banging himself as he did so?' Colin asked.

'It's one possibility,' Sammy said. 'But there's also bruising to his face, and you can see the knuckle marks.'

'Which suggests that he had a fight with someone at some

point before he climbed that ladder,' Colin said. 'Could it have been the previous night?'

'Possibly, but I'd say it happened not very long before he went into the tank,' Sammy said.

'So a fight, where someone landed a blow to his face – something that maybe upset him or angered him enough that he wasn't paying proper attention to what he was doing and didn't notice the fumes until it was too late,' Colin mused out loud, 'and he fell in. Or are there any signs that he was pushed?'

'There isn't any bruising to his back,' Sammy said. 'But the carbon dioxide would've taken up space in his lungs where there should've been air, which would've made him feel dizzy and faint. It wouldn't have taken much to make him lose his balance.'

'We need forensics to tell us how that ladder fell. Except we won't know exactly where it was, because Del Turnbull moved the ladder so he could climb up and look in the tanks,' Colin said.

'Unless it damaged the floor when it fell,' Larissa pointed out.

'Is there anything under his fingernails?' Colin asked.

'Nothing useful,' Sammy said. 'I've taken samples, and I'll email the report and photos over.'

'Thank you,' Colin said.

'We're no further forward,' Larissa said with a sigh when he ended the call.

No, and it was frustrating not to have any definitive answers. It could have been an accident; but he had a tingle in his gut that told him it was foul play. He just didn't have the evidence to back it up.

Just as Georgina didn't have evidence to back up her assertion that Doris existed... He shoved the thoughts away. Doris had nothing to do with this. And his gut feeling came from years of experience in his job.

'Let's go back to the station and look at the witness statements we collected from the farm,' he said. 'We can at least sort out a timeline of who was where and when, and see if any patterns emerge from the statements.'

'Right you are, guv,' she said.

NINE

After Georgina had dropped Sybbie back at the manor and taken Bert for a long walk, she spent a while at her desk in the office, working on the photos she'd taken of Gaby and writing up the notes she'd taken. The young winemaker had been full of brightness that morning, as she'd shown them round the vineyard. But then they'd come back to find tragedy at the winery: one brother dead and the other missing. Georgina hoped that Ashley would turn up safe and well, and that Nick and Diana could reach some kind of truce – even if only temporarily – to support Gaby.

Colin texted her to let her know that he'd just left the police station, and she headed for the kitchen to put together a one-pan chicken dish with plenty of vegetables, sun-dried tomatoes, garlic and orzo pasta. Bert started bouncing around the kitchen, wagging his tail, telling her that Colin's car had just pulled up; she added a couple of tablespoons of low-fat cream cheese to thicken the sauce slightly as Colin knocked on the kitchen door and walked in.

Bert greeted him rapturously and Colin made a fuss of him,

then handed Georgina a bunch of purple stocks: her favourite flowers, with their spice-and-clove scent.

'Thank you. You didn't have to do that,' she said, 'but they're gorgeous and I appreciate them. Sit down and I'll get you a drink.'

'A cup of tea would be wonderful,' Colin said, 'but I'll make it. What would you like?'

'Tea works for me, too, please,' Georgina said, and put the stocks in a jug of water on the windowsill.

She served up two bowls at the kitchen table and let him eat and decompress in a comfortable silence.

'That was fabulous,' he said when he'd finished. 'I don't think you've made me that before. New cookery book?'

'No. It's from an Instagram account,' Georgina said. 'By a young nutritionist who happens to be very photogenic – but her recipes definitely have substance as well as style. She takes some fairly traditional dishes and tweaks them to make them healthier on the heart. This one has a lighter sauce because it uses stock and couple of tablespoons of low-fat cream cheese instead of a small tub of crème fraîche.'

'You know me,' he said with a wry smile. 'If I'm left to my own devices, dinner will be a sandwich, beans on burned toast, or a takeaway.'

'You might find cooking relaxes you,' she said. Though his expression told her he doubted it. 'Thanks for sending me June Wood's details, by the way. She's having a chat with Sybbie and me tomorrow.' She paused. 'You haven't heard back from Rowena yet about the skeleton, by any chance, have you?'

'No,' Colin said, and his work phone beeped.

He glanced at the screen. 'Correction – that's her, now, so you're hearing this the same time as I am. She says we're looking at bones of antiquity.'

Georgina had already told him that, but didn't push the issue.

'Male, mid-thirties, and Rowena thinks he died somewhere between 1925 and 1935 – most of the clothing had decayed, but there were a couple of fastenings left which helped her to pinpoint the date.'

Georgina resisted the urge to say 'I told you so', though Colin clearly guessed what she was thinking because his face tightened slightly.

'There are two things she noted of interest,' Colin said. 'The first is a crack in the skull – she says it must've been around the time of death because there's no sign of the wound healing. She thinks it's the likely cause of his death. And she said his skull is thinner than normal – it looks like a case where the eggshell skull rule applies.'

'Eggshell skull?' she asked.

'But the principle of law is you take your victim as you find them – you can't say a death wasn't your fault because the blow you delivered wouldn't have killed someone who didn't have an eggshell skull.'

'If you hit someone and they die, of course it's your fault,' she said. 'But how sad that Percy survived all the nightmare of the trenches on the Western Front, all the shells and the snipers and the gas, but when he came home to the village where he grew up, someone hit him and he died.'

'And then whoever killed him hid the body in the pond – maybe weighing the body down with stones in the pockets, given that the body hadn't surfaced before,' Colin said.

Even the idea of it made Georgina shudder. What a horrible way to get rid of a body – not even allowing Percy a proper burial and a chance for his family to grieve. 'What's the second thing?' she asked.

'The left hand of the skeleton is missing,' he said. Then he frowned. 'Actually that *is* interesting. I'm sure Gaby said something about Ashley's artwork being based around hands, and he always drew or sculpted the left hand. She said it was probably because he was right-handed.'

'But then we find a skeleton at the vineyard with a missing left hand. It *could* be a coincidence,' Georgina said. 'Except I know you don't like coincidences.'

'I don't,' Colin agreed, and made a note. 'Though, until we actually talk to Ashley, we have no idea whether it's relevant or not.'

'Still no news?'

'Still no news,' he confirmed.

'Poor Gaby and Diana must be beside themselves.' She paused. 'Maybe Nick, too, in his own way.'

'Mmm,' Colin said, but his tone lacked conviction.

'You can still talk to me,' she said. 'Well – I know you're not supposed to talk to someone outside your team about a case, but I kind of *am* on your team.'

She could see the conflict in his grey eyes; he'd found talking things over with her helpful in the past, and he knew what he said wasn't going anywhere because she was his partner. Even though they'd had a bit of a bumpy road recently.

'If I lost Cathy,' he said, speaking about his daughter, 'I'd be off my head with grief. I don't think I'd have a British stiff upper lip at all. But Nick... he didn't seem in the slightest bit moved when he was told what had happened. One son dead, the other missing, and he just brushed it aside as if it were completely unimportant. He was more upset because I was interviewing Diana in his office.'

'Maybe he's one of these blustery men who doesn't know how to deal with their emotions,' Georgina suggested. 'From what Gaby said, Ashley has a habit of going missing. Maybe Nick doesn't let himself get upset about it because it's happened a few times before and he thinks Ashley will be back soon.'

'Maybe,' Colin said. 'But it chilled me a bit, the way he talked about his sons. So *cold*. I can't imagine you ever talking like that about Bea or Will. He said Nathan was careless and he drowned, and Ashley was a waste of space.' He blew out a breath. 'I can't understand any parent reacting like that about their children. Or maybe he said it just to hurt Diana – he said it in front of her,' he mused. 'I know they're divorced, but I really don't understand this idea of lashing out and hurting someone. It doesn't help anything.' He closed his eyes for a moment. 'I regret hurting Marianne. I'm truly sorry that I didn't cope with what was happening at work and I dragged her down with me. We've both moved on now – she married Michael, and he treats my Cathy as if she was his own – and I'd never dream of being vile to her just because she divorced me. I don't blame her at all. Even though I do feel a bit jealous of Michael,' he admitted with a wince, 'because he gets to do the job that should've been mine: being Cathy's dad.'

'This isn't meant to sound as harsh as it probably does, but you probably shoulder too much of the guilt about your marriage breaking up, Colin. You were ill, not an arrogant womaniser who didn't care about how anyone else felt,' she reminded him. 'Maybe Nick Edwards just can't admit that the breakup of his marriage was mostly because of his behaviour.'

'From what Diana and Kelly – Nathan's ex – said, it sounds as if Nathan had a very similar attitude to his dad's,' Colin said. 'But then again, Kelly said she and Nathan tried to keep things amicable because of the girls.'

'Nick didn't give me the impression that he'd tried to keep things amicable with Diana,' Georgina said. 'Either when the children were young, or now. Del said the tension between Nathan and Gaby was pretty much stirred up by Nick, too. Perhaps he was playing divide and rule.' She sighed. 'Which is so sad, for all of them.'

'I'm far from perfect,' Colin said, 'but I do try not to hurt people deliberately.' He paused. 'How did you get on with your research? I see from your texts that you've found out a bit about the people who lived at Willow Farm.'

'And Holm Farm, next door,' Georgina said. 'Percy Ramsey was born in 1899 to Fred and Mabel. Ivy was Nick's grandmother. Percy was the same age as Ivy's brother Len, and two years younger than her brother Sid. Sid joined up first, in 1915, and then Len and Percy in 1917. Sid and Len didn't make it back from the trenches, but Percy did.' She looked at him. 'I'm hoping June can fill in some gaps for me.'

'Do you have any theories about who killed Percy, or why?' Colin asked.

'Not yet,' she said.

He raised an eyebrow.

She sighed. 'I don't have evidence. Maybe June can put us on the right track. What I know from the census returns and parish records is that Percy lived at the farm next door to Ivy – I need to check if Holm Farm is still there, or if not what happened to it – and he married a girl who was the same age as Ivy, so presumably they were school friends. Her dad was the village innkeeper. And they had three daughters.'

'But you have theories without evidence,' Colin said. He took a deep breath. 'Doris.'

'Yes,' Georgina said, going very still. Were they about to have another fight?

'You told me you're on my team,' Colin said. 'I'm on yours. Tell me what... what Doris said.'

Georgina felt tears sting the back of her eyes. He was really making an effort, for her sake. 'Thank you,' she said quietly. 'All right. Percy was sweet on Ivy. He was friends with her brothers. The boy next door. I'd just bet everyone expected Percy and Ivy to end up together. Apparently they wrote to each other while he was in France.'

'But she married someone else. Why?'

'I think the war changed everything,' Georgina said. 'The

war, and then the flu epidemic. Len died at Ypres when he'd only been in the trenches for a couple of months – in a gas and shell attack. And Sid was a stretcher-bearer – he died a couple of months later, even though he'd survived more than two years by then. He was killed by a shell while he was rescuing someone. Douglas, their dad, couldn't cope with losing his sons. And then he lost Mary, his wife. She was the doctor's daughter, so it was second nature for her to help out when there was sickness in the village. She went to help people during the flu epidemic – except she caught the flu and died. And then Douglas started drinking.'

'Having been there myself, I get it,' Colin said quietly. 'You think it's the answer. Drink until the pain's blotted out. Except the next day the pain's still there, and you've got a headache on top of it.'

Georgina reached out to squeeze his hand. 'I'm sorry. I didn't mean to bring up bad memories for you.'

'It's fine,' Colin said, smiling at her. But he kept hold of her hand. 'What happened next?'

'Ivy pretty much had to run the farm, because her dad wasn't up to it,' she said. 'Between the 1911 and 1921 censuses, you could see that a few of the farmworkers had also died in the war. There was a new man at Willow Farm, though – Ernest Edwards, who was Nick's grandfather. He was the farm horseman – obviously back then they used horses for ploughing and what have you. He came from near London, but after the war he wanted to live somewhere quieter and he came to Norfolk.'

'And he and Ivy fell in love?'

'Maybe. Maybe not,' Georgina said. 'Percy tried to help Ivy with the farm, but Douglas accused him of trying to take over. He also refused to let Ivy marry Percy. The plan was, Percy and Ivy would wait until she was twenty-one and get married then.'

'But she married Ernest,' Colin said thoughtfully.

'Not just a different man: it was earlier than she'd planned to marry Percy, too. She married Ernest when she was twenty. So something obviously happened. Her dad was one of the witnesses to the wedding.' Georgina frowned. 'At the moment, it's just a theory, but maybe she thought if she married Ernest, it would make her dad happy and stop him drinking.'

'I assume Percy and Ernest didn't get on?' Colin asked.

'Right now I don't know. I'm guessing probably not. Ernest might have been the jealous type, especially if he knew that Percy had been Ivy's sweetheart before he went to France. And Percy obviously wouldn't have been happy about his girl marrying someone else. But he clearly moved on, too, because he married Winifred, the local innkeeper's daughter, in 1925 – a month before Douglas died.'

'Rowena said Douglas died somewhere between 1925 and 1935,' Colin said.

'I'm thinking the later end of that time period, because Percy and Winifred had three girls by 1930,' Georgina said. 'I've gone through the parish registers, and Percy's name isn't there. Which would fit, if he was killed and then the body was hidden.'

'Could the Ramseys have moved away?' Colin asked.

'I don't know. I'm going to check the 1939 register to see if they were still at Holm Farm,' she said.

'What about the 1931 census?' Colin asked.

'Apart from the fact that census records are closed for a hundred years, the whole of the 1931 census was destroyed in a fire during the Second World War,' Georgina told him. 'The 1941 census didn't happen because of the war, but a register of civilians in England and Wales was taken in 1939 to help the government produce identity cards and then ration books.'

'What about people in the forces?' Colin asked.

'They're in a separate register, but conscription wasn't introduced until 1940, so the register's almost as good as a census,' she said. 'I also need to check the newspapers, to see if Percy was reported missing at all.'

'Did Winifred have him declared presumed dead?' Colin asked. 'There's a procedure she would've had to go through. After he'd been missing for seven years, she would've had to apply to the court for a declaration, put an ad in the newspapers saying that she'd applied for a declaration presuming him dead and giving his last known address, and saying if anyone had an interest, they had three weeks to apply to the court. If nobody answered the ad, the court would declare him presumed dead, give her a certificate and then she could sort out wills and probate and what have you.'

'Let me make a note of that,' she said. 'I was going to ring Bea to see if she had any ideas, but by the time I got round to it, she would've been getting ready for tonight's show and I didn't want to distract her.'

'Is *Much Ado* still on at the Regency?' Colin asked.

Georgina nodded. 'It's been so popular that they've extended the run.'

'She was brilliant,' Colin said. 'I so wish her dad could've seen her. Your Bea playing the character she was named after.'

Georgina's eyes prickled again. 'Yeah,' she said, her voice cracking slightly.

Colin clearly noticed, because he winced. 'Sorry.'

'Don't apologise,' she said, feeling closer to him than she had done since she'd first told him about Doris and he'd walked away. 'I like that you're generous enough not to try to wipe Stephen out of my life.'

'You were together for thirty years,' Colin said. 'Of course I'm not going to try to eclipse him. Just as you don't try to remove Marianne and Cathy from my life.' He paused. 'I'd like you to meet them. Once this case is over.'

That was a huge step, Georgina thought. He was finally letting her into his life. 'I'd like that,' she said. 'And right now I'd really like to sit with you in the garden and listen to the birds singing, with a glass of elderflower.' She paused. 'And for you to stay, tonight.'

'I'd really like that, too,' he said. 'I've missed you, Georgie. Missed *us*. It hasn't felt right for months. And I know it's my fault.'

'Maybe you've been a little narrow-minded,' Georgina said. 'But I can be as stubborn as you are.'

'I'm trying to get my head round what you tell me,' he said. 'And with you telling me things before you can possibly have seen the evidence for them...'

'That isn't the same as me fitting the evidence to the narrative,' she said. 'It's just that Doris telling me things means I have somewhere to start to find the evidence. Which I guess some people might consider as being a bit lazy.'

'No. It's saving time,' he said. 'And you're bringing closure to people. Something I envy, actually, because I can't always do that.'

'I think all we can do is our best,' she said. 'Garden, I think.'

'Garden,' he agreed.

TEN

The next morning, when Colin had left, Georgina nipped out to buy some flowers for June.

'Are you coming with us to see June, Doris?' she asked.

'Sorry, I can't. Harrison's got a thing on,' Doris said. 'A gig. I said I'd be there. Sorry for letting you down.'

'You're not letting me down at all,' Georgina said. 'I don't expect you to be at my beck and call. I'm just grateful you help me as much as you do.' She smiled. 'Have fun. And give my love to Harrison.'

'I will,' Doris promised.

Sybbie came to pick Georgina up as arranged, in her vintage turquoise MGA.

'Scarf,' she said, handing Georgina a square headscarf.

Georgina had grown adept at tying a headscarf, under Sybbie's tuition, and added a pair of sunglasses.

'What *are* we like?' she teased.

Sybbie chuckled. 'You're quoting Jodie.' She made a fuss of Bert. 'Sorry, you can't come today because my car isn't safe for you. But we'll make it up to you. I have one of Cesca's special b-words, just for you.'

Bert gave two small barks, as if saying, 'Biscuit.'

'When we get back,' Sybbie promised.

Georgina slid into the passenger seat and did up her seatbelt. Sybbie had already put the soft top down. 'Ashingham,' she said. 'And then Holt.'

'Even though Holt's in the opposite direction,' Georgina teased.

'She needs a little run out – don't you, girl?' Sybbie patted the dashboard with one hand, and Georgina suppressed a smile, knowing how much her friend loved her car.

'I didn't tell Colin we were taking your car. He's a bit twitchy after what happened at Hartington.'

Sybbie rolled her eyes. 'That wasn't the car's fault. I'll have to take him out in her to prove to him that she's perfectly safe. Though I draw the line at offering to let him drive it. Even Bernard doesn't drive it.'

'And he'll respect that. Actually I think he'd probably enjoy it,' Georgina said.

'Did you find anything else about Percy in the records?' Sybbie asked.

'No, but I have some notes about what I want to check next.' Georgina paused. 'Colin stayed over, last night.'

'Mmm-hmm,' Sybbie said, her voice sounding carefully neutral.

'We talked about Doris. He, um, asked what she'd said.'

'He *asked* you? Seriously?' Sybbie turned her head to stare at Georgina for a moment.

'He's trying,' Georgina said.

'Well, if he's opening his mind a bit, that's a good thing.'

'Rowena sent him her initial findings on the skeleton, and it matched what I'd already told him. Male, in his thirties, died somewhere between 1925 and 1935, and the likely cause of death was a crack in his skull.'

'None of which you could've known without Doris telling

you. And Cesca and I are witnesses to the fact that nobody knew the skeleton was in the pond until Bert started digging,' Sybbie said.

'Evidence,' Georgina said. 'It's going to make life a lot simpler if he can accept what I tell him. He's trying to.'

'Good.' Sybbie paused. 'What we don't know is who hit Percy, or why. Hopefully June will be able to give us some more background. I have one of Cesca's Victoria sponges in the footwell behind me, which should help.'

'I brought flowers,' Georgina said.

'Then we're all set,' Sybbie said with a smile.

June Wood lived in a granny annexe in her daughter's house in the village of Ashingham, and was delighted with both the flowers and the cake. 'How lovely! Thank you. The nice thing about being eighty-four is you can eat cake as much as you like and nobody gives you a hard time about it,' she said with a grin, bustling round the small kitchen-cum-living room to put the flowers in water and make a pot of tea.

Georgina would've guessed that June was a good decade younger than she'd said she was; her pearl-grey hair was in a pixie cut and her blue eyes were very bright. She seemed full of energy, and clearly kept herself active. Georgina noticed the flyers pinned on the corkboard next to the kitchen table, with class times for Pilates and aqua aerobics and a knit-and-natter group.

June settled them all down at the kitchen table with tea and cake, and looked enquiringly at them. 'Our Tyler told us what happened at Willow Farm yesterday. It's a bad business. Poor Rosemary would be so upset to know her grandson had died like that. And Ty says you found a skeleton in the fields, to top it all off.' She spread her hands. 'Not what you'd expect in a quiet place like Ashingham. So what can I do for you?'

'As I said yesterday, we're looking into the skeleton, for Gaby and her mum,' Georgina said. 'We were at Willow Farm to take photographs of Gaby for a magazine, but I dabble a bit in family history research.'

'So you've got a good idea where to start looking,' June said.

'Yes, but it helps to have a bit of background. It's not the best of times to ask Gaby or Diana – they've got enough on their plate. And, as you've got a long connection with the farm, we thought you might be able to help us with some background,' Sybbie added.

'I can do that, all right,' June agreed. 'Lovely girl, that Gaby. She's very like her gran – and her mum. I can't say the same for the menfolk in that family, I'm afraid.' She shook her head sorrowfully. 'I know you shouldn't speak ill of the dead, but those Edwards men are all the same – well, apart from young Ashley,' she added, rolling her eyes, 'but he's not on the same planet as the rest of us, either. They're charming as the prince asking Cinderella to dance when they choose to be, but they just can't keep their bits in their trousers. I wouldn't want to be married to one of them.'

'Did you know Gaby's grandad?' Sybbie asked.

'Terence?' June nodded. 'And her great-gran, Ivy. I worked for Ivy as a dairymaid. Though Ivy's husband, Ernest, died when I was still a toddler.'

'Tyler said your family had worked at Willow Farm for generations,' Georgina said.

'They worked at Holm Farm,' June corrected. 'My dad worked for Fred Ramsey, and my granddad worked for Fred's dad until Fred took over. My dad worked with the horses,' she said. 'He was the ploughman. But after Fred died – well, with young Percy gone missing, it was up to his wife, Winnie, to keep the farm going. And she had them three kiddies to look after, as well. Run off her feet, she was. No wonder she sold up to the Edwardses as soon as she could.'

Georgina and Sybbie exchanged a glance. It sounded like quite a story to unpick. And it was only a small thing, but it seemed that Winifred had been known in the village as 'Winnie'. Maybe that was the name they should suggest Doris used to Percy.

'What was Fred like?' Georgina asked.

'Salt of the earth, my dad always said. Firm but fair. And young Percy was just like him. Do anything to help anybody, he would. He changed a bit after the war, Dad said, but all of them who came back from the trenches changed. I know my granddad did. Flinched at loud noises, got upset – but they wouldn't talk about it, back in those days. They thought they had to be men and just shut up and carry on. You just knew to leave them be when they had a fit of the black dogs. When you think how young those boys were when they went out to fight, and the terrible things they must've seen in the trenches... Well, it's no wonder half of them came back with shell shock.'

'You said Percy went missing?' Sybbie asked.

'He disappeared one night, before the harvest in 1934,' June said. 'It must have been around late June, early July. Nobody had a clue where he went. I heard my mum and dad talking about it, years after. Dad was still a boy when it happened – he'd left school by then and was working as a farmhand for Fred. He reckoned Percy was worrying about what was happening in Germany. Always reading the newspapers, Percy was. And he thought trouble was brewing. Times were hard. People were hungry and poor and miserable, and they were looking for someone to blame. Hitler gave people someone to blame. Percy thought it'd end up with another war, and he couldn't bear the idea of that, of having to go and fight again. All the injuries and the deaths...' She shuddered. 'And he was right, because that's exactly what happened, wasn't it? And it was over here, this time, with bombs dropping on London and Norwich and everywhere else.'

'Percy never came back?' Georgina asked.

'No. People thought he did himself in. Terribly sad. Mind

you, at least he did it away from the farm, so Winnie and the kiddies wouldn't have to find him,' June said. 'There was a search. The whole village turned out, and every man over school age combed all the ditches and the woods, in case he'd fallen somewhere or got caught in a poacher's trap. But there was no sign of him, hide nor hair.'

'That's so sad,' Georgina said. People had at least tried to find Percy, which was a comfort; but either the pond had been much deeper in those days or it hadn't been searched properly, because now she knew his body had been at the bottom of the pond when they'd looked for him.

'Fred never got over him vanishing like that,' June continued. 'My dad reckoned he became an old man overnight. Percy would've been in his thirties when he disappeared, so that would've made Fred in his late fifties, maybe early sixties. That's no age at all. He died just after the war started – from a broken heart, my mum thought – and it left Winnie in a difficult spot. If Fred had only changed his will and left the farm to her, it wouldn't have been a problem. But he left it to Percy, and nobody knew where Percy was.'

Another echo with the present, Georgina thought: just as Rosemary hadn't signed her will and it had left Gaby in a difficult position. And Ashley had gone missing, just as Percy had; hopefully the outcome of any search would be much less heartbreaking.

'I suppose Fred didn't want to give up hope that his boy had just gone off somewhere, and he'd got help from an asylum or something and would come back one day,' June said. 'But it left everything up in the air. With the farm passing from Fred to Percy but him being missing, Winnie's hands were tied. She couldn't inherit it without proof of Percy being dead, and she was struggling to get things done. In the end, once he'd been missing seven years, she went to see a solicitor and had him declared presumed dead, so she could inherit the farm. It was in the middle of the war, so the potatoes and wheat they grew were needed. The land girls helped her keep things going – my mum was one of them, and that's how she met my dad,' June said. 'He came home on leave, fell in love with her, and they got married on his next leave.' She smiled. 'I was a honeymoon baby. 1943. Then, after the war ended, Winnie sold Holm Farm to Ernest Edwards and it all became Willow Farm. I suppose it made sense, with the Edwardses having the farm next door, but my dad always said he didn't think Fred would've been happy selling Holm Farm to him. He was a bit of a chancer as well as a charmer, that Ernest.'

'Were Percy and Ernest friends?' Georgina asked.

'I don't think so. They were chalk and cheese. Though I heard Percy was sweet on Ivy, before the war. Nothing came of it, and to be fair Ivy had a lot on her plate. Douglas basically had her running the farm. I suppose marrying Ernest meant she'd got someone to help her, at least. I get the impression he made himself indispensable.'

'Why didn't she marry Percy, I wonder?' Sybbie asked. 'If they were sweethearts before the war, and he was the neighbour and could've helped with the farm, surely it would've made sense for her to marry him?'

'I reckon there must've been some kind of falling-out between the Ramseys and the Coopers,' June said. 'Maybe Fred lost patience with Douglas and told him to pull himself together for Ivy's sake, and Douglas didn't like it. If Percy asked for his permission to marry Ivy, maybe he said no because he didn't want her marrying Fred's son. Men can be funny old buggers like that. Get an idea into their heads and it won't shift, and they'll cut their noses off to spite their faces.'

'It's such a shame. If Ivy and Percy loved each other and they'd got married, maybe they would've had a happy ending,' Georgina said. 'And maybe Douglas would've come round, after the wedding.'

'And maybe he wouldn't. Maybe Ernest warned Percy off. We'll never know,' June said. 'Anyway, Ivy ended up marrying Ernest, and Percy married Winnie.' She spread her hands. 'And then Percy went off somewhere. Never came back. Winnie's girls wanted to move to Norwich, and selling Holm Farm to Ernest meant Winnie could go with them. After the war, Dad came back here to work for the Edwardses – well, it was really working for Ivy, because Ernest died a few months after they bought the farm, and she was in charge until Terence was old enough to join her. She never married again, mind. I think Ernest put her off matrimony for good. But she had a good daughter-in-law in Rosemary.'

'I'm glad something nice happened. It sounds as if Ivy had a tough life,' Georgina said.

'Do you think it was Percy's skeleton you found, then?' June asked.

'Maybe,' Sybbie said cautiously. 'But you said the area had been searched, so surely they would've found his body in the pond?'

'Not if it was right at the bottom. Looking back, that pond was always quite deep,' June said. 'I remember being told to keep away from it when I was little. It would've been a lovely place to swim in the summer, but all the village kids were warned not to go in because it was too dangerous. A couple did – you always get kids who just have to show off and kick against what they're told – and one of them got cramp and nearly drowned, so the rest of the kids steered clear of it after that. The Edwardses used to use it as a watering hole for the cattle, before Rosemary planted the vineyard. She kept it because it was good for local wildlife.'

'Would the pond have been on Holm Farm land, or was it always at Willow Farm?' Georgina asked.

'I couldn't rightly say. It's been so long since the farms were joined,' June said. 'There's probably maps in the library that'll tell you.'

'Or on the internet,' Georgina said. 'Thank you, June. You've really helped us.'

'I hope you find out who it is so you can lay him or her to rest properly,' June said.

'We're going to do our best,' Georgina promised.

ELEVEN

Halfway through the morning, Colin leaned back in his chair in the police station; Mo and Larissa's desks abutted his, and he could see both of them working away at their computers, checking and cross-checking information against the statements they'd taken at Willow Farm yesterday.

'I'll do the coffee run,' he said. Partly because he didn't believe in always making the most junior of the team to make the drinks, and partly because he was feeling creaky and needed to stretch his legs. 'Usual?'

'Please, guv,' they chorused with a smile.

'We'll have a catch-up in five minutes,' Colin said, and headed for the kitchen.

Larissa was on a health kick and drinking green tea; Mo drank his coffee strong and with only a splash of milk. Colin briefly longed for chocolate biscuits, but he was meant to be watching his sugar intake. He headed back to his team and handed out the drinks.

'Cheers, guv,' Larissa said. 'You know, you could give this a try. It's better for you than all that caffeine.' She lifted her mug of tea in a toast to him.

'That's kind, but to me green tea tastes like it's been through a lawnmower,' Colin said with a shudder. 'I'll stick with my coffee.' Though maybe he'd switch to decaf for the rest of the day. His sergeant definitely had a point about the amount of caffeine he consumed. 'How are we doing with the timeline for Nathan's death?'

'Most of the workers arrived at about ten to eight and were either in the bottling plant or the fields by eight a.m.,' Mo said. 'Gaby said she arrived at eight forty-five – later than usual, because she wanted to avoid any arguments with Nathan before the photography session. She went straight to the fields to get some samples, then went to the office for a shower and changed clothes at about nine forty-five. Nobody was in the office, so she assumed everyone was either in the fields or the bottling plant. Georgina, Sybbie and Cesca arrived at ten on the dot, and they went to the fields with Gaby, for a tour of the vineyard and to take photographs.'

'Del Turnbull, the production manager, went back to the office at quarter past ten; when Nathan wasn't there, he went to find him. He discovered the ladder out of place, flagging up that something was wrong; he checked the fermentation tanks and discovered Nathan's body. As he went to the bottling plant to get help to pull the body out, he called the emergency services,' Larissa said. 'The paramedics got there at ten fifty and pronounced life extinct. Gaby, Georgina, Sybbie and Cesca were back at the office a couple of minutes later, and we arrived at ten past eleven.'

'I'm still waiting to hear from Alexsy about most of the forensics, but the pathology report came back this morning. Sammy says Nathan's death is consistent with drowning – there was fluid in his lungs,' Colin said. 'Which means he fell or was pushed into the vat either before everyone arrived at ten to eight, or between eight, when everyone had started work, and nine forty-five, when Gaby came back to shower and change.

Sammy says he wasn't in the tank overnight; she thinks it was maybe three hours.'

'Which ties in with the timeline,' Larissa said.

'Del also said that Nick, Nathan, Gaby and himself had a set of keys to the office and knew the code to the alarm. Whichever of them arrived first opened up. Nick was apparently at a breakfast meeting with a client. Del says the office was unlocked when he arrived so he assumed either Gaby or Nathan were in, and Gaby says she arrived late,' Colin said. 'So either Nathan unlocked the office, or someone isn't telling the truth.'

'The CCTV doesn't cover the offices, and Willow Farm Wines is only open to the public by appointment,' Mo said. 'From their website, they run tastings and tours at the weekends in the summer, and although you can buy wine at the farm if you're on a tour, it's by card only. No cash. There wouldn't be anything to bank; nothing was kept in a safe.'

'Which means it's unlikely that Nathan's death is connected to any kind of robbery. Unless someone was taking wine from the warehouse,' Colin said.

'There's nothing on the CCTV,' Larissa said.

'I don't think it was an accident,' Colin said. 'Nathan's mother says he wouldn't have been reckless about the way he took the samples. My gut tells me it was foul play. So it comes down to who has a motive for killing Nathan.' Colin drummed his fingers on the table. 'We know someone hit Nathan, because of the pattern of bruising on his face. Sammy thinks it's likely to be just before he went into the vat, but she also said it's possible it happened the previous evening, so it might be completely unconnected with whatever happened in the winery. All we know about the person who hit him was that they were right-handed, and must've been reasonably tall to land a punch to his face.'

'We need to know who trashed Ashley's studio, whether he

was hurt, and where he is now. Did he leave of his own free will, or did someone abduct him?' Mo asked. 'In which case, what would the motive be for taking him?'

'Alexsy in forensics told me a couple of things,' Colin said. 'The pool of liquid in the studio is a mixture of blood and wine. Gaby also told me that, but Alexsy confirmed that the blood was frozen rather than fresh.'

'You can tell the difference?' Mo looked surprised.

'According to Alexsy, yes – under a microscope.' Colin checked his notes. 'With frozen blood that's been thawed, the erythrocytes are lysed.'

'Translation out of scientist-speak?' Mo asked.

'It means the red blood cells have broken open,' Larissa said.

'How did you know that?' Colin asked.

'Tsk, guv, call yourself a detective?' Larissa teased. 'My wife's a nurse, and I'm the one who tests her when she's revising for exams. She's interested in pathology, but specialising means she wouldn't be working with patients anymore and she'd miss the actual nursing side too much.'

'Maybe we ought to let you do the liaison with Alexsy, in future,' Colin said.

Larissa chuckled. 'I could, but you'd miss doing all the middle-aged male grumbling with him.'

'True,' Colin admitted. 'Anyway, we know that most of the blood in the studio was frozen as part of the artwork. Alexsy said there's some fresh blood, but not much – more or less what you'd get with a graze to the skin. If Ashley's been badly hurt or killed, it didn't happen at the studio.' He checked his notes again. 'There are fresh footprints outside, and Alexsy says some of them are of a size consistent with other shoes in Ashley's cupboard. Obviously the prints right by the door have been blurred by other people going in, but the evidence says he walked out of the studio. We just don't know if he was on his own at the time.'

'I checked with Gaby, and there's no CCTV at Ashley's studio – not even a video doorbell,' Larissa said. 'Ashley's the only one who can tell us if he had a visitor. Without him, we're stuck.'

'I've talked to the people on the list Gaby gave me of Ashley's friends,' Mo said. 'Some of them seemed to find it a bit awkward, talking to the police, but I think I've made them all aware now that we're worried about Ashley's safety and that's the only thing we're interested in. They all claim they haven't heard anything from him. I asked them to tell him to get in touch with us, with Gaby or with his mum, just to let them know he's all right. Obviously we can't rule him out for being involved in Nathan's death until we've spoken to him, but I didn't think saying that would make anyone want to give us information, so I focused on the fact his family's anxious in case he needs help and they don't know if he has his medication with him. Hopefully he'll get in touch with his mum or his sister and they can persuade him to talk to us.'

'Good work, both of you,' Colin said. 'I'm hoping that Alexsy's team will come up with a forensic lead from the fermentation tank area. In the meantime, let's look through the interviews again and see what needs following up.'

When Georgina and Sybbie had taken their leave of June, Sybbie drove them both to Holt. As Georgina suspected, Sybbie had her eye on a pair of Staffordshire china dogs in one of the antique shops, and after a bit of fierce negotiating, she had her prize.

'You're a horror, Sybbie,' Georgina teased.

'I haven't bought any china dogs for *ages*,' Sybbie protested. 'And look at their sweet little faces. How could anyone possibly resist?'

'It's Bernard you need to convince, not me,' Georgina reminded her with a grin.

Since they were in the area, they called in to Webster's Fine Art, the gallery owned by a sculptor they'd both got to know when Georgina had been investigating a cold case from the lighthouse at Summerstrand a few months before.

'Lovely to see you both,' Niamh Webster, the owner, said. 'What can I do for you?'

'I need some cards,' Georgina said. 'Sybbie's already bought Staffordshire dogs today, so she's not allowed any of your bronzes.'

Niamh chuckled. 'Faye' – Niamh's daughter, a potter who co-owned the gallery – 'has a new range of bowls, though...'

'Ooh – we need to see them,' Sybbie said. 'How's she getting on?'

'OK,' Niamh said. 'It's school holidays, so she's juggling childcare and work a bit more than usual. But I'm looking after the kids tomorrow and she's here.'

'Grandchildren.' Sybbie smiled broadly. 'Did I tell you that I'm going to be a grandmother in about three months?'

'It's wonderful, being a gran,' Niamh said, her own smile just as broad.

In the end, it was Georgina who couldn't resist the bowls, and while she paid for her purchases, Sybbie made a fuss of Niamh's Westie, Poppy. 'Georgie's as bad as I am, at heart,' she whispered with a chuckle.

Niamh deftly protected the delicate bowl with bubble wrap. 'So you're just on a lunch and shopping trip today?' she asked.

'We're actually researching a case from Ashingham,' Sybbie said. 'We've been talking to an old lady who was born in the middle of the war, about people she could remember her parents talking about – something to do with the First World War.'

'Bert discovered another skeleton,' Georgina said.

'Well, good luck with finding things out for the family,' Niamh said. 'I know we appreciated what you did for us.'

'You're very welcome,' Sybbie said.

When they'd finished chatting, they found a café and ordered lunch. While Sybbie went to the loo, Georgina quickly texted Colin.

> Had a very useful talk with June. She confirmed a lot of my theories. And you were right about presumption of death. Hope you're making headway. G x

A few moments later, he texted back.

> Not much. Ashley's friends aren't talking. C x

> Come over this evening.

> I'll buy dinner at the Feathers. And a sausage for Bert.

Sybbie came back to their table. 'So what are our thoughts on Percy?'

'We know Winnie had him declared presumed dead, so there'll be a paper trail, both in the newspapers and in the register office records,' Georgina said.

'Newspapers?' Sybbie asked.

'Winnie would've had to put an ad in the newspaper, according to Colin, before she could get the court to issue a certificate of presumption of death,' Georgina said. 'I'd guess it'd be in *The Times*, and possibly the local paper as well. I'll add that to looking at the 1939 register, checking the local maps to see whether the pond was originally part of Holm Farm or Willow Farm, and finding Percy's death certificate.'

'Sounds like a solid plan,' Sybbie said. 'The other question is who hit him. My money's on Ernest. He must've known that

Percy and Ivy were sweethearts at one point. Maybe he was jealous. Nathan sounded hot-tempered, and we've seen Nick is. If that temper runs all the way back to Ernest, perhaps he hit Percy to warn him to stay away from his wife.' She rolled her eyes. 'Considering June reckons all the Edwards men are unfaithful, that's pretty hypocritical.'

'I agree,' Georgina said. 'Though Ernest might not have meant to kill Percy. According to Rowena, Percy's skull was quite a bit thinner than a normal person's – Colin says it's an eggshell skull. A blow that might just give you or me a headache would've done a lot more damage to him.' She frowned. 'The killer must've panicked when he realised that Percy wasn't going to get back up. He couldn't tell anyone what he'd done, because he knew he'd go to prison for murder. So he had to cover it up. The pond must've seemed like the answer to his prayers. Fill Percy's pockets with stones, and the body would stay at the bottom. The village kids were all told to stay away from the pond because it was deep and there was a risk of drowning, so they wouldn't go in and accidentally find him.'

'We need to fill Doris in on what June said,' Sybbie said, 'and ask her to talk to Percy.'

'And we need to look at Rosemary's boxes. There might be something in there,' Georgina added.

'I think I know what we're doing tomorrow, then,' Sybbie said. 'Little Wenborough's the other side of the city from Ashingham, so I doubt if any of Bernard's maps will be relevant – but he might have sneaked something into that cabinet. He's as bad with maps as I am about Staffordshire china dogs.'

Georgina smiled. 'I'm not sure that's possible. But it's definitely worth asking him Thank you.'

Back at the farmhouse, when Sybbie had gone, Georgina caught up with Doris. 'How was Harrison's gig?'

'It was a jam session with some of his old mates,' she said. 'He was on guitar and backing vocals. And I have to say he was really good.' Her voice sounded bubbly with joy. 'He played "My Sweet Lord" for me, and "Here Comes the Sun".'

Georgina thought Doris sounded like a star-struck teenager, though it wouldn't be fair to tease her – not given that Doris had died at the age of eighteen but, had she lived, would now have been seventy-two. 'I'm glad you had fun,' she said instead, and told Doris what June had said.

'I need to talk to Percy,' Doris said. 'We need to know why Ivy married Ernest, and whether Percy did anything to try and persuade Ivy to wait until she was twenty-one and marry him instead. I'm guessing he married Winifred afterwards because Ivy was out of reach, but it'd be helpful to confirm it. And you're right – if June says everyone called her Winnie, maybe that will jog Percy's memory a bit more. Plus we need to know how he got on with Ernest. Were there any rows? Was Ernest the one who hit him and killed him?'

'I think he'll be upset when he finds out that Ernest bought Holm Farm,' Georgina said. 'I need to check exactly when Ernest died, but June said it wasn't long after he'd bought the farm.'

'So he didn't get to enjoy taking Percy's place for long. Good,' Doris said.

'And also tell him that everyone over school age in the village helped to look for him when Winnie said he was missing,' Georgina added. 'People didn't forget him. He was definitely loved.'

'I'll make sure he knows that,' Doris said. 'I'll have a word and report back.'

'Thank you,' Georgina said. 'I'm going to look up newspapers.'

It took a bit of searching, and one quick video call with Bea about navigating a particularly complicated website, but she found Percy's presumption of death certificate; it was dated July 1941, which she knew was seven years after Percy had last been seen. But it was the presumed death date which surprised her, because it was also July 1941; she made a mental note to ask Colin about it. Working backwards from the date of the death certificate, she discovered the ad that Winnie had placed in the newspaper. Nobody had applied to the court to say that Percy was still alive, so the court had granted the certificate.

When she checked back to July 1934, the local newspaper had a couple of paragraphs about missing farmer Percy Ramsey, but the mentions quietly faded out during the next couple of weeks.

Poor Winnie. And poor Ivy; had *she* ever wondered if Ernest had been involved in Percy's disappearance? Had she felt to blame?

The other deaths were more straightforward to find. Fred Ramsey had died in October 1939, and Ernest Edwards had died in 1945.

'As Doris said, I'm glad you didn't get to enjoy Holm Farm,' Georgina said quietly. 'You didn't deserve it.'

A page from the 1939 register for Ashingham showed her that Ernest and Ivy were living at Willow Farm. There was a thick black line across the record beneath them where she expected to find Terence's name, saying 'this line is officially closed'. She knew from talking to Beatrice, her daughter, that records of anyone born less than hundred years before who was still alive would be closed; the register was updated with deaths, but the updates had stopped in 1991. Terence had died in the 1990s, clearly too late for his record to be updated.

Fred, Winnie and three more 'records closed' lines that Georgina assumed were Winnie's daughters were at Holm Farm; Percy wasn't listed, and clearly Percy's mum had also passed away at some point in the previous two decades because her name didn't appear either.

At Number 2, Holm Cottages, Georgina found June's family. George Wood, aged forty-seven, farm labourer; Ruby, his wife, whose occupation was listed as 'household duties unpaid'; Robbie, aged nineteen, farm labourer – June had said he was the ploughman – and Violet, aged seventeen, dairymaid. Thinking that the old lady would probably enjoy seeing this and reminiscing about it with her family, Georgina took a screenshot of the page.

She was about to start checking online maps when Sybbie sent her a text.

> B has relevant maps. Says would be delighted to help.

Putting Bernard in a good mood would help Sybbie charm him into not minding that Sybbie had added to her collection, Georgina thought with a smile – even though she thought that Bernard secretly liked indulging his wife.

> Fabulous! Thank you. Would tomorrow be convenient?

> Come for coffee at ten and bring Bert. And bring Gaby's boxes. We can spread the papers over the dining room table.

Just as they'd done when looking at Timothy Marsden's case, Georgina thought. She'd enjoyed working with her daughter and Sybbie to uncover the truth. Bea wouldn't be able to come and help them, this time, because she was working, but maybe they could co-opt Bernard after they'd checked the maps.

Later that evening, Colin picked Georgina up and they went for dinner at the Feathers, the pub in Great Wenborough that they thought of as 'their' place ever since their first date. Bert, as usual, sat at their feet under their usual quiet table in the corner, and Hannah, the chef, sent a sausage out for him.

'June was helpful, then?' Colin asked as he tucked into the steak and ale pie that he'd been unable to resist ordering.

Georgina explained about everyone thinking the rumours of upcoming trouble in Europe had upset Percy and brought back the memory of his time in the trenches; he'd had shell shock when he first came back from the front, and was prone to bouts of depression. When he'd gone missing, the men of the village had mounted a search, but nobody had found him. As the weeks went by, they'd all assumed he'd taken his own life. 'You were right about the presumption of death,' she said. 'Winnie's hands were a bit tied when her father-in-law died, because he hadn't changed his will. He didn't want to believe that Percy was dead; he thought maybe Percy had gone off somewhere, out of his mind, and one day he'd get better and come home. Winnie inherited the farm from Percy, but without proof that he was dead, she couldn't sort out his will or probate. What I didn't understand was why his presumption of death certificate was dated 1941, when he went missing in 1934.'

'If there's no body found – no proof that someone died – then the presumption of their death is dated seven years after the last day they were known to be alive,' Colin said.

'And you said whoever applied for it had to place a newspaper ad. I found it in *The Times*,' she said, and showed him the photograph she'd taken with her phone.

'A claim has been issued in the High Court of Justice, for a declaration that Percy Ramsey, whose last known address was Holm Farm, Ashingham, Norfolk, is presumed to be dead. Any person having an interest may apply to the court to intervene in the matter. If you wish to apply to the court, you should do so as soon as possible, and if possible within twenty-one days of the date of this notice. Delay may harm your prospects of being able to intervene,' Colin read. 'Obviously nobody replied, because you said there's a certificate.'

'And then Winnie was able to sort out Fred's will leaving everything to Percy, and Percy's will leaving everything to her. When she inherited Holm Farm, she sold it to Ernest Edwards, and then she moved to Norwich with her daughters,' Georgina said.

'Are you saying that Ernest was responsible for Percy's death?' Colin asked.

'We don't know, but it's the strongest possibility,' she said. 'He must've known that Percy was once Ivy's sweetheart, and apparently they weren't friendly even though they were neighbours. He might not have meant to kill Percy, just intimidate him and knock him down.'

'Except we know from Rowena that Percy had an eggshell skull, and that blow was enough to kill him,' Colin said.

'Poor Percy,' Georgina said. 'But the one thing I can't quite work out is the timing. Ernest came to work at the farm at some point after the war; he's listed on the 1921 census, and he married Ivy in 1922. Surely then would be the time when he'd want Percy to stay away from Ivy, before they were married? Plus Percy married Winnie in 1925 and they had three girls. Why would Ernest wait until 1934 before attacking Percy?'

'Maybe Ivy wasn't the reason for the fight,' Colin said. 'I'm sure we've talked about this before and I said I've found the most common motives for killing someone are love, money and revenge.'

'Love and revenge could both be tied up with Ivy,' Georgina said. 'It would make more sense if Percy was the one attacking Ernest, and maybe Ernest tried to defend himself. After all, Ernest was the one who married Ivy, with her father's blessing. But again, why wait until 1934? Why not when he first found out that Ivy was going to marry Ernest?'

'Maybe it was all tied up with the war,' Colin said. 'You said

Percy suffered from shell shock. If he was upset about the probability of a second war, it might have made old resentments surface, too.'

'I really don't think Percy was the aggressor, though,' Georgina said. 'June said everyone described his dad as the salt of the earth, and that Percy was just like him. Whereas the Edwards men were all – well, as she put it, couldn't keep their bits in their trousers.'

'That's one way of looking at it,' Colin said, his mouth quirking in a smile. 'Maybe that was it. Maybe Ernest was having an affair and Percy told him to treat his wife better, and Ernest took exception to it and hit him.'

'You're right – that would make sense of the timing,' Georgina said. 'It's something else to investigate. There might be something in Rosemary's papers.'

'Or, if money was the cause of the row, perhaps a gambling debt?' Colin suggested.

'Maybe. Or was Ernest trying to make Percy sell up and move away? He bought Holm Farm after the Second World War,' Georgina said thoughtfully. 'But in 1934 it still belonged to Percy's dad, who was in good health – though, having said that, June says he died just after the start of the war. I think I need to do some more digging. Bernard has some local maps, apparently, so he's going to help us pore over them tomorrow and find out whether the pond was on Holm Farm land or Willow Farm land.' She looked at him. 'There seem to be a lot of echoes with your case. A missing son, a body that – had it been discovered soon after it had been put in the pond – could have seemed like an accidental drowning. And we don't know who the killer was, though one has a strong motive.'

'Too many echoes,' Colin said gloomily. 'I'm looking at motives, means and opportunity. And they're becoming muddled. Nathan was making life difficult for Gaby, interfering with her part of the winery. She knows about the winemaking process and the effects of carbon dioxide. And she works there. That's motive, means and opportunity all tied to her.'

'For what it's worth, she doesn't strike me as a killer,' Georgina said. 'Bert liked her, and he's a good judge of character. You were saying that the common motivations to murder are money, love and revenge. It's well known that she and Nathan clashed, so she'd be the obvious suspect; she's bright enough to know that. I don't think she killed him. If it was revenge, I think she'd do it by really excelling at what she does and proving that she's a better winemaker than he is. That her grandmother's methods were right. Think about it – she's already won an award, and he hasn't. If anything, Nathan would've been jealous of her and wanted to take her out. That's why he was trying to interfere in the vineyard.'

'Maybe,' Colin said.

'And Ashley's missing,' Georgina said thoughtfully. 'Could he have been the murderer? Everyone says he was gentle – but you once told me that most people are capable of murder, given the right circumstances and motivation. I didn't really believe you, until someone threatened Bea. If love is the basic motivation, but it comes in the form of wanting to protect someone... What if Ashley was trying to protect his sister against Nathan's interference? Maybe he didn't mean to kill Nathan, just warn him off or something. Maybe it went wrong, and he's gone missing because he's panicking about the mess he's in and doesn't know what to do?'

'Until I get the forensics report back, and until I've spoken to Ashley to find out his side of what happened in the studio, that's a possibility,' Colin said. 'Who else would want to protect Gaby against Nathan – and Ashley, for that matter?'

'Diana,' Georgina said. 'And maybe Shaun, her partner. He worked at Willow Farm and supported Diana through the divorce.'

'Gaby said Shaun always had a soft spot for Diana,' Colin mused.

'And maybe that soft spot extended to Gaby. He would've known her since she was a small child. Plus this wasn't just Gaby's work that Nathan was threatening: it was Rosemary's legacy and Diana's, too.'

'Nathan and Ashley were also Diana's children,' Colin pointed out.

'But Gaby was the one who lived with Diana,' Georgina said, 'so he's likely to have had more to do with her than with the boys. Is he the protective sort, the kind who'd take things into his own hands?'

'Shaun's on my list of people to talk to,' Colin said. 'But you're right. There are a lot of echoes between your case and mine.'

TWELVE

The next morning, Georgina loaded Gaby's boxes into her car together with her laptop and camera bag, clipped Bert into his harness on the back seat and drove over to Little Wenborough Manor.

'Lovely to see you,' Bernard said when she walked through to the terrace at the back and knocked on the kitchen door. He kissed her cheek. 'And I presume this rascal's come to play with Jet and Max.' He made a fuss of Bert, who wagged his plumy tail madly. 'Sybbie said you have some boxes of documents?'

'They're in my car,' Georgina said.

'Let me help you bring them in,' Bernard said with a smile.

'Thank you for agreeing to let me pore over your maps,' she said.

He chuckled. 'It's the least I can do. You know I love my maps. I've fished out the ones that apply to the case, and you're welcome to take photographs and share them with the Edwards family.'

'That's great,' she said. 'I was hoping that we might be able to co-opt you into joining the team and looking through the boxes. If you can spare the time, that is.'

'I can spare this morning,' he said, and took the heavier box. 'Sybbie's way ahead of you. She asked me last night, and she filled me in on your conversation with June yesterday.' He smiled. 'And I think Cesca's relieved that you're going to be taking Sybbie's focus off her today – otherwise Sybbie would be checking up on our daughter-in-law every ten minutes to make sure she's taking breaks instead of rushing round.'

'Considering the pair of them only have one speed – full pelt – that must be a bit tricky for you and Giles to negotiate,' Georgina sympathised. 'Even though Sybbie means well.'

'Francesca and Sybil are both trying,' Bernard said ruefully. For a moment, he looked even more mournful than his beloved Labradors and Bert put together. 'In all senses of the phrase.'

'I'll distract Sybbie,' Georgina promised, unable to hide her smile completely.

'I found some more information in the records, yesterday, so I can tell you both a little bit more,' Georgina said, following him through to the dining room.

Sybbie had clearly called Bert in to join her with Max and Jet. The three dogs were all sitting patiently on the rug next to the stone fireplace, facing Sybbie, and their gazes were fixed on a cream-coloured enamelled tin marked *Dog Treats*. They didn't even look round to see who had entered the room.

'I swear they think if they stare hard enough at the tin, the lid will start levitating and the biscuits will be free to fly over to them,' Sybbie said, laughing. 'Good boys, the three of you. Let us have our coffee in peace, and then you can have a treat.'

The huge oak dining table had been mostly cleared, ready for the contents of the boxes. In the middle was a large map; and at one end, at a safe distance from the map, there was a tray containing a cafetière, three mugs and a small jug of milk. 'Coffee, dear girl?' Sybbie asked.

'Yes, please. And I can show you what I found. There's the ad Winnie put in *The Times* before the High Court hearing in

Norwich, and the presumption of death certificate for Percy – and a couple of small articles about Percy going missing,' she said, getting the screenshots up on her laptop. 'And the 1939 register showing the Edwards family, the Ramseys, and June's family.'

'The evidence is stacking up,' Sybbie said. 'I still think Ernest did it.'

'I do, too. But the timing's odd. If he was motivated by jealousy over Ivy, surely he would've done something to get Percy out of the way before he married Ivy?' Georgina asked. 'And he was the one to marry Ivy, not Percy. Surely there wasn't actually any need for jealousy?'

'In his head, he might still have feared that Ivy thought she should've married Percy instead of him – that Percy was the better man,' Bernard said. 'Insecurity's a funny thing.'

'Something must have happened to make Ernest snap,' Sybbie said.

'Has Doris managed to find out anything?' Bernard asked.

Georgina choked on her coffee and almost dropped her mug.

'Sorry,' she said, when Sybbie had given her a napkin to mop up the spill. 'I wasn't expecting you to...'

'Know about her? Sybbie and I don't have many secrets from each other,' Bernard said. 'She told me about Doris after we laid Timothy to rest. And I gather this particular issue has caused a bit of tension between you and Colin.'

'It has,' Georgina admitted. 'And... I'm sorry, I know this is going to sound really offensive, but I didn't expect you to be so – well, *accepting* about something like this.'

'To quote your favourite author, there are more things in heaven and earth,' he said, giving her a wink. 'Not everything can be easily explained. And it makes a kind of sense of how you always know exactly where to look. I mean, obviously Bea's taught you about the kind of documents available, but you need a name to be able to start looking in the first place.' He paused. 'I know about our Grey Lady here visiting Sybbie, too. I didn't know, back in the day, but she told me a couple of months ago. Again, it makes sense of a family tradition.'

'I'm sorry, Bernard,' Georgina said. 'It must've been so hard for both of you.'

'It was,' he agreed. 'And I made the mistake of thinking that burying myself in work would make things better. It didn't, for either of us. But you come to terms with things, over the years. And I'm glad Sybbie had the comfort I couldn't give her at the time. She's my world.' He reached out to squeeze his wife's hand briefly. 'Which is why I forgive her for adding yet more Staffordshire spaniels to the mantelpieces in this house. Including yesterday's pair.'

'Oh. You noticed,' Sybbie said.

'Of course I noticed,' he said with a grin. 'I notice everything, even if I pretend I don't. Just as you do when a cardboard map tube arrives in the post.'

'Hmm,' she said. 'So *did* Doris come back with anything, Georgie?'

'Not yet,' Georgina said. 'You'll be the first to know when she does.'

'Thank you.' Sybbie turned to Bernard. 'Your maps.'

'It's the six-inch Ordnance Survey map from 1929,' Bernard said. 'This came as part of a job lot in an auction. Not strictly relevant to Little Wenborough, but I never quite had the heart to take it to a dealer – I just put it with the others. Just as well, because it's come in handy now.'

The two farmhouses on the outskirts of Ashingham were clearly labelled: Willow Farm and Holm Farm. There was a scattering of barns near each farmhouse, and a small strip of terraced houses marked as *Holm Farm Cottages*. On the border of the two farms, but a distance from both farmhouses, was the pond, labelled *Holm Pond*.

'That's fairly clear, then,' Georgina said. 'The fight happened on Holm Farm land, and Percy was buried on his own farm.' She took photographs of the two farms.

Sybbie gave the dogs a biscuit each, then took the tray back to the kitchen.

'Right. What are we looking for?' she asked on her return.

'Correspondence or diaries, particularly if it's to do with Ivy,' Georgina said. 'And especially from 1915 to 1934.'

'We're looking for mentions of her dad's health and his drinking, her relationship with Ernest and the wedding, any pregnancies or miscarriages before Terence's birth, and Percy's disappearance, yes?' Sybbie asked.

'And the sale of Holm Farm.' Georgina paused. 'We think Winnie and Ivy were friends at school. But I'm guessing Ernest tried to squash that friendship after Winnie married Percy, because he wouldn't have wanted Ivy anywhere near Percy.'

'Let's see what we come up with,' Bernard said.

'I've got some scrap paper so we can make notes and bookmark things, like we did last time,' Sybbie said. 'Also HB pencils and a pencil sharpener.'

'You've definitely been listening to Bea,' Georgina said with a smile. 'Thank you. That's great.'

'You brought exactly the same stuff with you, didn't you?' Sybbie asked ruefully.

'I did,' Georgina admitted. 'Better to have too much than not enough.'

They worked methodically through the papers in the first box, making the occasional note and replacing the papers that weren't relevant to their search.

'Hello,' Bernard said. 'I've found a pile of letters tied in a velvet ribbon.' He undid the bow very gently, and looked at the first envelope. 'It's addressed to Miss Ivy Cooper, Willow Farm, Ashingham, Norfolk, England,' he said.

He slipped the letter out of the envelope – cream paper,

ruled with feint lines, written in brownish-coloured ink – and squinted at it. 'The writing's reasonably clear. Shall I read it out?'

'Yes,' Sybbie said.

'It's dated 11 August 1917, from Ypres,' Bernard said, and began to read the letter.

My dearest Ivy

Thank you for your letter, which as always I keep close to my heart. I think you must be my good luck charm because your letters have kept me safe so far, my dearest.

Thank you also for sending a pound of tea. I am sharing it with the boys here in my dugout and it tastes of home, which is a comfort to all of us.

It has been raining every single day, and some of the trenches are two feet deep in water. The wounded men in the trench next to ours yesterday had to get rid of their kilts before they could get out of the trench, because the pleats were covered in slime which made the material so heavy it was weighed down. The shell holes are so deep, you have to be careful you don't fall in, and mind when you're walking on the duckboards.

The din of the guns never seems to stop.

And always, always the rain. It feels as if we will never be dry again.

I miss Len and Sid. They were the best friends I could have asked for. It must be so hard on you all at home. Give my regards to your parents. Tell them we remember their boys here. Len and Sid were brave, right to the last.

One day this will all be over and I'll be back home. And it's the thought of you keeping me going, dearest Ivy. Being back home with you in Norfolk, seeing the oak trees on my farm and the willows on yours. We'll hear the cows lowing in the meadow and see them kicking up their heels with joy as they go out to pasture in the summer. We'll see the wheat grow tall and turn gold. And, God willing, one day our children will grow up and never, ever see the things that I have seen out here.

My love to everyone back home.

Ever yours, dearest
Percy

Sybbie blinked hard. 'That's so sad. I can't imagine what those poor men went through on the front.'

'Women, too,' Bernard said. 'They were just as brave. The nurses who had to patch the soldiers up, sometimes do the anaesthetic and even the surgery, and then sit with the dying and hold their hand, give them sips of water and talk to them, and record their final moments and last words for their families so they had something more than just the official military telegram. And all the while the hospitals were being shelled, and the hospital tents were leaking, and the rats were squeaking everywhere.'

Georgina looked at him in surprise. 'It sounds as if you know an awful lot about the hospitals of the First World War, Bernard.'

'I did A level modern history, and the First World War was one of the topics. My mother told me her great-aunt Amy had been a nurse out in Ypres. The personal connection made me want to know a bit more about what Amy's life would've been like on the Western Front,' he said. 'Mum asked her cousin if there were any photos or anything I could borrow, and it turned out that Amy kept a diary. They lent it to us and I had the privilege of reading it. The details were pretty humbling, but at the same time they were fascinating. Amy said they used to treat shock with a mixture of brandy, saline and coffee. When supplies ran out, they had to improvise. And they just had to ignore the constant scream and boom of the shells and the din of the gunfire as they worked. Amazing women.'

'They were,' Georgina agreed.

Bernard read out the rest of Percy's wartime letters to Ivy, and it was very clear that he planned to ask her to marry him when he returned from the war.

'In every single one of them, he asks her to send his regards to her parents,' Sybbie said. 'Which surely he wouldn't have done if there was any tension between them. He was very good friends with her brothers. So what made Douglas refuse to let Percy marry Ivy?'

'Grief can make you behave in unexpected ways,' Georgina said quietly. 'And remember that Mary died during the flu epidemic. By the time Percy came back from the trenches, Ivy was the only family Douglas had left. Maybe Douglas was scared that Percy would take his daughter away and he didn't want to lose her.'

'What, take her all the way to the farm next door?' Sybbie shook her head. 'More likely, Percy would've moved in with Douglas and Ivy instead of having a cottage on his parents' farm. Percy's roots were there in Ashingham. Of course they'd stay close after the wedding. Yet Douglas let Ivy marry Ernest, whose roots were near London. Surely there was a bigger risk of her moving away if she married Ernest?'

'Then there must've been some kind of falling-out between Douglas and Percy,' Bernard said. 'And you mentioned shell shock. Maybe Douglas was worried that Percy wouldn't be a good husband to Ivy – not deliberately, but because the war had affected the way Percy thought and felt and acted. Going through something like that would change you. A lot of the soldiers struggled to fit back into life here again; even the ones who were physically unscathed were mentally affected by what they'd been through. Plus we didn't understand about PTSD back then.'

'Or maybe, because Douglas was drinking to blot out the pain of losing his sons and his wife, his judgement was clouded,' Georgina said.

'We only have part of the story here,' Bernard said. 'Can we trace Winnie and her girls?'

'We know they moved to Norwich, just after the Second World War,' Georgina said. 'And the girls were most probably alive in 1991, because their records on the 1939 register are closed. If they're still alive now, they'll be nearly ninety.'

'If the girls had children, they'd probably be around our age – mine and Bernard's, that is,' Sybbie said thoughtfully. 'That's often when people get interested in family history. Maybe it's worth trying to find them, to see if they have diaries or letters that their grandmother kept.'

'I'll ask Bea if she can give us some help, when she's not on stage or rehearsing,' Georgina said.

They managed to finish going through the boxes, that morning, but didn't uncover anything else that shed light on Percy or Ivy's story.

'It might be worth asking Gaby if she has access to the farm's title deeds, because they weren't in these records,' Bernard suggested that afternoon, before he left for a meeting. 'Or if she knows what happened to the farmhouse at Holm Farm – that's assuming her family still live at the original farmhouse at Willow Farm.'

'Or even,' Georgina said as she made a note, 'if Winnie and Ivy stayed in touch after Winnie moved. Even if they didn't at first, if Winnie's family was still in Ashingham, maybe she heard through them that Ernest had died and sent her condolences, and she and Ivy reconnected their friendship from there?'

'It might be worth asking June if she knows anything more, too,' Sybbie said.

'I'll add it to our list,' Georgina said with a smile. 'Thank you for your help, Bernard.'

'Pleasure,' Bernard said. He kissed Sybbie goodbye. 'I'll see you for dinner.'

Colin went to see Alexsy Nowak, the head of the forensics team dealing with the Willow Farm case. Alexsy's office was much like Colin's own, full of desks with people working away at computers, but at the back of the room, there was a section where the staff wore white lab coats and latex gloves, with microscopes and light boxes and racks of laboratory glassware.

'I'm not intending to hassle you,' Colin said when he reached Alexsy. 'I was just coming to see how things are going – and wondering if you'd uncovered anything that might be useful,' he admitted.

'Because you're stuck and you could do with some information?' Alexsy asked.

Colin grimaced. 'You know what it's like at this stage of a case. We've hit a wall, both with the death and the missing person. There's so much we don't know – how Nathan ended up in that tank, who had a fight with him and when. You told me earlier that the evidence shows Ashley walked out of the studio, but we still have no idea whether he was on his own or left under duress, or where he is now.' He felt his hands tighten in frustration. 'My boss is complaining because his wife goes to Diana's yoga class, and she's pushing him to hurry up and get some answers for her friend.'

'We're not quite there yet, but I can tell you the preliminary findings. Though obviously you know the scene was compromised,' Alexsy added.

'They didn't have a lot of choice.' Colin gave him a rueful smile. 'If there was a chance that Nathan Edwards could be resuscitated, they had to take it.'

'True,' Alexsy agreed. 'But it means that there are extra prints all over the place, and we can't make assumptions about when those prints were made on the ladder, for example – were they before Nathan went into the tank?'

'If you want to hide your involvement in a crime scene, make sure your prints are there when you're helping to clear up after the event,' Colin said. It would be worth having another look at Del and Harry, and any tensions there had been between them and Nathan.

'From your notes, it seems Del and Harry were both on the platform together, lowered a loop of rope over the body and tightened it, then pulled him up,' Alexsy said.

'If he was unconscious, that would've been enough to make him a dead weight. It sounds as if using a rope to pull him up was the quickest way to get him out of the vat,' Colin said. 'Once he was out, Harry went down the ladder to the bottom and Del lowered him off the platform so Harry could ease him gently to the ground and start CPR.'

'That sounds like the easiest way to handle it,' Alexsy agreed. 'OK. In the winery, there are scrapes in the floor by the fermentation tanks. They could have been caused by the ladder falling on Monday, or they could have happened at any time.'

'Do you think the ladder accidentally fell, or was it deliberately moved?' Colin asked. 'And are there any prints on it?'

'We have prints – but they belong to several people,' Alexsy said, 'all of whom have a good reason for the prints to be there. As for the ladder itself, it's possible that Nathan accidentally kicked it away as he fell into the vat. It's also possible that someone moved it deliberately. My team asked Del Turnbull to do me a sketch showing the position of the ladder on the floor,' Alexsy continued, 'and he did his best, but he wasn't completely sure.'

'Pulling someone's body out of a vat and trying to resuscitate them would throw anyone into a spin,' Colin agreed. Or was it more sinister than that? Had Del been the one who climbed up to the platform and pushed Nathan into the vat in the first place? Though, so far, Colin hadn't been able to uncover a reason for Del to want to murder Nathan.

'Without CCTV or anyone else to corroborate what Del saw, we're limited,' Alexsy said.

'It could have been an industrial accident,' Colin said. 'It could have been as simple as it sounds: an experienced winemaker leaned over an open fermentation tank to take a sample of the wine; perhaps he was distracted by something and didn't take any of the usual precautions.'

'Which were what? Masks?' Alexsy asked.

'Apparently they either had someone with them or they let someone know what they were doing, so if they took longer than expected, then whoever they'd told would know something was wrong,' Colin said. 'For whatever reason, he did the sampling on his own and didn't tell anyone what he was doing. He leaned over the tank; when the carbon dioxide he breathed in made him dizzy, he fell into the tank and drowned. Which means the Health and Safety people will expect changes in the winery's procedures to make sure nothing like this could happen again.' Even as he spoke, though, Colin knew he didn't believe what he was saying.

Clearly Alexsy could read the doubt in his face. 'But you think there was more to it than that?' he asked.

'Sammy Grainger said Nathan had bruising to his face – you could see the knuckle marks, so it would've happened within the last twenty-four hours. There were tensions in his work life and his personal life. His brother's studio is smashed up and the artist has disappeared,' Colin said. 'Is there a connection between Nathan's death, whatever happened in the studio, and Ashley's disappearance?'

'One narrative could be that Nathan smashed up the artwork. Maybe there was a fight; or maybe Ashley was too shocked by his brother's actions to do anything at the time, but later perhaps went after him, pushed him into the vat and let him drown,' Alexsy suggested.

'We need to find where he went next,' Colin said. 'He hasn't been in contact with his family or his friends. I'm hoping he hasn't harmed himself.' He frowned. 'Did you get anything else from the studio?'

'The papers,' Alexsy said. 'Torn up and scattered, but we pieced them together. They include a letter from the government saying that Willow Farm had been turned down for a grant, because the inspector wasn't sure the criteria were reached. Biodiversity, protecting species and habitats, and managing the land to benefit the environment were all under question. I'll send you the file.'

'Thank you,' Colin said. 'And that's interesting. Gaby's the one who's trying to get organic status for her fields, and that fits in with everything that letter describes. Why was the letter in Ashley's studio, and who tore it to pieces?'

'We have prints,' Alexsy said.

'Any matches?' Colin asked.

'There are four sets,' Alexsy said. 'We took prints from Nick Edwards, Gaby Edwards and Del Turnbull yesterday, simply so we could exclude them from the studio and the fermentation tanks. I checked, and Nick's and Gaby's fingerprints are on the letter. The other two sets both match prints found at the studio. We dropped in to see Sammy and took prints from Nathan.'

'Hang on – are you telling me you can take prints from a dead body, one that has been in liquid for a while?' Colin interrupted.

'The hands were still in good condition, so yes,' Alexsy said. 'If there's rigor mortis, you press just above the knuckle, and it straightens the finger so you can take a print. But don't be fooled by the TV dramas using a corpse's fingers to unlock a phone. It can't happen.' He rolled his eyes. 'When you're dead, there isn't any electrical activity in your fingers, so the phone sensor won't work.' He gave Colin a rueful smile. 'Sorry. I imagine medics complain about TV hospital dramas as much as I do about TV forensics.'

Colin thought about Larissa's comment about middle-aged male grumbling. She had a point. 'And don't start me on crime drama stereotypes,' he said, smiling back. 'So were Nathan's fingerprints a match?'

'For the prints on the letter? Yes. You mentioned about the body being in liquid; it wasn't for long enough to make the epidermis swell, so I'd say he was in there for less than three hours. Sammy says that timing matches her observations, too,' Alexsy said. 'I think the fourth set of prints is most likely to be Ashley's. It's a pity his sculptures were melted. It would've been interesting to see if they included the fingerprints.'

'It might be worth asking Gaby or Diana if they have anything that might show Ashley's prints – a book at their house, or a mug,' Colin said. 'In the meantime, Alexsy, if you can send me a copy of that letter, I think I need a chat with the Edwardses.'

Alexsy pulled up a file on his computer. 'I'm emailing it to you now,' he said, tapping the keyboard.

THIRTEEN

Georgina texted Bea.

> As you know, am embroiled in another cold case. Know you're busy at the Regency, but if you get time between rehearsals, can I ask for help finding the descendants of the family, please? Will email you what I have. Love you xx

She sent Bea an email including screenshots of the entries of Percy and Winnie's daughters from the births registers, along with Percy and Winnie's dates of birth, their wedding, and the information June had given her that Winnie had moved to Norwich with their daughters.

Bea texted back quickly.

> Will do my best tomorrow! Please stay out of trouble. Don't eat or drink *anything* you haven't made yourself. Love you xx

'That's telling you,' Sybbie said wryly. 'I think she'd have Colin on her side about that, too. And Will.'

'It's fine,' Georgina said. 'Doris has been very quiet. We're pretty much stuck until we hear from her, and I'd prefer to go back to June with a decent list of questions rather than risk annoying her by doing it in dribs and drabs.'

'Maybe we need to talk to Gaby and Diana,' Sybbie suggested. 'Shall I call Gaby and see if we can drop in?'

'Yes, please,' Georgina said. 'We can return Rosemary's boxes, too.'

She'd just finished repacking the boxes when Sybbie ended the call and said to her, 'Gaby says she'll meet at us her mum's place – Chalk Valley Wines.'

'I'll drive us,' Georgina said. 'Should I drop Bert home, first?'

'Leave him here. He'll be fine with Max and Jet,' Sybbie said.

They were halfway to Chalk Valley Wines – this time, heading north of Norwich rather than south of the city – when Doris said, 'So where exactly are we off to?'

'The vineyard where Gaby's mum works,' Georgina said.

'Oh, is that Doris joining us? Hi, there,' Sybbie said. 'We're returning Gaby's boxes. We found some letters from Percy to Ivy, written from Ypres. It's very clear that they were in love with each other, but we can't work out what went wrong and why they didn't get married. If you don't mind Georgie repeating everything you tell her, I'm all ears.'

'That works for me, too, if you don't mind, Doris,' Georgina added.

'Let's do that,' Doris said. 'I've been talking to Percy, and he's remembered a lot more. He said he was suffering from shell shock at the end of the war. He was demobilised just before Christmas 1918; he was one of the lucky ones, sent home relatively quickly from the trenches. But it took a while for him to adjust, and nothing felt real when he got home. All the things he'd been longing for while he was away, all the bits of home he valued most – the peace and the quiet, seeing the cows and hearing birdsong – he said they felt as if they were happening to other people, not him. He wasn't connected anymore. He felt lost.'

Georgina relayed the information to Sybbie.

'That's so sad,' Sybbie said. 'Wanting to come home, missing those you love, and then it doesn't feel the same anymore when you finally get there.'

'My granddad fought in the First World War, too,' Doris said. 'He'd never talk about it. He said he wouldn't want the things he'd seen giving nightmares to his wife or his parents or his children. Percy gave me the impression it was the same for him. It was a struggle for him to open up to me, at first, until I reminded him that this was the only way his family would finally get closure. He said he kept dreaming that he was back in the trenches, with all the mud and the noise and the gas and the stench of blood. He'd wake himself up screaming in the middle of the night, and it woke everyone else, too. In the end, he moved out to one of the farm cottages so his family could get some sleep, but he was so tired, every minute of every day. And he flinched every time he saw a rat – which, on a farm, happens quite a bit.'

'Poor man,' Georgina said.

'Because he was still trying to settle back to a normal life, it took Percy a while to notice what was going on with Douglas's drinking and Ivy being left to fend for herself,' Doris continued. 'By then, Douglas had hired Ernest to help out at the farm – they'd lost half a dozen of the farmworkers at Willow Farm in the war, so Douglas was pleased to find the extra help. But Percy couldn't stand Ernest. He thought he was out to marry Ivy and then take over the farm.'

'Which is pretty much what happened, isn't it?' Sybbie commented when Georgina passed on what Doris had said.

'But he built up to it. He charmed all the women in the village – the baker's wife always slipped him a bit of shortcake, the butcher's wife would give him an extra slice of bacon or a sausage, the greengrocer's wife would hand him an apple for the twinkle in his eye. Ernest went out of his way to be nice to Ivy – who'd been under a lot of strain for the last couple of years. He brought her a bunch of wildflowers he'd picked, or a ribbon for her hair, or something sweet from the fair. He paid attention to her and he made her laugh, whereas Percy brooded about the trenches and made her feel she'd always be stuck in the shadows between him and her dad. Then Ernest told her he could see what was happening with her dad, and if it would help, he'd play cards with her dad every evening and try and distract him from the bottle of whisky,' Doris said.

'Couldn't Percy see he was losing her?' Georgina asked.

'He just saw Ernest trying to get his feet under the table. He was too wrapped up in his own head to think properly about Ivy. It was almost Christmas, 1920, and Percy tried to warn Douglas that Ernest only had his own interests at heart, but he got nowhere – Douglas wouldn't hear a word against the man who'd made himself indispensable. Instead of realising that it'd be better to back off and think up a strategy to win Douglas over, Percy came straight out with it,' Doris said. 'He told Douglas he'd been in love with Ivy for years and they planned to marry now the war was over. Douglas retorted that his daughter was nineteen years old and he would refuse permission for her to get married until she turned twenty-one. And even then he absolutely refused to give his blessing to any marriage between her and Percy; he'd lost his beloved sons, and he couldn't forgive Percy for coming home when Sid and Len didn't. It made him wonder if Percy was some sort of coward, to have survived when so many didn't. Percy was furious and they had a stand-up row.'

'Oh, Percy – why didn't you wait instead of rushing in and having a fight with Douglas?' Sybbie asked, when she heard the next bit of the story. 'I know he was damaged by what happened in the war, but going head-to-head with a stubborn old man is never going to work. There's pride, there's... Oh!' she said crossly. 'For goodness' sake. Why on earth didn't he let Ivy do the talking for him?'

'That was part of the problem,' Doris said. 'Ernest obviously saw how neglected Ivy was, and he turned on the charm. Starved of love and attention by both her dad and Percy, she blossomed under Ernest's words.'

'The poor girl was a sitting duck,' Georgina said.

'When Ernest asked her to marry him, she said yes. They got married in 1922 – the year before she turned twenty-one,' Doris said. 'Percy was devastated when he found out she'd accepted. Ironically, considering what actually happened to him, he thought about drowning himself in Holm Pond, because he couldn't bear to see Ivy with Ernest. Winnie found him sitting brooding there, on her way to see his sister Millie.'

'Was Winnie friends with his sister, then?' Sybbie asked.

'Winnie was working with her aunt as a dressmaker, and Millie wanted to talk to her about making a wedding dress,' Doris explained. 'Winnie talked to Percy and stopped him doing something rash. She pointed out how devastated his family would be to lose him after he'd made it home from the war. Over the next few months, they got closer, and eventually he fell in love with her, though he never quite forgot his first love.'

'That's so sad,' Georgina said. 'But I'm glad he managed to find some happiness with Winnie.'

'After Douglas died – the month before Percy's wedding to Winnie – Percy noticed how unhappy Ivy seemed,' Doris said. 'Not just because she'd lost both her parents; she'd been married to Ernest for three years, by this point, and there was still no sign of a baby. They met up when she was walking the boundary of the farm with the dog, checking if any of the fences needed fixing. She admitted to Percy that she thought she'd made a mistake marrying Ernest, and said she was sure Ernest had another woman because things weren't right between them. Percy urged her to leave Ernest; there had been a change in the divorce laws, a couple of years before, so if she could prove Ernest's adultery, she could get a divorce. He said he'd never forgotten how he felt about her. And, even though he didn't want to hurt Winnie and he loved her, it wasn't the same as the way he felt about Ivy. Percy said he was prepared to break it off with Winnie and marry Ivy, if that was what she wanted.'

Again, Georgina passed on what Doris had said. 'Whatever he did, at least one person was going to be hurt,' Sybbie said, wincing. 'If he left Winnie, he'd break her heart; if he didn't marry Ivy, it'd break his heart and Ivy's, too. This situation was never going to have a happy ending, was it?'

'Ivy turned him down. She said she wasn't going to break up a marriage before it had even started. Winnie was her friend, and no way would she hurt another woman like that,' Doris continued. 'Though she admitted she'd always loved Percy, too. But she'd found it so hard to cope when he came home from the war – when he seemed to shut off from her, and her dad was going rapidly downhill. She felt the only chance of happiness she had was with Ernest, and her dad seemed to approve of Ernest where he'd rejected Percy. She thought maybe Ernest would help her stop her dad drinking. In hindsight, she knew it had been the wrong decision, because it hadn't worked out that way, but she'd made her bed and now she had no choice but to lie in it. Ernest was clever, and he'd never give her the chance to prove he was committing adultery.'

'Poor Ivy,' Georgina said. 'To be stuck in a loveless marriage would be hard enough, but then she learned the man she'd always loved still loved her, too. She must've been so tempted to agree to go away with him and have the life she'd always wanted. Though, at the same time, I get why she didn't want to take her chance of happiness at someone else's expense. And I'm proud of her for not treading over Winnie's dreams.'

'I agree. And in those days there were so many "surplus women" who'd lost their loved ones in the war,' Sybbie said, making quote marks with her fingers. 'Weren't there nearly two million more women than men?'

'Something like that,' Georgina agreed.

'If Percy had walked away from Winnie,' Georgina said thoughtfully, 'Winnie would've had more choices in her career. She would've had a lot more independence than she'd had before the war. But if she was in love with Percy and wanted to settle down and make a family, it wouldn't have been fair to take that choice from her.' She paused. 'What happened when Ivy turned Percy down? Did he try to change her mind?'

'I think he accepted her decision,' Doris said, 'because he carried on with Winnie's wedding plans. Though Ernest must've found out from somewhere that Ivy had talked to Percy, and he wasn't going to take any chance of letting her get away,' she added. 'The night before Percy's wedding, Ernest came over to Holm Farm and made it very clear that Percy was to stay away from his wife – he didn't want Winnie being friends with her when she moved to Holm Farm, and he didn't want Ivy within a hundred yards of Percy. And if Percy didn't stay away from her, Ernest would make very sure he regretted it. Percy could hardly tell Winnie about the situation, or even his sisters or his parents. Len and Sid were dead, so he didn't have his closest friends to confide in; and he didn't dare risk talking about it to any of his other friends. Not because he was scared for himself,' Doris said, 'but he thought gossip was bound to leak out, as it clearly already had, and he worried that Ernest might take it out on Ivy. The way he saw it, Ivy was already unhappy enough and he didn't want to make it worse. So Percy did his best to stay away from her. He tried to be a good husband to

Winnie, and when the girls were born, he tried to be a good father.'

'I sense there's a "but" coming,' Sybbie said dryly.

'Sadly, there is,' Doris said. 'It got to 1930. Ivy had been married to Ernest for nine years now, and still there was no baby. One night, Percy went for a walk around the farm boundaries, and he found Ivy sitting by the pond, crying. Ernest wasn't home, and she thought he'd taken his fancy woman to a hotel or something in Norwich, but she couldn't prove it. Percy tried to comfort her, and one thing led to another,' Doris said. 'He felt terrible, afterwards. He'd betrayed Winnie, the woman who'd unfailingly loved him and supported him. And when Ivy gave birth to a baby boy, nine months later...'

'Hang on. Was Terence actually Percy's son?' Georgina asked.

'Percy wasn't sure. But if a couple try to have a baby, and nearly a decade later there's still no baby, there's obviously a problem somewhere,' Doris said. 'The thing is, Percy had red hair. And by the time Terence was a toddler, his hair colour had changed and it was obvious that he had red hair, too.'

'That doesn't mean Percy was definitely Terence's father,' Sybbie said, when Georgina told her what Doris had said. 'You can carry the gene for red hair and not have red hair yourself.'

'Ivy said her brother Sid had auburn hair,' Doris said. 'But Ernest didn't believe her. All he saw was that his wife had been barren for nearly ten years, and then finally she has a baby. By the time the baby's a toddler, his hair's red – and the man she'd once been going to marry had red hair, too. In his eyes, it was obvious that Percy was Terence's dad. Percy wondered about it, too, though he avoided Ivy because he didn't want to stir up any rumours and give Ernest an excuse to make her unhappy. And it made him think about what might have been if Douglas hadn't refused to let them get married. Yes, he was upset about what he read in the newspapers about Europe, worrying that war would come again; but half his melancholy was about the boy he thought might be his son, and that Ernest might be taking things out on Ivy and making her even more miserable in her marriage than she already was,' Doris said. 'It went on for a good few months, but then Ernest got drunk one night and pitched up at Percy's door. Percy suspected Ernest was finally going to tackle him about Terence's paternity, and he didn't want Winnie to overhear anything and find out he'd had a one-night stand with Ivy – he didn't want to hurt her – so he took Ernest away from the house.'

'By the pond?' Georgina asked.

'By the pond,' Doris agreed. 'There was an argument. Percy said that Ivy was too good for Ernest, and Ernest just lost his temper. He hit Percy; Percy went down and hit his head on a flint. And that was it.'

'But if Ernest turned up at the house, drunk and angry, wouldn't Winnie have overheard him yelling at Percy? She could've pointed the police in Ernest's direction as someone who'd fallen out with Percy, and came to the house and threatened him. Surely that made him a suspect?' Sybbie asked.

'Apparently their youngest daughter was poorly and Winnie was nursing her in the back bedroom. She didn't hear a thing. And the older girls would've been in their rooms, asleep,' Doris said. 'Nobody knew Ernest had been to Holm Farm. Everyone in the village knew there was no love lost between Ernest and Percy, but thought they stayed away from each other for Ivy's sake.'

'Didn't Ivy wonder if Ernest might have had something to do with Percy's disappearance, because he suspected Percy was Terence's father?' Georgina asked. Then she sighed. 'Sorry. Of course Percy won't be able to answer that. He won't know about anything that happened after his death.'

'Percy being Terence's father would explain a lot,' Sybbie said thoughtfully. 'Ernest wouldn't really have been able to denounce Ivy as a cheat, because there was red hair in her family. Plus there weren't DNA tests back then to prove paternity. But he would've held his suspicions against the boy. Nothing Terence did would ever make Ernest approve of him or think of him as his son. And if Ernest constantly rejected the boy, it's no wonder that Terence became the kind of man who had affairs all the time. He'd be looking for love, and no one person would ever have been enough for him.'

'Even if Ivy tried to make up for Ernest, she would've felt guilty every time she saw him, not knowing whether he was Ernest's or Percy's. Terence might've picked up on that subconsciously,' Georgina said. 'Maybe she did worry that Ernest was behind Percy's disappearance, but she couldn't follow it through; if she admitted what had happened between her and Percy, too many innocent people would be hurt by the fallout – Winnie, the girls, and Terence. How tragic, for all of them.'

'It's going to be hard to explain this to Gaby and Diana,' Sybbie said.

'We'll give them the short version, with lots of "maybes" in it,' Georgina said. 'Without the proof of a diary, letters or family hearsay, it's still only a theory.' She paused. 'But Percy does know now that he was missed, Doris? That people cared?'

'I told him the village turned out to look for him,' Doris said. 'He was humbled. And also very sad. He says his dad would've remembered Percy's nightmares after he came home from the trenches, and Winnie would've remembered him thinking about ending things when Ivy got married, so he's not surprised people thought his mind had been turned by the news from Europe and his conviction that war would start up again. But his biggest sadness is that he didn't get to see his girls grow up, or be the husband Winnie deserved.'

'All of them lost out,' Georgina said sadly.

FOURTEEN

As with Willow Farm and Rosa Wines, the land around Chalk Valley Wines was covered with rows and rows of neat vines. Georgina turned into the driveway and parked by the office; Diana and Gaby both came out to meet them.

'Welcome to Chalk Valley,' Diana said. 'Would you like some wine, or would you prefer tea or coffee?'

'I'm driving,' Georgina said, 'so coffee would be lovely, thanks.'

'Coffee for me, too, please,' Sybbie said.

'Come into the house,' Diana said. 'We can be a bit more comfortable there.'

'I'll just get Rosemary's files from the back of the car,' Georgina said.

'I'll give you a hand,' Gaby offered.

'And I'll help with the coffee,' Sybbie said. 'Georgie, I'll take your laptop.'

'Thanks, Sybbie.'

'Did you bring Bert with you?' Gaby asked.

'No,' Georgina said.

'That's a shame, because Monty would've enjoyed playing with him.'

'How are you doing, Gaby?' Georgina asked, turning to the younger woman.

'It's all pretty grim at the moment,' Gaby admitted. 'We can't really do anything until the police have finished investigating and the coroner's been involved. Dad's not talking to anyone – he just stomps around, and everyone's keeping out of his way in case he has a hissy fit on them. Including me,' she said.

'Is there any news about Ashley?' Georgina asked.

Gaby shook her head. 'We're pretty sure he hasn't been badly hurt – the blood in his studio was definitely from the melted sculptures. But he's really gone to ground, this time. We've tried everyone we can think of. Nobody's seen him – well, if they have, they're not telling. I just hope that wherever he is, he's got someone looking out for him and he's taking his meds.' She grimaced. 'At least, we think he took his meds with him – they're not in his bedside cabinet or his bathroom.'

'I'm sorry. It must be so worrying for you,' Georgina said. The bright, sparkling young woman she'd met a couple of days ago looked pale, with deep shadows beneath her blue eyes; no doubt she was finding it hard to sleep.

'Mum suggested I came and stayed with her and Shaun for a bit. I couldn't face going back to an empty house at the end of the day,' Gaby said. 'Though I feel a bit guilty, because that's what Dad's doing. But I don't want to put myself in the firing line of his bad moods.'

'That's completely understandable,' Georgina said.

When they brought the boxes into the kitchen, a handsome liver-and-white English springer spaniel trotted over from where he was being fussed by Sybbie, to sniff at Georgina's knees.

'You must be Monty. Hello. You're a beauty. And Gaby's right, you do look like my Bert,' Georgina said, scratching behind the dog's ears and earning an enthusiastic wag of his plumy tail. She accepted a mug of coffee gratefully from Diana and sat at the kitchen table next to Sybbie, while Gaby took the fourth chair and Monty wriggled under the table to lie at everyone's feet. 'This is lovely,' she said. 'Thank you. How are you doing, Diana?'

'Not great,' the other woman admitted. 'I can't do anything to help Nathan, now, and Ashley's vanished. It feels a bit horrible of me, but I'm glad you're here to talk about the skeleton, because it means I can block out what's happening at Willow Farm and not think about it for a little while.'

'It's not horrible at all,' Sybbie reassured her. 'Distraction's a good thing. The only thing you can do right now is wait, and that's very hard to do.'

'It is,' Diana confirmed. 'Did you manage to find out much?'

'A bit, but some of it's speculation,' Georgina warned. 'Some of it's through official archive records and newspapers, and some of it's from someone who worked for Ivy back in the 1950s and remembered her parents talking about the Ramseys at Holm Farm. Her great-grandson works at Willow Farm now.'

'Oh – would that be Tyler Wood?' Diana asked. 'I remember working with June in the fields. She always had a wicked sense of humour. It's good to know she's still around.'

'Yes, we went to see June,' Georgina confirmed. Some of her information was directly from Percy; not that she could explain that easily. 'Plus we found some letters to Ivy in Rosemary's papers – from Percy, the son of the farmer next door, written from Ypres,' she said instead.

'And Ivy kept them all those years?' Diana said. She looked thoughtful. 'I guess he must've died in the war, then, because she didn't marry him.'

'It's a little bit more complicated than that,' Sybbie said.

Georgina explained what they'd found out about Percy, Ivy

and Ernest, and showed Diana and Gaby the screenshots she'd taken from the records.

'Winnie had to have Percy declared presumed dead?' Diana asked.

Georgina nodded. 'She had to wait for seven years; provided there was no evidence he was still alive, he hadn't contacted the people most likely to hear from him – which would've been his parents, his wife and his daughters – and all the enquiries she'd made about him were unsuccessful, the court could declare him presumed dead. Obviously if he reappeared after then, they could reverse it and declare him no longer dead.'

Gaby and Diana glanced at each other, and Georgina could guess what they were thinking. *Would they have to do that with Ashley?*

'Sorry. That wasn't meant to be quite so tactless,' she apologised. 'I'm sure you'll hear from Ashley soon. He's close to you both.'

'I just hope he hasn't done anything rash,' Gaby said. 'And I keep thinking, what if I was the last person to see him alive? That is, apart from whoever smashed up his studio. I had my usual cup of tea with him on Sunday morning.' She bit her lip. 'I honestly thought he was on an even keel. He was planning to do some sketching, later – he was doing a series of the vineyard, sketching the same bunch of grapes every day so you could see the change over the course of harvest, and he'd got interested in the wildlife. He likes the birds, and he reckons we have skylarks – which is wonderful. I asked him to try and video a skylark on his phone, next time he hears one; even if he only gets the song and the video is of the vineyard rather than the birds, it'd be lovely on the vineyard's blog. Plus it keeps him involved in the vineyard.' She shook her head. 'But what if he was starting to have a wobble and I missed the signs?'

'I don't think you missed anything, sweetheart,' Diana said.

'You've always supported his art, and he appreciates that. The police need to find whoever smashed up the studio.'

'Trust in the forensics,' Georgina said.

'I guess,' Gaby said, looking miserable. 'Do you think the skeleton Bert found in the vineyard is Percy?'

'I think it's very likely. From what Rowena – the finds liaison officer – said, he's the right age and from the right time period,' Georgina said.

'God, that's awful. Poor man.' Gaby's eyes widened. 'But was it an accident?'

'There's a crack in his skull,' Georgina said. 'He might have tripped and fallen; or, yes, I do think someone might have pushed him.' It was easier to explain it that way than to say that Ernest had punched him. 'What we do know is that his skull was thinner than most people's, and that's why the impact caused a crack in his skull.'

'And whoever did it realised he was dead, panicked and rolled him into the pond?' Diana shook her head. 'Poor man. And his poor wife and children, never knowing what happened to him.'

'Do you think,' Gaby asked carefully, 'my great-grandfather Ernest was the one to kill him?'

'It's one theory,' Sybbie said. 'And the most likely motive there was jealousy. Maybe he believed Percy was Terence's father. After all, Ernest and Ivy had been married for nearly ten years and they hadn't yet had a baby. If Percy and Ivy were still in love with each other, what if they got carried away and Terence was the result?'

'And if Ernest suspected that,' Diana said, 'he would've been vile to both Ivy and Terence, as well as wanting revenge on Percy.' She blew out a breath. 'Ernest died in 1945, and I know Ivy never remarried. Maybe it was Percy she was mourning, rather than Ernest.' She looked thoughtful. 'It makes a bit of sense now about how Terence was with Nick. If his own dad was always difficult with him — because he wasn't sure if Terence was actually his son — then that could be why Terence was always so hard on Nick. Following the same pattern.'

Gaby blinked. 'You actually sound sympathetic towards Dad.'

'I loved your father, once. Enough to marry him,' Diana said. 'It's a lot of years since we split up, enough for me not to resent him as much as I did at the end of our marriage. I think it's a shame your dad's never found happiness, either in his personal life or his work. I've been lucky — I've had both.'

Gaby frowned. 'Hang on. I thought Dad loved Willow Farm?'

'Yes and no,' Diana said. She sighed. 'It all comes back to Terence. I have to admit, your grandmother was an incredible woman, but I didn't like your grandfather very much. He could be really charming when he wanted something from you, but he could also be a bully. Your dad tried so hard to please him, but nothing Nick did was ever good enough for Terence. Nick had to prove himself to his dad over and over and over again. Which I'm guessing is the way Terence's father was with him — I can see the pattern.'

'Me, too,' Gaby said thoughtfully. 'It's the way Dad's always been with Ash and Nathan.'

'Your dad wanted to be an engineer, when he was younger,' Diana said. 'But your grandfather said Nick was the only child, so he had to carry on the family business. I think your gran tried to intercede, but Terence was adamant. Carry on with the farm, or get out. When Terence died, Rosemary said she'd sell the farm and Nick could retrain and do what he really wanted — but by then we had two small children and he didn't feel he was in a place where he could give up work and go back to being a student, even though I would've supported him to do it. I just wanted him to be happy, but he said it was too late to change career.' She sighed. 'I wish now that I'd pushed harder. Maybe we'd still have been together, Ash wouldn't have been so fragile, and Nathan would've been less... I don't know, *angry* all the time.'

'I never knew about any of that,' Gaby said. 'And it explains an awful lot.' She looked shocked. 'I never thought I'd feel sorry for Dad, but actually I do.'

'It was his choice,' Diana reminded her. 'When his dad died, he took over the farm, and Rosemary set up Rosa Wines. Over the years, your dad got more and more difficult to live with. He didn't even bother hiding his affairs, towards the end. By the time you were five, I'd had enough, and that's why I walked out. I wish I'd managed to take the boys with me as well as you.'

'Nobody blames you, Mum. It sounds as if Dad made the same mistakes his own father made,' Gaby said. 'OK, so he lets Ash do his art, but nothing Ash does ever pleases Dad – even though Ash is really talented.'

'And no amount of love is ever enough for the Edwards men,' Diana said softly. 'After Ivy died, Rosemary told me Ernest died in a car being driven by one of his mistresses. Terence wasn't faithful to Rosemary. Your dad wasn't faithful to me. And Nathan wasn't faithful to Kelly. It's just a long, long line of anger and resentment, and nobody's been able to break it.'

'That's really sad. Maybe some talking treatments might've helped them all deal with things a bit better.' Gaby grimaced. 'Mind you, I can imagine Dad's reaction if anyone suggested that to him. He'd go spare.' She sighed. 'So where do we go from here?'

'We wait for Ash to contact us, unless the police find him first,' Diana said. 'And hopefully the police will find out what happened to Nathan.'

'I'm sorry we couldn't bring you anything more positive,' Georgina said.

'But at least you've found out who the skeleton is, even if his story's really sad,' Gaby said. 'He can at least be buried properly now.' She paused. 'Can we find out if he definitely was my great-grandfather? You know, DNA testing or something?'

'That's definitely possible,' Georgina said, remembering the previous cases where they'd tested skeletal remains and discovered the link to present-day relatives. 'I can talk to Colin and get that arranged, if you'd like me to.'

'Thank you,' Gaby said. 'That'd be great.'

'I also brought the photos from our shoot over for you to have a look at,' Georgina said. 'I'd like to finish off with a few shots in the winery, as well as the wildlife shots I suggested to Gaby, but only when the police have said it's OK.'

'I'm almost tempted to suggest you doing the winery shots here,' Diana said, 'but Nick will see it as evidence of me trying to poach our daughter.' She rolled her eyes. 'At least here she'd be supported with using sustainable methods. Not to mention she'd get the chance to learn more about sparkling wine.'

'Mum,' Gaby said, putting a hand on her arm. 'I'd love us to work together again – and we will, one day. But right now I need to make sure Gran's legacy carries on.'

'I know, love.' Diana put her hand over Gaby's and squeezed it. 'I'm sorry. I don't mean to pressure you.'

Gaby and Diana were both pleased with the photos.

'I know this is really cheeky, because you're doing them for the magazine, but this one of her with the fields behind her – it's gorgeous. Could I buy a copy so I can frame it?' Diana asked.

'I'm sure the magazine won't mind you having a copy,' Georgina said. 'Obviously there's copyright involved, so I'll need to clear it with them, but I don't think it'll be a problem at all.'

Georgina and Sybbie were about to leave when the kitchen door opened and a man walked in. He was tall and muscular, with grey-blond hair that had been cropped short, and the kind of tan that said he spent most of his working life outdoors. Monty bounded over to him and twined round his legs.

'Oof, Monty, mind my poor knees,' he said, but he bent to pet the dog. 'Hello,' he said with a smile, and turned enquiringly to Diana. 'I didn't realise we had visitors today, Di.'

'We're actually just on our way out. Georgina Drake and Sybbie Walters,' Georgina said, introducing themselves swiftly.

'Shaun Phillips,' he said, shaking her hand and then Sybbie's. 'You're the photographer and her friend who've been looking at the skeleton, right?'

'Right.' Georgina smiled, but she'd noticed the livid bruise on Shaun's face.

He clearly realised that she'd seen it, because he winced. 'Given what happened at Willow Farm, I know this looks suspicious – but it's not. It's just a bit embarrassing,' he said. 'I was taking Monty for a walk through the vineyard early on Monday morning – which I like to do, to listen to the birdsong – when I tripped over my own feet, fell over straight onto my hands and knees, and banged my face on one of the supports for the vines. It really hurt, and I thought I might've broken my wrist, so I limped back home with the dog and got Di to drive me to the hospital so I could get it checked out.'

Georgina thought how convenient Colin would think that excuse was, and it must've shown in her expression because Shaun grimaced. 'I promise you, I had nothing to do with whatever happened to Ashley or to Nathan on Monday. I like Ashley, and I feel sorry for him because Nick and Nathan always give him a hard time. I admit, I'm not so fond of Nathan – he's too much of his dad's mini-me for my liking, and I really don't like the way he treats our Gaby. But I would never have done anything to hurt him. That's not who I am.'

'What he's not telling you,' Diana said, slipping her arm through his, 'is that his dad had Parkinson's, and it started when he was the age Shaun is now. Shaun's been really clumsy lately, tripping all over the place, and he's half convinced himself that he's got Parkinson's. But will he go to see the GP to get some reassurance?'

'I'm all right,' Shaun said. 'Don't make a fuss over nothing, Di. There are plenty of people who need an appointment far more than I do.'

'Hmm,' Diana said.

'We'll let you get on,' Georgina said. 'Nice to meet you, Shaun. Let me know when you're able to finish off the photo session, Gaby.'

'Actually, could I ask a huge favour?' Gaby said. 'Some of Ash's friends might be a bit – well, wary of the police. And they might not want to talk to us in case Dad muscles in. But I've been thinking about it. You're a fellow artist, so they might talk to you. Especially if they know you've taken my photo for that magazine.'

'And perhaps I've suggested to you that another magazine might be interested in an article about your older brother, who does rather unusual artwork?' Georgina asked, cottoning on.

'I know it's a big ask,' Gaby said. 'Just... I'm really worried about Ash. If he doesn't want us to know where he is, that's all right. We just need to know he's OK, and that his friends will get help if he's having a wobble.'

'All right,' Georgina said. 'Let me have a list of names and phone numbers. And if you know they have a website, that'd be handy, too.'

'I'll message you,' Gaby promised. 'Thank you so much, Georgie.' Her eyes filled with tears. 'I just want to know my brother's safe.'

On the way back to Little Wenborough, Georgina was thoughtful. 'Do you think Shaun was telling the truth about how he got that bruise on his face, Sybbie?'

'Possibly. Are you thinking he's involved?' Sybbie asked.

'I don't think Gaby killed Nathan – I've already said to Colin that if she wanted revenge on him for interfering in her vineyard, she'd do it by excelling and proving she's better than he is,' Georgina said. 'But what if there was a row between her and Nathan, and Shaun decided to stand up for her?'

'And the bruise on his face and any damage to his hand was from a fight, rather than from falling over?' Sybbie asked. 'Maybe. But if he did go to the hospital to be checked out, it means there's a record of his visit with a time and date – and they'll also have an idea about what actually caused the damage to his hand.'

'I think I should mention it to Colin,' Georgina said, 'so he can check it out and rule Shaun out.'

'Or,' Sybbie said grimly, 'rule him in.'

FIFTEEN

Colin steeled himself as he parked on the gravel outside Willow Farm Wines. Given his previous behaviour, Nick Edwards was likely to be aggressive and difficult. And, even though Colin had little patience with adult tantrums, he had to remain professional.

'Ready?' he asked Mo.

Mo nodded. 'I think we have to grit our teeth and just get on with it. And,' he added, 'make sure your bodycam's switched on.'

'Good call.' Even though Colin wasn't planning to make an arrest, he thought that this could potentially be tricky and recording it would be the best way to make sure there was a proper record of what happened.

They climbed out of the car – the only one parked there, Colin noticed, so there were no visitors today – and Colin pressed the intercom.

'Yes?' The voice sounded slightly tetchy, and Colin winced.

'DI Colin Bradshaw and DS Mo Tesfaye, here to see Nicholas Edwards,' he said.

'You don't have an appointment. What do you want?' the voice demanded.

Colin raised his eyebrows at Mo. If one of your sons had died and the other was missing, would you insist that the police made an appointment to see you?

'To speak to you about your sons, Mr Edwards,' Colin said.

'Oh, for... All right. But I'm busy.' The intercom crackled and went silent. A few moments later, the door was pulled open and Nick stood there, glowering at them. 'Have you found Ashley?' he demanded.

'Not yet,' Colin said. 'We have a few questions we'd like you to answer, please. And please be aware that my bodycam is currently recording.'

Nick glowered at him. 'Why? I haven't done anything wrong. Or are you' – he turned to stare at Mo – 'and that Black b—'

'I strongly advise you not to continue with that sentence, Mr Edwards,' Colin said quietly. 'Racial abuse is unacceptable and it's an arrestable offence.'

'Are you threatening to arrest me?' Nick demanded, narrowing his eyes at Colin. 'You haven't got any grounds. You're supposed to be finding my missing son. Why are you wasting time instead of doing your job?'

'We're investigating the death of your son Nathan,' Colin pointed out, making the effort to keeping his tone even. 'I'd like to interview you under caution, Mr Edwards – which isn't the same as arresting you. It simply means I think you may have information that's relevant to this case, and interviewing you under caution protects your rights.' When Nick said nothing, Colin clarified, 'I'm asking you to come to the station for a voluntary interview under caution. If you prefer, I can arrest you, and we'll still end up at the station.'

'Do I need a solicitor?' Nick asked.

'You have the right to legal representation if you wish to

have it,' Colin said. 'You can either use the duty solicitor or instruct a solicitor of your choice.'

'I'll call my lawyer,' Nick said, scowling.

'Good. Nicholas Edwards, you do not have to say anything. But it may harm your defence if you do not mention, when questioned, something which you later rely on in court. Anything you do say may be given in evidence,' Colin said.

Without letting them past the front door, Nick phoned his lawyer and arranged for a solicitor to meet him at the police station. Without comment, Mo sat with Nick in the back of Colin's car, and they drove to Norwich in silence.

Nick's solicitor was already waiting for them at the police station. Colin ensured he and Nick were given a hot drink while they conferred in one of the custody rooms.

'I think it might be better if Larissa sat in rather than me,' Mo said. 'He might have fewer issues with her.'

Colin rather thought that Nick was a misogynist as well as racist, but he understood. 'Talk to Larissa and decide between you,' he said. 'Whichever of you comes to the interview, you'll have my full support.'

'That goes without saying. And it's appreciated,' Mo said.

In the end, Larissa was the one who sat in. As soon as Nick and his solicitor had finished talking and the solicitor indicated that Nick was ready for the interview, Colin took them through to the voluntary interview room. It was very similar to the main interview rooms – painted blue, with a table bolted to the concrete floor, four chairs and the recording equipment.

He introduced the four of them for the benefit of the recording, re-cautioned Nick, and reminded him that he had the right to free and independent legal advice, he wasn't under arrest and he could leave at any time.

'So what did you want to talk to me about?' Nick asked.

'Our forensic team has investigated the area where Nathan

died, and also Ashley's studio.' Colin paused. 'We found a letter that had been torn up.'

'What's that got to do with me?' Nick asked.

He wanted to drag this out and do it step by step? Fine. 'The letter was addressed to you,' Colin said.

Nick frowned. 'And?'

'For the benefit of the recording, I'm showing exhibit 1A to Mr Edwards,' Colin said, and passed a printout of the letter to Nick. 'Do you recognise this letter, Mr Edwards?'

'What's that got to do with my son going missing?' Nick demanded.

It was definitely going to be one of *those* interviews, Colin thought resignedly. 'I'll ask you again, Mr Edwards. Do you recognise this letter?'

After a prompt from his solicitor, Nick nodded.

'For the recording, please, Mr Edwards?'

'Yes.' Nick's voice was full of exasperation.

'Could you explain to me what the letter means?' Colin asked.

Nick scowled. 'It means we didn't get the government grant we applied for.'

'Which particular areas of land did the proposed grant relate to?' Colin asked.

'My late mother's vineyard,' Nick bit out.

'Is that the land your daughter Gabrielle looks after?' Colin asked.

'Yes.' Nick raked a hand through his hair. 'She was the one who made all the fuss about doing it. Obviously she didn't fill in the form properly.'

'I believe that you own the title to the land, so your name is the one that would've needed to be on the form,' Colin pointed out. 'And that's also why the letter's addressed to you, rather than to her.'

'What's your point?' Nick demanded.

'I was wondering why the letter was ripped into small pieces and scattered in your son's art studio,' Colin said mildly.

'How the hell am I supposed to know that?' Nick stared at him in outrage.

'Your fingerprints are on the letter,' Colin said.

'So?'

'As are Gabrielle's fingerprints.'

'I gave it to her, so she could see for herself she'd messed up,' Nick said.

'Nathan's fingerprints are also on the letter,' Colin added.

'And?'

'Gabrielle had an interest in the outcome, because she looks after that piece of land. What interest does Nathan have?'

'Are you telling me how to run my business?' Nick asked.

'Merely asking,' Colin said. 'We have a letter which concerns you and Gabrielle. I was wondering why Nathan's fingerprints are on it, why it was torn into pieces, and why it was scattered in Ashley's studio.'

'I really have no idea about any of this.' Nick gave him a steely gaze. 'You said this is a voluntary interview and I can leave any time I choose. Unless you arrest me – and I can't see what grounds you have for that – I'm going.'

'As you wish. I'll be in touch, Mr Edwards,' Colin said.

'Just do your bloody job and find my son,' Nick ordered, and stormed out of the room, followed by his solicitor.

'He's very upset about that letter,' Colin remarked to Larissa when he'd turned off the recorder. 'But he wasn't the one who shredded it. According to Alexsy, the prints on both sides of the paper show that Nathan was the one who shredded it. But why would Nathan have been angry about a letter that would put something in the way of Gaby's plans? Surely, if anything, it was what he'd been aiming for, so he had an excuse to take over her fields and turn them over to the way he produced wine in the Willow Farm fields?'

'I think Nick knows more than he's telling us,' Larissa said. 'What I can't work out is whether he thinks Ashley was involved in Nathan's death and he's trying to protect him. The evidence points to some kind of fight in the studio. Was Ashley there at the time, or did Nathan smash up the place in frustration because his brother wasn't there? And why did he take the letter to Ashley anyway?'

'There are only two people who could answer that,' Colin said. 'One's dead and the other's missing.'

He was about to suggest talking to Gaby again when his phone pinged with a text.

'It's Georgie. She's just been to see Gaby about the skeleton,' he said, scanning the words swiftly. 'This is interesting. She says that she met Diana's partner, Shaun, who has bruising to his face and wrist. He claims he fell over in his own vineyard on Monday morning and thought he'd broken his wrist. Diana drove him to the hospital to get it checked out.'

'Does she think he's telling the truth?'

'She hasn't commented. But it would be useful to get that confirmed before we speak to him,' Colin said.

'Do you want me to talk to the hospital or arrange to talk to Shaun and Diana?' Larissa asked.

'If you can arrange for us to see Shaun and Diana,' Colin said, 'I'll speak to the hospital.' He'd need to navigate the tricky line between patient confidentiality and public interest.

The conversation proved useful only insofar as the emergency department receptionist confirmed the time and date of Shaun's visit. To check that he was telling the truth and the damage to his hand and face were caused by a fall in his own vineyard rather than in a fight with Nathan, Colin would need Shaun's explicit consent for the hospital to share the information.

'We can ask for his written consent when we see him, guv,' Mo said. 'If he has nothing to hide, he'll be happy for the hospital to share the information. If he's not prepared to do that, it suggests we need to bring him in for questioning under caution.'

Larissa and Colin drove over to Chalk Valley Wines.

'If you don't mind, Ms Murray, Larissa will ask you some questions while I talk to Mr Phillips,' Colin said.

'Of course,' Diana said. 'Gaby's not here, I'm afraid – I know she needs to get on at Rosa. It's coming up to the busiest time of year in our industry.' She paused. 'Can I make you some coffee, before we start?'

'That's very kind of you, but I'm fine,' Colin said, smiling.

Monty pushed his nose against Colin's knees, and Colin bent to make a fuss of him. 'Obviously you can smell Bert,' he said with a smile. 'That's Georgina's dog. Also a springer,' he added to Diana.

'I met him,' Diana said. 'And he has a nose for old bones, from what Georgie tells me.'

'He does,' Colin confirmed.

Larissa accepted a mug of coffee, and Diana took her through to another room, the dog padding behind them.

'How can I help, Inspector?' Shaun asked when Diana and Larissa had gone.

'If you wouldn't mind answering some questions, Mr Phillips?' Colin checked.

'Of course. And Shaun will do,' Shaun said.

'When did you last go to Willow Farm, Shaun?'

'I can't remember the exact date, but it's roughly four years ago, a few months after Rosemary died and when Nick had got the probate through. The day he got the paperwork sorted, Nick terminated Diana's employment and evicted her from the cottage,' Shaun said. 'I helped Di and Gaby move their stuff. When we see Gaby nowadays, it tends to be either here or at her cottage in Ashingham – never at Willow Farm.'

'Could you tell me about your relationship with the Edwards family, in your own words?' Colin asked.

'I took a job with Rosemary when she started Rosa Wines,' Shaun said. 'It was 1995, after Terence died – I didn't know him at all. I helped her set out the fields and plant the vines. I didn't have much to do with Nick, because Willow Farm was still a mixed farm – there were cattle as well as the arable crops. Diana worked on the dairy side, making artisan cheese. Nathan was at preschool, and Ash was a baby.' He sighed. 'I fell in love with Di the minute I saw her. Obviously I wasn't going to do anything about it. For a start, I knew she was married; even though Nick wasn't a good husband to her, I wasn't going to break up a home. I dated other women, but nobody made me feel the way Diana did. The months went by, and my feelings for her didn't change. So in the end I was honest with her. I asked her to leave Nick for me. I said I'd be happy to take on the boys. She said she couldn't offer me anything but friendship – I didn't realise it at the time, but she was pregnant with Gaby, and clearly she was trying to make a go of her marriage.'

'Go on,' Colin said quietly, making notes.

'I couldn't stay working there, seeing her unhappy but not being able to do anything to help, so I left to work for Chalk Valley Wines. I stayed friends with Diana and Rosemary, but it was completely platonic. I ended up buying Chalk Valley when my boss decided to retire. A couple of months after that, Diana finally left Nick, and Rosemary let her and Gaby have one of the farm cottages. I know she was devastated that he was awarded custody of the boys, and she wanted to stay near in the hope she could have some influence on them. I always hoped that maybe one day she'd change her mind about me and marry me, though I knew Nick had pretty much put her off marriage for good.' He rolled his eyes. 'When Rosemary died and Nick pushed Di out of Rosa Wines, I offered her a job here. No strings. She's good at her job and I knew she'd be an asset to my business – which she has been.' He shrugged. 'A couple of years ago, we finally got together, and she moved in with me. Gaby and Ash were fine about it, but Nathan wasn't quite so happy.'

'How did you get on with Diana's children?' Colin asked.

'For the most part, fine. Gaby and I are friends, and I respect what she does at work. She knows she can have a job here any time she wants it,' Shaun said. 'I feel sorry for Ash – he doesn't fit in with his dad and his brother, and they give him a hard time because he's not like them. Again, if he needed a bolthole here and wanted to be near his mum, it wouldn't be a problem.' He paused. 'It feels wrong, speaking ill of the dead, but I didn't have much time for Nathan. He's too much like his father, and I don't like the way Nick treats people, either.'

'Have you clashed with Nick in the past?' Colin asked.

'No. I'm polite to him if we meet at some do or other in the winemaking world, but that's as far as it goes. The rest of the time, I avoid him. Diana doesn't need any more hassle from him, and I'm not going to give him any excuses to have a go at me so he can upset her.'

'Fair enough,' Colin said. 'What do you know about Gaby's relationship with Nathan?'

'They clash,' Shaun said. 'But it's not my place to interfere. Gaby's perfectly capable of looking after herself. She's a better winemaker than Nathan or Nick could ever hope to be. At the end of the day, everyone knows that, so it doesn't matter that Nick micromanages her and Nathan's been trying to ruin her plans for organic status. As I said, I'd be more than happy to give her a job here – not just because she's Di's daughter, but because she's talented. But she's stubborn and she wants Rosa Wines to carry on being Rosemary's legacy instead of being swallowed up by Willow Farm.'

Shaun's account was open and honest, and Colin thought he was telling the truth. 'Do you want to tell me about the bruising on your face?' he asked.

'It's very simple: middle-aged man makes a complete fool of himself,' Shaun said dryly. 'Even though nobody at the vineyard saw it happen, they all know about it and I've been ribbed mercilessly since Di took me to the emergency department.' He gave a wry smile. 'I go for a walk in the fields every morning with Monty, Di's dog, around sunrise. It's the best time of the day, and we've got some skylarks in our fields here – just hearing them really sets me up for the day. Anyway, I was trying to get a video of them so Di could hear. I was looking up at the sky instead of concentrating on where my feet were; I tripped over, landed on my hands and knees and smacked my face against a vine support.'

'You're sure the bruising wasn't caused during a physical altercation with Nathan Edwards?' Colin asked.

'I'm sure.' Shaun turned his palms over so Colin could see the bruising to his right palm, then back again to show there was nothing on the back of his hands. 'You can check with the hospital, if you want,' he added.

'I was hoping you'd say that,' Colin said. 'We'll need your written permission for them to share the data with us. I'll ask you to sign the consent form before I leave, if you don't mind.'

'Fine by me,' Shaun said. 'But I can assure you I didn't have a fight with Nathan. I'm reasonably fit, but I'm not stupid.' He shrugged. 'Nathan's thirty years younger than I am. No way would I stand a chance of beating him in a fight.'

'Fair point,' Colin said.

'Even if there wasn't the age difference, I still wouldn't have had a fight with him. That's not the way to sort out a problem – it might work temporarily, but then it'll all start up again and there'd be added resentment on both sides,' Shaun said. 'It's better to talk things over, negotiate and reach a fair solution, one where you're both happy.'

'Was Nathan the sort to negotiate?' Colin asked.

'With Gaby?' Shaun thought about it. 'Probably not.' He suddenly looked uncomfortable.

'What aren't you saying?' Colin asked quietly.

Shaun sighed. 'It feels a bit like throwing Gaby under a bus – but I assure you, that girl isn't capable of killing anyone.'

'But?'

'Rosemary was going to leave her vineyard to Gaby,' Shaun said. 'Except she died before she could sign her new will. She had a stroke. It feels a bit... Well, if I was Gaby, I would've asked questions, that's all. What if Nathan and Nick had a go at Rosemary when they found out her plans, and that's what brought on the stroke?'

'I'm not sure that stress necessary causes strokes,' Colin said.

'It's still worth asking the question,' Shaun said. 'Though for Gaby it wouldn't be losing the vineyard that upset her – it'd be losing her gran. They were really close.'

'And if she learned that her brother's actions had led to her grandmother's last illness, it could've made her confront him?' Colin asked.

'I don't know,' Shaun said. 'Like I said, she's not the violent type. She wouldn't fly off the handle. I think she'd go head-to-head with him at work, and prove to her dad that she did a better job than Nathan did. She was the one who won an award, after all, not her brother.'

Colin made a note. 'Did you know her application for organic status was turned down?'

'No, but I'm not surprised because Nathan was always threatening to spray her fields. I think he just said it to wind her up, but I wouldn't be surprised if he made sure he was around for any inspection and had a quiet word with the inspector,' Shaun said dryly. 'Enough to cast some doubt.'

'Would she have any redress?' Colin asked.

'If she could provide facts and figures – and she'd need to

get her dad on side. I'm not sure which of them Nick would back,' Shaun said. 'You'd be better off asking Gaby that.'

'Noted.' Colin took the consent form from his file, and gave it to Shaun. 'If you wouldn't mind reading that through and signing it, I'd be grateful,' he said.

'No problem,' Shaun said. He took his time reading the form, signed it, and handed it back. 'For what it's worth, I didn't like Nathan, but I wouldn't have wished him dead. And especially not like that. I know I said Gaby clashed with him, but Di and Gaby are both devastated, because they loved him,' he added quietly. 'And with Ash being missing, too... they're going through hell. I hope he turns up unharmed, and soon. If there's anything I can do, you can count on me to do it – just let me know what you need from me.'

It was easy to tell why: for Diana's sake, and Gaby's, too.

'We'll be in touch,' Colin said. 'Thank you for your frankness.'

Larissa didn't have any extra information from her informal chat with Diana. But they went home via the hospital, with the signed consent form, to check what Shaun had told them.

'I'm pretty sure he's been honest with us,' Colin said. 'He didn't kill Nathan.'

When Colin spoke to the nurse who'd examined Shaun, she confirmed that Shaun's injuries were consistent with his description of how they'd happened.

'Not from punching someone?' Colin checked.

'If you punch someone, you're more likely to break your fifth metacarpal, just underneath the knuckle,' the nurse said, running her finger along the bone that connected her little finger to her wrist to show Colin where she meant. 'Mr Phillips fell onto his hands and knees. There's bruising on both knees, and broken skin. The way he described his fall, I expected him to have a Colles fracture to his wrist – that's where the end of the radius breaks and is bent backwards. They're common in winter when people slip on ice and land on their outstretched hands,' she explained. 'I gave him an X-ray, and he was lucky to get away with just bruising and soreness to his palms. I advised he should wear a sling for a couple of days to give a bit of extra support to his wrist, and take paracetamol.'

'And the bruise to his face?' Colin asked.

'The poor man was a bit unlucky where he fell. But at least nothing was broken. I recommended icing his knees and trying to keep them elevated.'

'Thank you,' Colin said.

It was progress of sorts; they could rule out Shaun as Nathan's attacker. But progress was painfully slow. Until Ashley turned up, they were stuck.

SIXTEEN

Colin called Gaby when he left the emergency department. 'Can Larissa and I come and see you for a quick chat?' he asked.

'Does that mean you've found Ash?' she asked, her voice full of hope.

'Sorry, I'm afraid there's still no news about your brother,' he said.

'I'm at his studio at the moment,' she said. 'Alexsy from the forensic team said this morning they'd finished and I could clear up – he emailed me the paperwork.'

Colin thought there was probably a copy of the paperwork sitting in his own emails, too.

'At least then Ash won't come home to a complete mess,' Gaby added, 'even if most of his artwork's ruined.'

'I'm sorry,' Colin said, meaning it.

'If you need a reminder of directions when you get to the office,' she said, 'ask Del or someone in the bottling plant, and they'll show you where it is.'

'Thank you,' Colin said; he could remember the way, but guessed that Gaby needed to feel that she was doing something useful. Waiting for news was always one of the hardest things, and feeling helpless was particularly difficult for the kind of people who were used to just getting on with things.

He parked outside the Willow Farm Wines office, checked in with Del Turnbull over the intercom – relieved that Del rather than Nick answered – then headed over to the studio with Larissa. There were several black bin bags outside, neatly tied.

He rapped on the open door – which he assumed was Gaby letting fresh air into the studio to get rid of the smell of blood and stale wine – and called, 'Hello, Gaby? It's DI Bradshaw and DC Foulkes.'

Gaby called back, 'Come through.'

She was kneeling on the floor, putting torn-up paper into a box. 'There are Ash's drawings,' she said. 'I don't want to throw these away in case he can salvage something from them. Even if it's reusing bits for a collage or scrap paper.' She'd clearly been crying because her eyes were reddened and slightly swollen. 'I'm so upset for him. He put his heart and soul into his art. Who would've wanted to destroy his work like this?'

'Is there a chance he might have done it himself?' Colin asked gently.

Gaby shook her head. 'Ash doesn't get angry when he's upset – he goes in on himself, I guess. He can barely drag himself out of bed, won't even have the curtains open and everything's *dark*. It's like being in a cocoon. And that's when he gets obsessive about the hand stuff.' She gestured to the artwork in the box. 'These were mainly sketches and watercolours he'd done in the vineyard. Insects, birds, flowers – things that would've worked beautifully as cards. I'd been encouraging him to do some commercial art as well as his more out-there stuff – things where people would give him positive feedback because they could understand what they were seeing. This is the sort of stuff I remember him doing when I was little.'

'That dragonfly's incredibly detailed,' Larissa said, looking at one of the watercolours. 'The wings are beautiful.'

'It's a damselfly,' Gaby corrected. 'They're a bit smaller than a dragonfly and they hold their wings differently. Still beautiful, though. We see a lot of them by the pond.' She swallowed hard. 'Though I'm not sure I'd want to sit by the pond anymore, not now I know someone's body was hidden in there for nearly a century.'

'Georgina said she'd done some work to try and identify him,' Colin said.

'She thinks he's Percy Ramsey, who used to have the farm next door to my great-grandparents. What did you want to talk to me about?' she asked.

'We found a letter that had been shredded in here,' he said. 'It said you hadn't got the grant you applied for.'

She frowned. 'Why would *that* be in Ash's studio? And how come it was ripped up? Dad showed it to me, obviously, because he said it proved my plans were wrong and he threatened to let Nathan take over the Rosa Wines fields. I asked him to give me a couple of weeks to sort it out. I told him there must've been some kind of mistake, because I knew we met all the criteria for the grant or I wouldn't have suggested applying for it in the first place, and I double-checked everything before I filled in the forms. He agreed to let me have a few days to ring the government department, ask them where things had gone wrong and see if I could get them to change their mind.' Her frown deepened. 'That letter should have been in Dad's desk, not here.'

'Do you think,' Colin asked, choosing his words carefully, 'Nathan might have had anything to do with whatever went wrong?'

'He went behind my back and told a pack of lies to the inspector, you mean?' Her frown deepened. 'I mean, he wanted to be top dog and in charge of everything, but even he wouldn't have been that much of a snake.' Doubt filled her expression. 'Would he?'

'What if he did,' Larissa asked, 'and Ashley found out? Say, Nathan showed him the letter?'

'And gloated that he'd managed to stop me getting the grant for Rosa Wines, you mean?' Gaby asked. She sighed. 'That makes a horrible kind of sense.'

'How would Ashley have reacted?' Larissa asked.

'I don't know,' Gaby said. 'The thing is, Nathan is – *was*,' she corrected herself, 'the oldest, so he always thought that made him in charge of Ash and me. He bossed us around all the time when we were little. Things changed a bit when we were teenagers. He didn't go to uni because he said there was no point; he knew he was going to inherit the farm, so he might as well work here and learn on the job instead of getting in debt with a pile of student loans. When Ash went to art school, Nathan wasn't very nice about it, saying Ash was arty-farty and useless and he'd always be dependent on Dad for money.' She gave a small huff of disgust. 'And of course there was me, with my degree, which according to him made me think I was better than him when I wasn't.' She rolled her eyes. 'I always reminded him it wasn't about my degree: I learned a lot of stuff at Gran's knee and from Mum, and I'd been around the vineyard for longer than he had. Every time he had a go at me, I just said he'd do himself a favour if he kept up to date and learned a bit about sustainable farming methods, because that's the way the future's going. It didn't go down well with him, but...' She broke off, shaking her head. 'Ash would've tried to stand up for me. But Nathan would've squashed him and made him feel bad about himself, the way he always did.'

'Could it have finally pushed Ashley to the point where he snapped and hit back?' Colin asked.

'No. That isn't Ash. Ever,' Gaby said. 'As I said, he burrows in. If it's really bad, he might go off somewhere on his own. But I've tried all his friends and they're stonewalling me.' She bit her lip. 'I asked Georgie if she'd try talking to them. They might talk to her, with her being a photographer. They might see her as a fellow artist.'

'Georgie's really good with people,' Colin said. 'They often open up to her when they won't talk to anyone else.'

'I hope so,' Gaby said. Her eyes filled with tears again. 'I just want Ash home, and safe.'

'We'll let you get on,' Colin said. 'If we find anything out, we'll be in touch.'

'OK,' Gaby said. 'And if I hear from him, I'll let you know.'

Larissa waited until they were back in the car before turning to Colin. 'I don't think she was involved – either in Nathan's death or Ashley's disappearance.'

'I agree,' Colin said. 'And I know she says Ashley wouldn't have finally snapped, but everyone has their limits. Did he finally lose his temper? Is she covering up for him, or does she really not know?'

'We need to do more digging,' Larissa said.

'Hello, is that Marty Lennox?' Georgina asked.

'Who's asking?' the voice on the other end of the phone asked cagily.

'My name's Georgina Drake. I'm a photographer,' Georgie said. 'I've been doing a job for *Veritas* magazine, photographing Gaby Edwards for a feature, and she showed me her brother Ashley's artwork. I was quite struck by it, and I wanted to have a chat with him with a view to putting together a feature on his work.'

'Sorry. I haven't seen Ash for months,' the man – who might or might not have been Marty – said.

Before he could hang up, Georgina said, 'One last thing; do you have any idea who might be able to help me find him?'

'No,' the man said, and ended the call.

The next two people reacted exactly the same way: refusing to tell her anything, just as they'd done to Gaby.

Then Georgina had a brainwave. She was friends with an artist and gallery owner whose name would be well-known in the local art community. Maybe that would be a better way of introducing herself. She rang Niamh as a courtesy first, not wanting to use her name without asking, and when she explained the situation, Niamh was sympathetic. 'I take it that's linked with the case you and Sybbie were talking about when I saw you?'

'Yes,' Georgina said.

'I don't actually know him, so I can't suggest anyone who might be helpful in finding him, but of course you can mention my name. You could say you'd been talking to me about showcasing local artists,' Niamh added.

'I don't want to make life difficult for you,' Georgina said.

'Not at all – it's not as if you're promising that I'll give someone a full display in the window. It's a way to open a discussion. And, actually, I do like to support young artists. It's tough for them in the early years.' She paused. 'I hope you manage to find him – and if I think of anything that might help, I'll give you a call.'

'Thank you,' Georgina said. 'I really appreciate that.'

The next person she rang, Hayley Kingston, was equally cagey at first when Georgina asked if she could possibly put her in touch with Ashley. 'I haven't seen Ash for ages.'

'That's a shame,' Georgina said. 'My friend Niamh Webster has a gallery in Holt, and we've been talking about supporting local artists – I'm a photographer,' she explained.

'Niamh the sculptor? Faye's mum?' Hayley checked.

'Faye who makes those amazing ceramics,' Georgina

confirmed. 'I bought one of her new bowls, recently. All those ocean colours are irresistible.'

Hayley paused. 'I know Niamh. She's really nice.' There was another silence. 'Can I call you back?'

'Of course you can,' Georgina said, feeling the first pinprick of hope. 'And let me give you my website details, so you can see that I'm really who I say I am and I'm not trying to scam you.'

There was a brief huff of laughter. 'I'm an artist. I don't have any money for anyone to scam out of me.' But, to Georgina's relief, Hayley took the website address anyway.

Twenty minutes later, Hayley called back. 'OK. He'll talk to you, tomorrow morning, if you bring your dog.'

Georgina hadn't mentioned Bert to them, but clearly they'd checked out her website and discovered Bert's page on it. Georgina smiled. 'I'm glad you said that before I had to ask you if he could come, because Bert and I are a package deal. Though I'd better warn you that he's a typical spaniel; he wants to be everyone's best friend and he's likely to demand plenty of tummy rubs.'

'That,' Hayley said, 'would do Ash a lot of good.'

'Where do you want to meet?' Georgina asked. 'Your studio, or a coffee shop somewhere? I'm paying, but obviously it needs to be a dog-friendly place for Bert.'

Hayley sighed. 'Ash isn't really up to going out anywhere, right now. My studio's probably the best place to meet.' She gave Georgina the address.

'Thank you. What time would you like me to be there? And I'll bring cake – do either of you have any dietary requirements?'

'Neither of us is gluten-free or vegan. Cake would be wonderful. For that, you'll get the decent coffee instead of the instant stuff that's gone hard in the bottom of the jar,' Hayley said. 'Does ten work for you?'

'Ten would be perfect,' Georgina said. 'I'll see you both tomorrow.'

She made a fuss of Bert, settled him in his bed, then called round to see Sybbie.

'Are you coming in for coffee?' Sybbie asked.

'If it's on offer, yes please,' Georgina said. 'But I'm really after a bit of advice.'

'You have my full attention,' Sybbie said, and switched the kettle on.

When they both had full mugs of coffee and were sitting at Sybbie's kitchen table with a Labrador leaning against each of them, Georgina said, 'I've been ringing round Ashley's friends. None of them would really talk to me until I had the bright idea of telling them I know Niamh Webster. Obviously I checked with Niamh first that she didn't mind me using her name.'

'And?' Sybbie prompted.

'He's staying with one of his friends, who happens to know Niamh and her daughter.'

'That's wonderful news!' Sybbie beamed at her. 'Have you told Gaby and Diana? Or Colin?'

'None of them yet,' Georgina said. 'The thing is, his friend was a bit cagey with me. She asked if she could call me back – and it seems Ashley would like me to bring Bert. I've agreed to meet them tomorrow, with Bert and cake.' She sighed. 'I get the impression that Ashley's not very well, at the moment, and I don't want to put additional pressure on him by taking Gaby or Diana with me. Or Colin, for that matter.'

'This isn't something you're going to be able to hide from Colin,' Sybbie warned.

'I know. Obviously Ashley's a person of interest in Colin's investigation, and I ought to let him deal with it. Going rogue means I'm getting close to obstructing his investigation – but I think Ashley needs a different approach to persuade him to talk to Colin. I'll tell Colin what I'm doing, but I need him to trust me to handle it.'

'What if Ashley's involved with Nathan's death? What if you're putting yourself at risk? What if he lashes out at you as soon as you mention Nathan's name?' Sybbie asked.

'I'm sure he won't. And he specifically asked me to bring my dog. I think the poor boy is in a muddle, probably worrying that there's a terrible family situation – he might not even know that Nathan's dead – and I get the impression that his friend is feeling a bit out of her depth,' Georgina said.

'Why don't I go with you, for backup?' Sybbie said. 'I'm a harmless little old lady, after all.'

Georgina grinned. 'With your secateurs?'

Sybbie laughed. 'Seriously. What's threatening about a middle-aged mum and a grannie-to-be?'

'Not forgetting Bert. All right. I'll ask his friend.'

'You're being a bit cagey,' Sybbie remarked.

'Protecting you,' Georgina countered. 'If she says no, and Colin wants to know your involvement, you can truthfully say that I didn't tell you any details whatsoever.'

'This isn't espionage,' Sybbie said.

'Even so. I don't want to drag you into any row I might or might not have with Colin. That wouldn't be fair.' Georgina sent a quick text to Hayley, asking if she could bring her friend Sybbie, on the grounds that her satnav was always playing up and it was helpful to have someone with her who could use a phone app and give her directions. She added that Sybbie was also friends with Niamh Webster and had more than one of Niamh's Labrador bronzes.

A few minutes later, Georgina's phone beeped with a text. 'She says yes.'

'Good,' Sybbie said, sounding pleased. 'Where are we off to?'

'Just outside Wells-next-the-Sea,' Georgina said. 'I arranged to be there at ten.'

'That's about forty minutes from here. OK. I'll pick up some cake from Cesca's and meet you here at quarter past nine – that gives us a couple of minutes' wiggle room,' Sybbie said. 'But you're still going to have to tell Colin.'

'I will. Later,' Georgina promised. 'And thank you.'

Back at Rookery Farm, she sent Colin a text. *Cooking veggie chili for dinner tonight, if you'd like some x*

Love to. Thank you. 7pm OK? he replied.

Bert made his usual fuss over Colin when he arrived.

'How's your day been?' she asked.

'I've been able to rule out some things,' he said. 'Thank you for your note about Shaun. It all checks out.'

'Good. He seems to think a lot more of Gaby than her own father does,' Georgina said.

'Sadly, I think you're right,' Colin agreed. 'How has your day been?'

'I talked to Diana and Gaby about Percy,' she said. 'Hopefully Bea can help me find Winnie and Percy's grandchildren, and they'll be interested in doing an DNA test.' She paused. 'Can I ask you something?'

'Sure,' he said.

'Do you trust me?'

He frowned. 'Of course I do.' He winced. 'Is this about Doris?'

'No, it isn't,' she said. 'I was thinking, if I had a conversation with someone without telling you until afterwards...'

His eyes narrowed. 'If it's connected with a case I'm working on, then I'd need to know about it beforehand, Georgie.'

Which wasn't the answer she wanted. 'In the past,' she said, 'I've talked to people involved in a case. I've persuaded them to trust you and tell you what they know. Do you trust me to do that?'

He rubbed a hand across his face. 'Of course I do. But I don't want to bend any rules, so let's not have this conversation. Just promise me you're not going to put yourself at any kind of risk – because you're important to me, Georgie, and I couldn't live with myself if anything happened to you.'

'I'm not going to do anything reckless. I'm taking Bert with me – and Sybbie,' she added.

'My unofficial team appears to be growing,' he said wryly.

'We'll see how it goes,' she said. 'But I think Bert's going to be the key, here.'

'Thank you,' he said quietly. 'And if I can do anything to help your case, just ask.'

'You already have. You put us in touch with June,' she said with a smile. 'She confirmed a few things for us.'

'Then I'll pretend we didn't discuss this, and I'll wait until you're ready to talk to me about the issue,' he said.

'Thank you,' she said. 'Are you getting any nearer pinning down what happened to Nathan?'

'Not right now,' he said. 'The problem is, the most likely person with the motivation, the means and the opportunity is Gaby, and the other most likely person Ashley – who happens to be missing.'

She blinked. 'You seriously think Gaby's capable of murdering her own brother?'

'Nathan was interfering with what she's trying to do at the vineyard, and he also doesn't treat Ashley very well. Could he have done something to finally make her snap?' Colin asked. 'Similarly, Ashley was protective of Gaby – even though everyone says he was gentle. Again, did Nathan do something that finally caused Ashley to lose his temper and act in a way nobody expected? Does Gaby know what happened and is she protecting Ashley?' Colin spread his hands. 'But until Ashley comes back to Willow Farm – or someone can persuade him to talk to me – I can't get to the bottom of it.'

'Noted,' Georgina said with a sigh. 'I can't see Gaby pushing Nathan into the tank, and I believe her when she says Ashley couldn't have done it, either. I think we're missing something.'

'Who had a fight with Nathan and landed that punch?' Colin asked. 'When we find the answer to that, I think it'll help us work out who's protecting who and why. Until then... we're stuck.'

SEVENTEEN

The next morning, Georgina met Sybbie as arranged and they headed for the coast.

'Is Doris with us today?' Sybbie asked.

'Harrison's got a gig. She's going to watch,' Georgina said. 'Actually, it's lovely that she can finally enjoy... I was going to say *live* music, but you know what I mean.'

'I do,' Sybbie said with a smile.

Hayley's studio was part of an art collective, based in an old Nissen hut that had been repurposed. The curved corrugated steel walls and roof had been painted green, the metal window frames had been painted white, and the wooden front of the hut had also been painted white and decorated with purple daisies, with the legend *North Norfolk Women's Art Collective* painted in purple above the door.

Georgina parked on a gravelled section at the side of the hut and called Hayley. 'We're here and I've parked on the gravel. Is that all right, or will I be in anyone's way?'

'It's fine. It's mostly visitors who park there, and unless it's Open Studios they normally only come here by appointment.

It's just me here this morning – and Ash, of course. I'll come out to collect you,' Hayley said.

By the time Georgina and Sybbie had got Bert out of the back of the car, Hayley had opened the front door to the studios. Georgina introduced them all swiftly. 'Thank you for persuading Ashley to talk to us,' she said.

'I hope it'll take him out of himself, a bit,' Hayley said.

'You've been friends for a while?'

'We met in art school in London,' she said with a smile. 'Ash moved back to Norfolk straight after graduation; I spent a few more years in London, but we stayed in touch. I came back a couple of years ago because I missed the sea. Come in and I'll put the kettle on.'

Ashley was a slight man who looked very like his sister Gaby, though his hair was sandy rather than blonde; he wore faded jeans and a black hoodie. There were deep shadows under his blue eyes.

'Hello, Ashley. Thank you for agreeing to talk to us. I'm Georgina and this is my friend Sybbie,' Georgina said. 'And this is Bert.'

Ashley made a fuss of Bert, who wagged his tail happily. 'He looks so much like my mum's dog, Monty,' Ashley said quietly. 'That's why I asked you to bring him. I miss having a dog around since Mum moved away, and Dad won't let me get a dog.'

Bert seemed to sense that the young man needed extra comfort, so he sat next to Ashley, rested his chin on Ashley's knee, then leaned against him. Ashley seemed to relax just a tiny bit and stroked the dog's coat.

'I think Hayley told you I'm a photographer?' Georgina checked.

Ashley nodded.

'And I'm a gardener,' Sybbie said. 'I hang out with Georgie because her work means she gets to visit gorgeous gardens that aren't usually open to the public. If I go with her to carry her camera bag or keep an eye on Bert, I get to enjoy them, too.'

'Sounds like fun,' Ashley said, his smile just a little bit watery.

'Work's always better with friends,' Georgina said. 'I believe you're an artist?'

He nodded. 'It's been hard, lately. I messed up, and everything went wrong.'

'Sometimes life gets like that,' Georgina said. 'But things tend to work themselves out. And there are always good people who'll help you.'

'Like Hayley. She's been good to me. She came and fetched me from Norwich and she's let me stay with her since...' He shivered, and huddled down into his hoodie.

Hayley brought them all coffee, and Sybbie produced the cake.

'I love lemon drizzle. Thank you,' Hayley said appreciatively. 'So what were you saying about Niamh Webster's gallery, yesterday, Georgina?'

'She's thinking about ways to support young artists,' Georgina said. 'And obviously I have connections with a lot of magazines because of my work. I wanted to talk to you about your work, Ashley. All the wildlife stuff you've done.'

Ashley shook his head. 'I can't show my work to anyone. It's all gone. But you should look at Hayley's stuff,' he added loyally. 'She's good.'

'How did you hear about Ash's work?' Hayley asked.

'My daughter-in-law Cesca – the cake-maker,' Sybbie said, 'runs the farm shop in our village. A magazine asked Georgie to take some photographs of one of Cesca's suppliers, for an interview.'

'When I do portraits, I like to put my subjects at their ease and get them to chat to me,' Georgina said. 'When they open up about things they love, I get better pictures. And Gaby told me about her brother, the artist.'

'Gaby,' he whispered. He shivered. 'She won't want to be my sister anymore. Not after what I did.'

Was he trying to tell her that he'd killed Nathan? Though somehow she couldn't see it. Ashley was slight, his build more like his mother and sister than his father.

'I promise you, Gaby loves you,' Georgina said gently. 'She's really worried about you. I met Monty this week, too. He's a lovely dog. And you're right, he's quite like my Bert. A tiny bit smaller, do you think?'

Bert shifted slightly towards Ashley, who stroked the top of his head. 'Yes, I think he is.' He looked at her. 'Did Gaby send you?'

'You lied to me,' Hayley said, standing up and looking angry. 'You said you know Niamh.'

'I do know Niamh,' Georgina said.

'So do I,' Sybbie said. 'I have some of her bronzes.'

'We called in to see her earlier this week and I bought one of Faye's bowls,' Georgina added.

'But you came here because of Ash's family, not because of his artwork,' Hayley said, folding her arms.

'I've been trying to find Ashley because his mum and his sister are worried sick about him. They're terrified that something's happened to him,' Georgina said.

Ashley closed his eyes. 'Sorry, Hayz. I didn't mean to bring trouble to your door.'

'You haven't brought any trouble.' Hayley glared at Georgina and Sybbie. 'But *they* have. You two need to go. Now.'

'I understand why you're angry, and I apologise. But please give us five minutes to explain, Hayley,' Georgina said.

'You already lied to us,' Hayley said. 'How do we know we can trust a word that comes out of your mouth?'

'My kids are just a bit younger than you,' Georgina said, 'and if either of them ever has a hard time and I can't be there within five seconds, I hope they have someone like you in their corner.'

'Just the one for me,' Sybbie said. 'Plus a daughter-in-law I love very dearly. Ashley, you might have met Cesca when she's gone over to see Gaby, in the past? She's having a baby in three months' time. Right now I'm trying to knit a baby blanket, but it's the most embarrassingly wonky, terrible thing in the history of blankets. I've unpicked it and reknitted it five times, and it's not looking any better.'

Hayley looked at her, and at Georgina, and then she sighed. 'I still think I ought to kick you both out, but OK. You've got five minutes.'

'Ashley, I'm not going to put any pressure on you, I promise,' Georgina said. 'I'm not looking to kidnap you and drag you back to Willow Farm against your will. All Gaby and your mum want to know is that you're OK.' She paused. 'Gaby's cleaning up your studio at the moment.'

Ashley somehow managed to make himself even smaller, and Bert pushed his nose into Ashley's hand. 'He smashed my hands,' Ashley whispered. 'He took them out of the freezer and smashed them.'

Wanting to know the identity of the man who'd smashed up the studio, but not daring to say a word in case it stopped Ashley talking, Georgina waited. Bert put a paw on Ashley's knee, as if encouraging him to continue.

'Nathan said it was my fault for talking to the surveyor. I didn't know the guy was a surveyor. I thought he was just one of the people who come to stay for the weekends at the vineyard – they stay in Gran's old cottage. They like to go for walks over the farmland. I was sketching in Gaby's fields. The flowers and the insects, and I'm doing a series for Gaby showing how the grapes grow week by week,' Ashley said. 'He liked my damselflies. He talked to me about what I was sketching, and I was telling him I always work in Gaby's fields because she doesn't spray and there's a lot more wildlife.' He bit his lip. 'If I'd known he was a surveyor, I wouldn't have said anything about Nathan trying to take over and threatening to spray her fields.'

'It's not your fault,' Georgina said gently. 'He was a nice guy, talking to you about art and wildlife. You chatted. There's no harm in that.'

'Nathan said it was my fault. That I'd opened my big fat mouth and blabbed, and that's why we didn't get the grant. And Dad was furious with Nathan. He punched him. There was this massive bruise on Nathan's face when he stormed into the studio.' Ashley shuddered. 'I thought he was going to hit me. I ran to the bathroom and locked myself in. He kicked the door and screamed at me, telling me how I'd ruined everything. And then I heard him smashing things. I knew he was wrecking my work and I hated that, but...' He shook his head. 'If I'd gone out to try and stop him, he would've hurt me. He would've broken my hands so I couldn't work for months. My *hands*.' He shuddered again. 'I have nightmares about hands.'

'Oh, sweetheart.' Georgina couldn't hold back any longer. She went round to his side of the table and wrapped her arms round him. 'Everything's going to be all right. Nathan isn't going to break your hands.' Ashley was clearly traumatised, and she realised that she was out of her depth. All she could do was try to persuade him – and Hayley – to let her get him to the help he needed.

'He broke the skeleton,' Ashley whispered.

'A skeleton you made?' Georgina asked.

Ashley shook his head. 'The skeleton in the pond.'

Percy's skeleton? Ashley had found it? When? 'Tell me about the skeleton,' she said gently.

'I can't,' Ashley said.

'If we don't talk about something that frightens us and try

and stuff it down out of the way, it doesn't actually go away,' she said, keeping her voice kind. 'It just gets harder to talk about and it feels bigger and scarier. But if you let the words out, you'll take away its power.'

Ashley gulped. 'I can't.'

'OK. Let me tell you what I know about the skeleton,' she said. 'Bert found him on Monday when he went to have a drink in the pond, and my friend Rowena came out to check the bones and said he'd died nearly a hundred years ago. I've done a bit with family history, so I promised Gaby and your mum that I'd look into it for them. I borrowed your gran's papers from Gaby to see if they'd help me trace him,' she added. 'He was a man called Percy Ramsey, and he was in love with your great-gran Ivy.' She told Ashley about Percy falling out with Douglas, and how Ivy had married Ernest – and how Ernest had ended up having a fight with Percy. 'Percy had a thin skull, so if the fight had been with someone else, he wouldn't have had been affected in the same way,' she continued. 'I think it was an accident and Ernest panicked when he realised what had happened.'

'Then he pushed Percy in the pond to hide him? And we found him, all those years later,' Ashley said thoughtfully.

Georgina wondered who 'we' was. Clearly not Gaby, who would've mentioned it earlier. Nathan, perhaps? 'When did you find him?' she asked gently.

'It was the summer Mum left us, and Dad wouldn't let me go to live with her and Gaby. I used to like sitting by the pond, watching the damselflies. I'd draw them.' Ashley's face tightened. 'Nathan said he didn't care that they'd gone, but I minded. A lot. I missed Mum and Gaby. I'd make myself sick so I could stay home from school and sit in the office with Mum and Gran instead. And I ran away to Mum's house a few times, but Dad said I had to live with him and he wouldn't let me stay with Mum. He always made me go back with him.' He dragged in a breath. 'The only time I was really happy was when I was out in the fields, drawing. One day, that summer, Nathan sneaked up behind me and pushed me into the pond. I managed to reach the side again, but when I tried to pull myself out, I stood on what I thought was a branch. I heard it crack. And then...' He put his hand to his face. 'Oh, God. And then these bones floated up. I saw it was a hand – and I realised I must've trodden on a skeleton's arm, not a branch, and I'd broken the hand off it. I was horrified. I wanted to tell Dad, but Nathan pulled me back before I could run home. He said I wasn't to tell anyone about what happened, and if I did, the hand would come and get me. It would strangle me in the night.' He shivered. 'I know that's a load of rubbish, but... Every so often, Nathan used to leave the hand under my pillow, or in my art box, where he knew it would upset me. It gave me nightmares.' He gulped. 'And he said, if I told anyone what he'd done, he'd say I was lying and they'd lock me in the loony bin, and I'd never see Mum and Gaby again.'

No wonder, Georgina thought, that Ashley had had a breakdown and was obsessive about hands. Nick had no doubt been too busy being angry and resenting Diana for divorcing him to notice that his oldest son was a bully and his younger son was suffering. And maybe Nathan's bullying had itself been a cry for help and attention.

Though Nick, too, had been damaged by his own father's behaviour – and in turn Terence had been damaged by Ernest. Families could be such dark, unhappy places, and some patterns repeated over and over.

'None of it was true, Ash,' she said quietly. 'If you'd told your mum, she would've helped you. She loves you. So does Gaby.'

'It still haunts me. The sound of the crack, and the way that bony hand floated up,' Ashley said.

'Is that why you draw all those hands, Ash?' Hayley asked gently.

He nodded. 'It gets them out of my head. I thought making the blood-and-wine hands would stop the nightmares, but they didn't.' He dragged in a breath. 'That morning, when Nathan came to have a go at me and I locked myself in the bathroom, I could hear things being broken outside. Things being ripped up. I knew Nathan was wrecking everything, but I didn't dare leave the bathroom. He's bigger than me, stronger. I wouldn't have been able to stop him, and he was so angry with me. He would've hurt me. So I waited until everything had gone quiet again. And then I stayed a bit longer, in case he was outside, lying in wait for me.'

Georgina stroked his hair, gently encouraging him to keep talking.

'Eventually I unlocked the door. He'd gone, but he'd trashed my studio. He'd pulled all the sculptures out of the freezer – the hands were melting, and they looked as if he'd stamped on them. I couldn't stand seeing what he'd done. I had to get out. I stuffed some things into a bag, and went to the office. Gaby hadn't come by for her usual cup of tea because she was doing a photo shoot, that morning.' He looked at Georgina. 'Was that with you?'

'It was with me,' Georgina confirmed.

'I hoped she might already be at the office and she'd help me. But her car wasn't even there yet.' He dragged in a breath. 'I was scared Nathan would see me and have another go at me. I was going to walk to the village and get the bus to Norwich, then see if I could stay with friends for a while.' He swallowed hard. 'Then I heard Nathan yelling. I thought if I hid in the room with the fermentation tanks, he might not see me and I'd be able to slip out when he'd gone. But when I went into the room, I realised that's where he was. In one of the tanks. There was a ladder on the floor. He'd obviously fallen in and was yelling for help.' He closed his eyes. 'I should've helped him, I know. But I thought of the hands. All the times he'd picked on me when I was younger, how he'd scared me to the point of wetting the bed so I'd get in trouble with Dad – if it wasn't for Rita, our housekeeper, catching me trying to wash my sheets and helping me, it would've been so bad. I thought of how Nathan had just smashed up my work in front of me – well, with me behind a locked door but he knew I could hear what he was doing. How he tried to ruin things for Gaby, too. And I thought, if I did try to help him, he'd only have another go at me, so what was the point? I thought Del or someone would be in soon anyway; they'd hear him and get him out of the tank. So I walked away.' He closed his eyes. 'And then the papers said he'd died. Drowned in the wine. It was my fault, because I should've gone and found someone to help me get him out. I killed him.'

'You didn't kill him,' Georgina said. 'There's evidence of Nathan having a fight with someone before he went into the tank. And we can prove that wasn't you.'

'How?'

'Because, apart from the fact you told me there was a fresh bruise on his face when he came into your studio, I'm willing to bet there aren't any bruises on the backs of your hands,' Georgina said.

Ashley's hands were shaking as he laid them on the table, palm down, but as Georgina had suspected there were no signs of bruises.

'See? Someone else was involved,' she said. 'It wasn't your fault.'

'It feels like it is, though. And I don't know what to do,' Ashley said. 'This is so *stupid*. I'm thirty years old and Nathan was right about me – I'm completely useless.'

'Nathan was wrong,' Georgina said. 'Everyone's good at something. Your talent's in art. It's beautiful enough for Gaby to want it on her website.'

'If we were all the same as everyone else, it'd be a very strange world – and not a very nice one to live in,' Sybbie added.

'My advice,' Georgina said gently, 'is to talk to the police.'

'I can't.' Ashley shook his head vehemently. 'They'll lock me up.'

'I promise you they won't,' Georgina said.

'Dogs are good judges of character, wouldn't you say?' Sybbie asked.

'Well – yes,' Ashley admitted.

'My partner, Colin, is a detective,' Georgina said. 'Bert adores him.'

'I have two black Labradors, Max and Jet,' Sybbie added. 'They adore Colin, too.'

'Talk to him on the phone, and tell him what you've told me,' Georgina urged. 'About your dad having a fight with Nathan, Nathan coming to see you with a bruise on his face and threatening you, then smashing up your studio. He'll listen, and I promise you he won't make judgements. He's always careful with facts.'

'Talk to him on speaker, so we can chip in and support you,' Sybbie suggested.

'What if the police arrest Ash?' Hayley asked.

'They won't,' Georgina said. 'There's a missing piece to the puzzle of what happened to Nathan, and I think Ashley can help solve that mystery.' She gave Ashley another hug. 'And please will you take a selfie and send it to your mum and your sister with a text, so they know you're OK?'

With the support from the three women and Bert, Ashley talked to Colin and told him what had happened.

'Thank you for talking to me, Ashley,' Colin said gently. 'I know it's been difficult, and I appreciate it. I'll need to do a formal interview with you, where you sign a statement, but we can do that anywhere you like, and if you need someone with you, we can arrange that. And I need to see your hands for myself, so I can testify there are no injuries and you weren't in a physical fight with Nathan.'

'I'm not sure,' Ashley said. He dragged in a breath. 'My dad...'

'Leave your dad to me,' Colin said. 'And I know your mum and Gaby will be relieved that you're safe. Can I have your permission to tell them you're OK?'

'No. I'll tell them myself,' Ashley said. He lifted his chin. 'On my way to seeing you.'

'That's great. I can arrange transport for you, if you want,' Colin said.

'Or I could drive you,' Georgina said. 'As long as you don't mind sitting with Bert.'

He gave her a shy smile. 'I'd like that.'

'And you're welcome to come, too, Hayley,' Georgina said. 'I'm more than happy to bring you back here, afterwards.'

'All right,' Hayley said.

Ashley looked as if the world had just been lifted from his shoulders; he was still pale and had shadows under his eyes, but there was a light in his eyes that Georgina hadn't seen before. Something that looked like hope – that his nightmare was finally over.

EIGHTEEN

Georgina had come up trumps, Colin thought – but then, she always did. She'd brought Ashley in to the station to give his statement, persuaded Ashley to call Diana and Gaby on the way in, and she'd brought Ashley's friend to support him during the interview.

Ashley's evidence had turned out to be the key to the case, and now Colin was about to make an arrest.

He and Mo headed over to Willow Farm. Del Turnbull answered the intercom and let them in.

'What can I do for you?' Del asked.

'Is Mr Edwards here?' Colin asked.

'Yes. He's in his office,' Del said.

'Thank you,' Colin said.

'Hang on – I think he's making an important phone call,' Del said.

'I'm afraid this is a tiny bit more important,' Colin said gently. He and Mo walked over to the office they'd used for interviews on Monday, and knocked on the door. Without waiting to be asked to enter, Colin opened it.

'Do you *mind*? I'm in the middle of something, here,' Nick said, glaring at Colin.

'I'd recommend ending the call, Mr Edwards. Unless you're intending to resist arrest, which I wouldn't recommend because it won't show you in a good light in court,' Colin pointed out.

'Arr—?' Nick muttered something into his phone and ended the call. 'What the hell is this about, DI Bradshaw? And rest assured I'm going to be having a word with the Chief Super about this harassment.'

'As you wish,' Colin said, knowing that Nick had no grounds whatsoever. 'Nicholas Edwards, I'm arresting you on suspicion of the murder of Nathan Edwards on Monday, August the 19th. We have evidence that shows you may have been involved, and your arrest is necessary to question you about your involvement.'

Mo followed up with the official words of the caution.

'We'd like you to come with us to the station, Mr Edwards,' Colin said. 'You can call a solicitor of your choice, or you can use the duty solicitor. But we will be interviewing you today about your involvement.'

'This is outrageous. You can't do this!' Nick said.

'As officers of the law, we can. You can choose to come with us quietly,' Colin said, 'or you can make a fuss and resist arrest – in which case we'll need to handcuff you to avoid the risk of violent behaviour on your way into the station. Up to you.'

Nick stared at him, and clearly realised that Colin wasn't going to back down. Then he sagged in his chair. 'Can I call my solicitor now? And I'll come quietly.'

'Sure,' Colin said.

Once Nick had made the call and arranged to meet his solicitor at the police station, Colin and Mo walked with him to the car.

'Del, you're in charge,' Nick said as they passed through the reception area.

'What? Why? What's happening?' Del asked.

'Mr Edwards is helping us with our enquiries,' Colin said. 'We'll be in touch.'

Mo sat in the back with Nick, and Colin made sure that the child locks were engaged. Nobody spoke on the way to Norwich, though the bluster seemed to have gone from Nick by the time they reached the station.

After Nick had spoken privately to his solicitor, the interview began.

'We know what happened on Monday,' Colin said. 'Your post tends to arrive early, before office hours. You received the letter saying that you didn't get the grant Gaby had applied for. You rang her and yelled at her about it, and she asked you to give her time to sort it out. The letter said her land wasn't conforming to the organic standards – that someone was spraying her fields. And you know Nathan had been threatening to do that.'

'You have no proof of this,' Nick said.

'Oh, but we do,' Colin said. 'Look at the back of your right hand. There's bruising along your knuckles.'

'Because I caught my hand on something at work,' Nick said, looking away. 'It happens. Occupational hazard.'

'We have a witness statement that you had a huge row with Nathan. That you punched him. Nathan's body has clear bruising to the face, with the imprint of knuckles. If we take a photograph of your right hand, I'd say it will be an exact match to those imprints,' Colin said. 'Nathan believed someone had spoken to the surveyor and told him about the threats he'd made to spray Gaby's crops. After you hit him and stormed out, Nathan went to see the person he thought was responsible for that particular conversation.'

Nick spread his hands, as if to deny it was anything to do with him.

'Nathan threatened Ashley, who locked himself in the bathroom; even though Nathan tried to kick the door down, it held. Nathan smashed up the studio and came back here, still furious and resentful. He decided to take some samples from the fermenting tanks. You came through to the winery and saw him on the platform at the top of the tanks. You were still angry with him because you blamed him for the fact you weren't going to get the government grant – even though you'd encouraged him to clash with Gaby in the first place – so you went up that ladder and pushed him into the tank, knowing he wouldn't be able to get out without help. Knowing that he'd be overcome by the fumes, and he'd drown.'

'That's not true,' Nick said. 'I didn't try to kill him. He was my *boy*. He – I...' His words stuttered to a stop.

'He died, Mr Edwards, as a direct result of falling into the vat,' Colin said softly. 'And you're going to have to live with knowing what you did.'

'I was putting him in his place, that's all,' Nick protested. 'I wasn't going to kill him. I meant to give him a fright, and make him remember that I've not retired yet – I'm still in charge. It was nearly time for everyone to start work, so there'd be enough people around to hear him. I knew someone would pull him out of the tank. He'd look a fool in front of everyone, and it would put him in his place.'

'Del told us that the workers in the bottling plant like to turn the radio up. Nobody heard that ladder fall. Nobody heard him yelling.' One person had heard him yell. But Ashley had been scared that if he pulled his brother out of the vat, Nathan would take out his temper on him again.

'I swear I didn't try to kill him,' Nick said. 'It wasn't deliberate.'

'Did you know how much Nathan bullied Ashley, as a child?' Colin asked.

Nick flapped a dismissive hand. 'Kids squabble. They get over it.'

'It was a lot more than a squabble. Nathan bullied his little brother. Enough that he used to wet the bed, the year their mum left,' Colin said quietly.

'He wet the bed? But he was ten! Way too old to be doing that sort of thing,' Nick said, sneering.

No wonder Ashley had been so reluctant at first to talk to him, Colin thought, fearing that he'd have to face his father's contempt. 'Enough that it caused him to have a mental breakdown when he was at college,' Colin continued. 'Enough to make him fragile. That's why you built the studio for him, isn't it? Out of guilt, because you knew you should've stopped the bullying years ago. He was your son, he was desperately unhappy and you should've protected him. Or at least let him live with his mum and his sister. You should've put his needs before scoring points against Diana.'

Nick looked as if he was at the point of losing his temper; but suddenly all the fight went out of him. 'Yes. I... I felt bad about Ash's breakdowns. And I knew Nathan had a go at him every so often. But I was angry at Ash at the same time, for giving in so easily. Why couldn't he have just been a man and fought back?'

Toxic masculinity at its absolute worst, Colin thought. *Be a man.* Why did that have to be equated with bullying and bluster and fighting? Why couldn't it be humanity and respecting other people's boundaries?

Nick's mouth tightened. 'If Diana had known about it, she would've gone to court to get custody of Ash, and I... God help me, yes, it's true about point-scoring. I wanted to make her miserable more than I wanted to make my son happy. I just didn't understand Ashley. And all that stuff with the hands freaked me out.'

Colin filled him in on the skeleton, and Nathan's role in it.

Nick went white. 'I didn't know about *that*. If I'd known, I would've stopped it.' He put a hand to his face in horror. 'Oh, my God.'

'Hopefully, now Ashley's finally started talking about it, he'll get the help he needs,' Colin said. 'Nicholas Edwards, I'm going to keep you in custody while I talk to the Crown Prosecution Service, and they'll decide whether to charge you with the murder of Nathan Edwards.'

'But I didn't kill my son!' Nick protested. 'He was *alive* when I left Willow Farm.'

'You're an experienced winemaker, Mr Edwards. How many years has Willow Farm Wines been going?' Colin asked.

'I planted the first fields twenty years ago,' Nick said. 'Ten years after my mother planted the fields for Rosa Wines.'

'So you're well aware of the gases produced during fermentation, and the risks of people being overcome by carbon dioxide,' Colin said. 'You knew Nathan wouldn't last long in that tank. That there was a risk of him losing consciousness and then drowning.'

'I thought someone would get him out in time,' Nick said. 'Other people were about. I tripped when I got off the ladder and it fell to the floor. I knew someone would see it lying there and realise something wasn't right.' A muscle worked in his cheek. 'He was still alive when I left. I heard him shouting.'

'But you walked away and let him drown,' Colin said, striving to keep his voice neutral when he wanted to shake Nick until his bones rattled and ask him what the hell he'd been thinking.

That was the thing he really couldn't understand.

Shoving Nathan into the vat in the first place, he could just about understand; father and son were both stubborn, both bad-tempered, and both used to pushing other people around verbally, if not physically.

But how could you walk away and leave your child to die?

OK, so Colin knew he'd let his own daughter down, when

the drink had taken hold; but even at his worst point he would never, ever, *ever* have deliberately tried to hurt her. He would've given his life for her. Still would.

The man in front of him clearly wasn't capable of that kind of love. His own interests came first, second and last.

'I'll need to keep you in custody,' Colin said, 'until the Crown Prosecution Service decide to charge you formally in front of a magistrate.'

NINETEEN

Bea had managed to find one of Winnie's granddaughters, Kathleen Rowan; Kathleen and her niece, Cheryl, had agreed to meet Georgina in Norwich.

'Thank you so much for agreeing to see me,' Georgina said when she arrived at the café where they'd arranged to meet.

'You're very welcome,' Kathleen said. 'So this is about my gran?'

'And your grandfather,' Georgina said.

'The one who disappeared,' Kathleen said. 'I wish Mum was still here. She always wondered what happened to him. Gran wouldn't talk about it very much.'

'It might be useful if we start with what you know about Percy,' Georgina suggested, 'and then I can fill in the gaps.'

'Just that he disappeared,' Kathleen said. 'My mum was his oldest daughter, Mabel. Gran moved in with Mum in her last few years. I did manage to get her talking about the past, a few times. She told us Percy fought in the First World War; when Hitler started his rise to power, Percy was worried sick about what was happening in Europe and that it would end in another war. It brought all the memories back, of his time in the trenches. He suffered from the black dog, and everyone in the village thought that he just couldn't cope and... well, ended things. They never found his body. Though Gran wondered what really happened, because she was sure he would never have left his girls.' She paused. 'And you found what you think is his skeleton, in a pond on the farm where my mum grew up?'

'Yes,' Georgina confirmed.

'So he did drown himself, then. Poor man,' Kathleen said.

'It's not *quite* as clear-cut as that,' Georgina said.

'Gran also let it slip once that she knew she was Percy's second choice for a bride,' Kathleen said. 'Before the war, Percy's sweetheart was the daughter of the farmer next door. The whole village expected them to get married, but after the war she married someone else.'

'Ivy,' Georgina said. 'Her great-granddaughter, Gaby, still has the letters that Percy wrote to Ivy from the trenches, and she let me make copies of them for you.'

'How amazing that the letters were kept safe, all these years,' Cheryl said. 'It'll be wonderful to see them.'

'Mum thought there must've been a big falling-out between Percy and his first love,' Kathleen continued. 'Though she says she can't imagine what, because she really loved her dad. She was five when he went missing, but she remembers him being kind and gentle. He used to read to her and her sisters, and she went with him everywhere. He taught her to recognise all the birds and butterflies. All she had left of him were a few photographs.' She picked up an envelope and removed a group of photographs. 'This is obviously my grandparents on their wedding day,' she said, revealing a larger black-and-white photo of a man in a suit and a woman wearing a wedding dress with a veil. 'And these are him with Mum and her sisters.' The smaller photos had a white border; Percy looked relaxed and happy with his three girls, one of them a babe in arms.

'How lovely that you still have them,' Georgina said.

'I wonder what caused the falling-out?' Cheryl asked. 'Is there anything in the letters?'

'No. We think the problem was Ivy's dad,' Georgina said. 'He couldn't accept that both his sons were killed in the war but Percy came home – Percy was in the same regiment as them. Then Ivy's mum died in the flu epidemic, and her dad started drinking to... well, blot it out, I suppose.'

'That's really sad,' Cheryl said.

'Even though my granddad made it home, he wasn't unscathed by the war,' Kathleen said. 'Gran said that he still had nightmares about the trenches and he'd wake up in the middle of the night, yelling.'

'I'm not surprised,' Georgina said. 'I think a lot of the soldiers struggled when they got home.' She paused. 'Do you know how they got together?'

Kathleen nodded. 'After the war, Gran pretty much resigned herself to never marrying because there were so many more women than men. But Percy's sister Millie was getting married, and Gran and her aunt were making her wedding dress. Gran went to see Millie about the dress; she walked by the pond, and there was Percy, all brooding and unhappy. She ended up sitting down and talking to him. Reading between the lines, we think she talked him out of doing something rash.' She looked at Georgina. 'I take it that was the same pond where the skeleton was found?'

'Yes,' Georgina said.

'But you said you don't think he drowned himself?' Cheryl asked.

'No,' Georgina said, 'because someone would have found him. I think there might have been...' She chose her words carefully. '...an accident. Maybe an altercation. Percy had a very thin skull, and there's a crack in it. My friend Rowena is the finds liaison officer, who analyses the remains when people find bones; she thinks that injury was the cause of death. Maybe he fell and hit his head.'

'Or maybe someone hit him?' Cheryl asked.

'And because his skull was thin, it affected him differently,' Georgina said. 'Though whoever hit him might not have intended to kill him.'

'Why didn't they run and get help?' Kathleen asked. Then she grimaced and answered her own question. 'I suppose that's obvious. If they thought it was too late, they would've worried about being hanged for murder.' She blew out a breath. 'My poor grandfather. Do you know who had a fight with him?'

'I think it might've been Ivy's husband, Ernest,' Georgina said.

'Actually, that would make sense,' Cheryl said thoughtfully. 'Gran once told me there was a bit of gossip in the village, before Percy went missing. Ivy and her husband had been married for ten years before they finally had a baby, and it turned out he had red hair.' She paused. 'So did Percy.'

'Gran held her head high. She said Ivy's oldest brother had had auburn hair, so obviously red hair ran on Ivy's side of the family. Fred, my great-granddad, supported her,' Kathleen said. 'But it must've been hard, listening to the gossip and wondering if there really was something in it. Did the little boy have red hair because there was red hair in Ivy's family, too, or was Percy his biological dad?'

'I would've asked Ivy straight out, if I were her,' Cheryl said.

'Maybe she decided she'd rather not know,' Kathleen said. 'Maybe she wanted to believe Percy hadn't been unfaithful to her and he really had put his first love behind him after she married someone else.'

'It must've been difficult living next door to his ex, though,' Georgina said sympathetically.

Kathleen nodded. 'Especially as Gran had never really

wanted to be a farmer's wife. But Percy was the only boy in the family and he was expected to take over from his dad. What Gran really wanted was to be a dressmaker and set up a workshop in the city, but then what would Percy have done for a living? She thought he would've been miserable in the city. Plus he would've felt guilty about letting his dad down. So she settled at the farm, and stayed there to support Percy's mum and dad after he disappeared. And then it was wartime, so she was really stuck.'

'Poor Winnie,' Georgie said.

'When Mum and my aunts moved to Norwich, after the war, Gran decided to sell up and join them. Her in-laws had died by that point, so she didn't feel she had to struggle on for their sake anymore, and someone offered to buy the farm. They gave her a bit less money than she thought it was worth, but it was enough for her to buy her a house in Norwich and a workshop to make her dresses. After she moved, she only went back to Ashingham on the first Sunday of the month, to see her parents.' Kathleen smiled sadly. 'She's buried in the churchyard at Ashingham, but that's simply because that's where her parents were buried, it's where she set up a gravestone for my granddad, and it was the church where she was married and Mum and my aunts were christened.'

'What happened to Ivy and her family?' Cheryl asked.

'They stayed at Willow Farm,' Georgina said, not wanting to stir up the fact that Ernest clearly hadn't given Winnie a fair price for Holm Farm. 'About thirty years ago, Ivy's daughter-in-law Rosemary turned part of the farm into a vineyard. Rosemary's granddaughter runs it now.'

'We saw in the news about the man who drowned in the wine,' Kathleen said. 'Terrible for them.'

'It's all just really sad,' Georgina said. 'Hopefully things will get better for the family, now.' She brought out the file with the printouts she'd made of the letters. 'If you can let me have your email address, I'll send you the digital files, but I thought you'd like to see these.'

Kathleen and Cheryl read through them. 'Even though they're to his first love, rather than to my gran, I'm glad to have these,' Kathleen said. 'He sounds a really lovely man. Kind and caring.'

Cheryl nodded. 'And he still lives on in all of us, Aunty Kath.'

'That's a lovely way to look at it,' Kathleen agreed. 'Please thank Gaby for us. It's kind of her to let us have copies.'

'What happens to Percy now?' Cheryl asked.

'He'll be interred properly,' Georgina said. 'Though we really need the definitive proof that it's him.'

'They can do DNA tests to check, right?' Cheryl asked.

At Georgina's nod, Kathleen said, 'Then I'm happy to give you a DNA sample to test against his.'

'Thank you,' Georgina said. 'I'll pass that on to the police, and they'll get in touch with you.'

EPILOGUE

Two months later, Colin went with Georgina to Willow Farm to deliver a copy of *Veritas* magazine to Gaby.

'Oh, my God! They've put me on the cover!' Gaby shrieked. 'That's amazing.' She flung her arms round Georgina. 'Thank you.'

'I didn't have anything to do with the layout. I just did the photographs,' Georgina said. 'And I've got that print your mum wanted, too.'

'Thank you. Can I offer you both a glass of wine?'

'I'm driving,' Colin said, 'so water or a cup of tea for me, please.'

Georgina glanced at Colin. She knew that even though he didn't drink any more, he didn't expect other people to be teetotal around him, but she still wanted to do him the courtesy of checking rather than taking it for granted. The tiniest of crinkles at the corners of his eyes told her that he appreciated that. 'I'd definitely like a glass of your wine, please, Gaby,' she said.

'I got the DNA results back, the other day,' Gaby said. 'I'm not a match for Percy.' She gave a rueful smile as she switched the kettle on and poured Georgina a glass of wine. 'I have to admit, I'm a bit disappointed. He sounded such a nice man – the kind of ancestor you'd be really proud of.'

'He's at peace, now,' Doris said. 'He remembers everything. And he's reunited with Winnie.'

Georgina dipped her head in acknowledgement, knowing that everyone else would think she was responding to Gaby – which she was, in part.

'But I guess Dad and Nathan – and the grandfather who died before I was born – all took after Ernest,' Gaby continued. 'Difficult men.'

'But you,' Georgina said, 'take after your mum, Rosemary and Ivy. And so does Ashley. How's he doing?'

'OK. He's responding really well to his new treatment,' Gaby said. 'We're going to turn his studio into a holiday cottage, and we're going to build him a new studio, where he can also do a bit of teaching.'

'That's good to hear,' Colin said.

'He still refuses to visit Dad,' Gaby said.

Georgina knew that Nick Edwards was in custody, awaiting trial for manslaughter by unlawful act, and Colin believed he'd be convicted.

'But we've agreed a way forward for the farm,' Gaby continued. 'Dad's signed everything over to Ash and me, and we're merging the two vineyards and turning them completely organic. We're going to sell the bits of Willow Farm that are still arable farmland. Half of the money from that will going to Kelly and the girls, to give them some financial security. With the other half, we're going to set up a trust in Percy's name to offer art therapy for local people suffering from depression.'

'That sounds really good,' Georgina said.

'I spoke to Kathleen and Cheryl about the DNA results,' Gaby said. 'They got Kathleen's back, too, and it confirmed the skeleton was related to her. The body in the pond was Percy.' She gave a rueful smile. 'It's a shame that we're not related to

Percy. But I feel that he has a kind of link to us, through Ivy. Kathleen said they're going to have him interred with Winnie in St Peter's, and she's invited us to go to the internment. I suggested we had lunch here, afterwards, and we can toast Percy with Rosa Wines' finest.'

'That sounds perfect,' Colin said.

'I think we should toast Percy now,' Georgina said. 'May he rest in peace, and may Willow Farm be a much happier place in its new incarnation.'

'To Percy,' Gaby and Colin echoed, raising a glass of wine and a mug of tea respectively.

Georgina's phone beeped with a text.

'Sorry,' she said. 'I'll pick it up later.'

'Check it. It might be urgent,' Gaby said.

Georgina looked at the screen and grinned as she saw the text flash up. 'I have news from Sybbie. I've never seen her type a text completely in capitals before.'

'News?' Colin prompted.

Georgina's grin broadened. 'I'M A GRANNIE!'

'That,' Gaby said, 'is brilliant. And I'm going to be sending two bottles of Rosa's best vintage back with you – one for her and one for Cesca. Congratulations!'

A LETTER FROM THE AUTHOR

Huge thanks for reading *The Body at the Vineyard*; I hope you enjoyed Georgina, Doris and Colin's journey. If you want to join other readers in hearing all about my new releases and bonus content, you can sign up for my newsletter.

www.stormpublishing.co/kate-hardy

If you enjoyed this book and could spare a few moments to leave a review, that would be hugely appreciated. Even a short review can make all the difference in encouraging a reader to discover my books for the first time. Thank you so much!

This series was hugely influenced by three things. Firstly, I grew up in a haunted house in a small market town in Norfolk, so I've always been drawn to slightly spooky stories. (I did research it when I wrote a book on researching house history, but I couldn't find any documentary evidence for the tale of the jealous miller who murdered his wife. However, I also don't have explanations for various spooky things that happened at the house – including the anecdote about Sybbie's dogs in *The Body at Rookery Barn*, which happened in real life with our Labradors and a tennis ball.) Secondly, I read Daphne du Maurier's short story 'The Blue Lenses' while I was a student, and... I can't explain this properly without giving spoilers, so I'll say it's to do with how you see people. Thirdly, I'm deaf; after I had my first hearing aid fitted, once I'd got over the thrill of hearing birdsong for the first time in years, my author brain started ticking. The du Maurier story gave me a 'what if' moment: what if you heard something through your hearing aids that wasn't what you were supposed to hear? (The obvious one would be someone's thoughts; but that's where my childhood home came in.) It took a few years for the idea to come to the top of my head and refuse to go away, but what if you could hear what my heroine Georgina ends up hearing?

And so Georgina Drake ends up living in a haunted house in a small market town in Norfolk...

The Body in the Vineyard started life when it occurred to me what a good setting it would be to hide a body. I also had a murder method in mind. Then I thought I really ought to go and have a proper look round an actual English vineyard, for research purposes, and dragged my research assistant (aka husband) on a tour of one near us (which also happens to make the most delicious wine – there's no reason why your job can't be fun, right?). Thank you to Lee Dyer of Winbirri Vineyard for a really interesting talk (and for answering the questions that weren't appropriate to ask in front of your other guests!). All mistakes are mine, and my vineyard is definitely fictional!

The cold case: like Bernard, I did A level history, and the First World War was one of the topics. I always thought how hard it must've been for returning soldiers to fit in to their old world and keep the horrors of what they'd seen from their family. And I think there are a lot of parallels between the 1918–20 flu pandemic and the Covid pandemic we lived through a century later.

Little Wenborough isn't a real place, but the name is a mashup of the town where I grew up and the river where I walk my dogs in the morning. Norfolk is an amazing place to live. Huge skies (incredible sunrises and sunsets), wide beaches (aka my best place to think, and the Editpawial Assistants are always up for a trip there), and more ancient churches than anywhere else in the country (watch this space!).

Thanks again for being part of this amazing journey with me and I hope you'll stay in touch – I have so many more stories and ideas to entertain you with!

All best,

Kate Hardy

www.katehardy.com

facebook.com/katehardyromanceauthor
x.com/katehardyauthor
instagram.com/katehardyauthor

ACKNOWLEDGMENTS

I'd like to thank Oliver Rhodes and Kathryn Taussig for taking a chance on my slightly unusual take on a crime series; Emily Gowers for being an absolute dream of an editor – incisive, thoughtful and a wonderful collaborator as well as being great fun; and to Shirley Khan and Maddy Newquist for picking up the bits I missed! I've loved every second of working on this book with you.

Gerard has been a particular star with location research (aka the vineyard trip), as have my sister-in-law, Nicki, and brother-in-law, Vernon – thank you for being so enthusiastic.

Special thanks to my family and friends who cheer-led the first Georgina Drake book, made useful suggestions on this one about wine/cake/ghosts, and are always there through the highs and lows of publishing: you know who you are and I appreciate you.

Extra-special thanks to Gerard, Chris and Chloë Brooks, who've always been my greatest supporters; to Chrissy and Rich Camp, for always believing in me and being the best uncle and aunt ever; and to Archie and Dexter, my beloved Editpawial Assistants, for keeping my feet warm, reminding me when it's time for walkies and lunch, and putting up with me photographing them to keep my social media ticking over while I'm on deadline.

And, last but very much not least, thank *you*, dear reader, for choosing my book. I hope you enjoy reading it as much as I enjoyed writing it.

Printed in Dunstable, United Kingdom